Lost Morning

by DuBose Heyward

POETRY

JASBO BROWN AND SELECTED POEMS
CAROLINA CHANSONS (*with Hervey Allen*)
SKYLINES AND HORIZONS

PLAYS

PORGY: A PLAY (*with Dorothy Heyward*)
BRASS ANKLE

FICTION

PETER ASHLEY

PORGY

ANGEL

THE HALF PINT FLASK

MAMBA'S DAUGHTERS

LOST MORNING

DU BOSE HEYWARD

Lost Morning

ଯଯ

A man does not reach any stature of manhood until like Moses he kills an Egyptian (i.e., murders some oppressive prejudice of the all-crushing Tyrant Society or Custom or Orthodoxy) and flies into the desert of his own soul, where among the rocks and sands, over which at any rate the sun rises clear each day, he slowly and with great agony settles his relation with men and manners and powers outside, and begins to look with his own eyes, and first knows the unspeakable joy of the outcast's kiss upon the hand of sweet, naked Truth.—*from* POEM OUTLINES *by* SIDNEY LANIER.

ଯଯଯ

FARRAR & RINEHART
INCORPORATED
New York   *Toronto*

Lost Morning

$\mathcal{I}$T WAS half past eight of a sultry August night when Felix Hollister left the Exeter Country Club. This was a part of the routine into which he had fallen during the absence of his wife, Miriam, and his children, Felicia, aged eighteen, and Aubery, aged twenty-one, who were away on a ninety-day European tour.

The summer was a busy time for Hollister, so he had remained at Wingfields, the model estate that lay on the other side of town from the club. It was, however, his custom to dine every evening at the club. Although he did not play golf, and was frankly, almost defiantly, sedentary in his mode of life, the hour or two each evening on the broad veranda, the comfortable let-down of the desultory gossip, and the highball or two that he allowed himself furnished a relief from the tedium of the day's routine.

Driving, for Hollister, was never more than a necessary means of transporting himself from one place to another. By nature absent-minded to a fault, and of an apprehensive and imaginative temperament, he always drove under high nervous tension, wheel gripped in his long, sensitive fingers, and leg muscles taut and ready for instant action at the pedals.

The day, while not oppressive, had been hot with that light, baked-out, brittle quality character-istic of the Piedmont region of Carolina. To the west a thunderstorm was making up, and when the car topped a gentle hill overlooking the lights of Exeter, Hollister saw it building steadily toward the zenith in a vast architectural design of superimposed levels surmounted by lofty domes. From time to time the resonant air vibrated in response to distant thunders, and against the last red stain of the after-glow the lightnings sketched their hieroglyphics in a hard, metallic blue.

As the car swung between the imposing gate-posts of his drive the storm broke. He was driving the roadster and had, of course, forgotten to put up the top. In the short distance to the garage he was drenched. He closed the garage and locked the door, then started toward the house, suffering the deluge, as he concluded that it would be impossible for his clothing to take up any more water than it already contained.

When he was passing the large building that housed the studio, and that stood in the grounds at some distance from the house, he noticed that the lights were on. It surprised but did not alarm him. It could only be Leslie Morgan, his studio assistant and secretary, but he had told her that she could go, before he had left for the club. Now he wondered with a familiar pang of contrition if he had forgotten something that had caused her to stay and get caught by the storm.

When he opened the door the roar of the rain and the earthy, acrid, smell from the thirsty garden entered with him. Leslie turned her head and looked over her shoulder at him. She was standing at the far side of the room mixing the ink for the morrow's printing.

Hollister was a tall man with a loose, angular frame and broad thin shoulders carried slightly forward in a premature stoop; and yet this spareness, this manner of carrying the shoulders, the slight thrusting forward of the head, all of which should have suggested an age greater than a man's mid-forties, contributed to an impression which was, paradoxically, quite the reverse. The effect produced was that of adolescence, of a co-ordination not yet mastered rather than one which was breaking down. And this illusion was heightened by the suit he wore—short in sleeve and leg, leaving wrists and ankles exposed.

And now Leslie Morgan, watching him, and puzzled as always by this incongruity between appearance and effect, struck upon a solution. As he closed the door and turned toward her, the gesture, casual and devoid of self-consciousness, gave her the key. The forward thrust of the figure, eager, gauche, almost wistful, was instinct with youth, but a youth that had grown weary almost to the point of surrender.

His face, she noticed, was pallid, but the pallor was clear and healthy, and the muscles behind it were firm and high, and behind these again she sensed, as she always did, a bony structure that, starting with the firm line of the jaw and building up into the broad, high forehead, touched nobility. She had told herself that some day she would model that head. She would start with the completely articulated skull, then lay the muscles over it, and the skin should be a transparent veil, and not an opaque masque. Done in only that way could it be expressed in its full integrity. Only in that way could she bring out its potential power and subordinate the growing note of frustration that was commencing to mar the finely chiseled mouth.

She watched him while his eyes were finding her, their clear blue piercing the veils of his preoccupation and centering on her, lifting her from the background of the studio and bearing down upon her with their half-quizzical, half-tragic regard. It would be those eyes that would baffle the artist, she thought. What they told of Felix Hollister lay beyond the range of pigment or clay. They showed the man's fatal vulnerability. They were too credulous. They would believe anything, accept anything. They would never doubt anyone, except, possibly, Felix Hollister.

She said: "Why, you're soaked to the skin. I suppose you were caught in the open car. It certainly is high time Mrs. Hollister came home to look after you and make you behave."

He saw then that a fire was burning in the high, Gothic fireplace, and he realized suddenly that he was chilled through. He sloshed over and spread his hands to the blaze.

Without looking up, Leslie said: "You'll have to look after yourself. I'm ink to the elbows. I was about to leave when I realized that we had none for tomorrow's printing, so I stayed to get a batch up. Now the storm's caught me."

Hollister said: "It was sweet of you to think of this fire. Do you know, I think I'd have bloomed out with a first-rate chill if I hadn't got warmed up right away."

"You'd better get into your work clothes," she told him, practically, "and hang those wet rags to dry. I'll get you a hot toddy, too, as soon as I emerge from this mess."

In a few minutes Hollister was back from the dressing room, clad in a pair of ink-stained white duck trousers, a white shirt V'd in at the throat, and with his bare feet in the light leather sandals that he always wore in the studio.

Leslie was absorbed in her task. She had reduced the Frankfort black to a paste and was engaged at that moment in adding the exact proportion of raw sienna that would impart the warm glow which was characteristic of Hollister's etchings. Then very delicately she added burnt linseed oil, rotating the muller with her other hand, and gradually reducing the consistency until the ink reached the precise texture required.

Hollister stood admiring the smooth and apparently effortless competence that she brought to all her work. What a find she had been. Miriam had got her, four years before, from an art school in New York. They had said that she had a quite remarkable talent, but her father had died and, with an infirm mother to support, she had had to give up her studies and find a paying job. The mother had, in due course, been brought to Exeter, and Leslie had made a home for her at the Gresham Arms, a small walk-up apartment house at the edge of town where one could look out over the rolling, open land to the west, and away from the great tobacco and cotton mills that bit into the eastern horizon with their serried smokestacks.

Hollister had always taken everything that Miriam did for granted, and Leslie had been no exception. She had been "Leslie" from the first. She was only eighteen then, and in the informal air of the studio "Miss Morgan" would have been ridiculous. She was a paragon of adaptability, but Hollister, in the rare intervals when he thought of her as an individual, had invariably felt that this pliant quality was the result of constant mental effort, and that beneath it there was always the pull of a strongly marked, and at times almost antagonistic, personality. There were rare moments when, engrossed with some phase of the elaborate scheme of life that had involved him, he would get a definite sense of her disapproval. His eyes would pick her up in a way they had, as though they were setting her on the model stand, looking over and through her with their intense, paradoxical regard. Then their conversation would go after this fashion:

"I'm sorry, Leslie, but families must live."

"And sons must go to Yale."

"And daughters to Vassar."

"And the women who bear them for us must ride in motorcars."

"And so it goes."

"And so it goes."

Now Leslie had finished her work and was washing up at the sink, while Hollister stood watching the smooth play of her hands as she soaped then rinsed her rounded forearms. For a moment she disappeared in the alcove that served as her dressing room, and when she returned she had changed her smock for the slim undistinguished street dress that she always wore to work.

An iron kettle was singing on the hearth, its high cheerful note vying with the roar of the rain on the vaulted roof. When Leslie set the kettle on a tile on the small table, it brought a pleasant, homey smell of wood smoke into the room. From a cupboard she fetched a china mug, a decanter of whisky, and a brass bowl of sugar. Then she mixed a toddy and handed it to Hollister.

He was sitting on the deep divan that flanked one side of the fireplace, and as he took it he smiled his thanks absently up at her. Becoming aware of her, he said: "You're looking awfully tired. Where's your drink?"

She hesitated, and he announced with finality: "I shan't touch a drop unless you join me."

While she was mixing the toddy, he moved to the end of the divan in implied invitation, but Leslie crossed the hearth and took a deep leather chair facing him. It occurred to Hollister that this was in character, and that Miriam would have approved.

Leslie emptied her mug quickly, placed it on the floor beside her chair, and lay back with an air of extreme fatigue. "As soon as I feel that," she said, "I must get on home. I'm worried about Mother tonight."

"You must wait for the storm to let up," Hollister told her. "It can't hold this pace long. Then I'll run you home in my car."

The chair in which Leslie was sitting was covered with night-blue suède leather, and the dark cloud of her hair was lost in it as shadows are absorbed into deepening shade, and from this background her face looked out, startling in its pallor and in its extraordinary purity of both spirit and line.

Hollister felt a pang of pity for her, but when

he spoke he kept it resolutely out of his voice, as he knew that it would instantly kindle that pride of hers which amounted almost to disdain. Raising his voice above the roar of the rain, he said: "Sit over here, won't you? I don't want to shout at you across this howling chasm."

She got up submissively, crossed the hearth, and settled herself in the far corner of the divan.

Hollister felt vaguely irritated at the way in which she deliberately depersonalized her acceptance of the invitation, giving it somehow the air of obeying an order. He said, a trifle tartly: "That wasn't a command, you know. It's after hours, and you can do as you please."

She smiled a little wanly, and said without warmth: "Thank you, this is lovely. I like it here."

"Tell me about your mother," Hollister asked. "It is odd that having known you for so long, I know so little of her."

"There's not much to tell. She's small, and dark, and—brave."

"Like you."

"Small like me, and dark like me; but that's all."

Wisely Hollister let the obvious opening pass, and she continued in her small beautifully-modulated voice: "And if she were to die tomorrow I suppose that it wouldn't make the slightest difference to anybody in the world but me."

"But it would matter to you."

"Terribly. I want her to live until I can make up to her for all of the rotten tricks that life has played on her. Physically life has almost broken her, but her spirit is whole, untouched, almost like a child's. If I can win through in time, I'll know exactly what to give her."

Hollister said: "That's the woman in you. Women always know what they want. But in this case—just for instance?"

"The country," she answered promptly. "A simple little place somewhere where I could paint or perhaps model again, and she could have her trees and sunsets, maybe a few flowers. It doesn't sound like much, does it?"

Leslie's eyes were fixed on Hollister, but he had a feeling that they were not looking at him, and this impression was heightened when he got abruptly to his feet and they continued to look at a spot that was now the fireplace.

Always when he moved he went into angles, the lift of a bony knee, a sharp, thrusting shoulder, the lean profile of the jaw. He strode across the studio and back, then flung out: "Ridiculously little, yes, but the real thing. And look what I've got. I should think you'd hate me, Leslie. Come, what do I look like to you, anyway—Simon Legree? Go ahead, say it, get it off your chest. It will do us both good."

A change came over her face. Its disciplined calm broke and it was suddenly reckless, but her voice was low and controlled. "I ought to warn you," she said, "that I shall take that invitation seriously. Are you sure you want me to go ahead?"

His left eyebrow lifted and the corners of his mouth twitched, giving his face a comical and disarming expression. You could see that he counted on that expression and that women especially would be subject to its appeal. "Oh, dear," he complained, "and it's such a gloomy night, too. Well, go ahead, but I'll warn you, if you're too free with personal truths, I'll assume that you're out for revenge, and are merely settling up old scores."

She sat forward, fingers linked tensely together and locked about her knees. When she answered, she spoke rapidly and a little breathlessly, as though fearing that her courage would fail her. "Good. That gives you a beautiful out, and at the same time frees me;—so here goes:

"From January to April, when you are out with the exhibits, you look like one of Mr. Maxton's tobacco drummers—a very poor one. In the spring when I first came down, and you used to go hiking off by yourself and do your sketching, then came home and put yourself into your plates, you were often cross as hell, but there were moments when you looked a little Abbey's Sir Galahad."

Hollister raised a hand in mute protest.

"Oh, you don't any more," she assured him, a faint note of scorn creeping into her voice. "You don't, any more, so you needn't be frightened. Then all summer while we're sweating it out here together, piling up prints against next season's harvest, there's nothing to describe. You're at Capri, or on the top of an Alp, or lying on the beach at Samoa, or most likely just cruising through space. But that doesn't matter really, because I'm not here either. There's nothing in all of this to keep us at home.

"There!" She smiled a little wearily. "You asked for it. Now I suppose I'm fired."

Hollister blurted: "God, you're young! You really care, don't you? Things matter. Life has teeth, and you are not afraid of being torn by them. From the bottom of my heart I envy you."

"No, you don't. You think you do, but you only like the picture of yourself envying youth. You've made a jolly comfortable bed, and naturally enough, I suppose, what you really like is lying in it."

"No," judicially, "that's not quite it. One lives and one becomes a philosopher. The graveyards are full of corpses that have battered their brains out against stone walls. The successful man is one who has realized his limitations early enough, and has spent himself within those limits instead of breaking himself to pieces trying to get out."

"Of course," she said, "of course, that would be the answer." Then suddenly she was on her feet before him, her fists clenched at her sides. "No. It isn't the answer. It's damned rot, and some day before you die you'll know it. But then it will probably be too late. You could have been great. You could still be great, but you have sold out."

Hollister turned his back on her and stood looking down into the fire. He lit a cigarette and smoked it through before he faced the room again. In the low, indirect lighting of the studio his face was pale, distressed. Against the ruddy background of the fireplace his body, legs wide apart and arms akimbo, showed in gaunt, almost spidery silhouette. He essayed an unsuccessful tone of badinage:

"What are you anyway, Leslie,—just a plain sadist? Were you one of those horrible children who skin live mice and pull off flies' legs? Or am I being chastened in a thoroughly Christian manner for the good of my soul?"

She said very soberly: "You are being chastened for the good of your soul."

"Oh, but this is too horrible!" he exclaimed.

"One can exterminate a sadist with impunity. He's outside the pack. But a missionary has the backing of society."

She interrupted him. "Please, please don't laugh me off. I didn't think I'd ever have the courage to speak to you about it, but tonight it came. It has taken me so long, and I'm so sure I'm right. Please don't make it sound ridiculous. I will promise never to speak of it again if you will listen to me this once."

With abrupt, angular movement Hollister seated himself in the chair opposite the girl, elbows on knees and face buried in hands.

"Go ahead," he said in a tight, controlled voice.

There was a silence, then Leslie said: "Now I don't know where to begin—what to say. It is so hard because I am humble before the real you, and so small." Then she asked: "Do you mind talking about yourself seriously just this once? Have you any belief? I don't mean in God, but in your destiny—yourself. Have you a philosophy?"

"Oh, yes," wearily, "I have a belief. I believe that every man finds his level. And I have a philosophy. Only the great, the completely realized personalities can do without a philosophy. It is the little people who always have them tucked handily into their sleeves. They are the pitiful, private systems of acceptance and justification by which we explain our presence in a certain level after we have found ourselves fixed in it. By the time we are, say, forty-five, life has made the pattern. Then we formulate our philosophies. In the light of them we evaluate the past. We say: 'Because I believed thus and so I took that particular turning.' It gives us the illusion of having been free agents. It bolsters up our self-respect. We can always say: 'I could have been great. I could have been rich. But fame and wealth were not consistent with my inherent modesty, my simplicity. Therefore I am still poor and unknown, but no one can deny that I am still triumphantly modest and simple.' "

Hollister lifted his face from his hands and looked across at Leslie. With that rapt quality of his he was already escaping from a distressing personal emotion into an intellectual elaboration of his theme.

"But such a philosophy as that is really scarcely worth its name," he went on. "It is negative instead of positive. There is nothing creative about it. Now the real philosopher will carry it further. He will say: 'I am happier than either the famous or the rich.' Or, reaching supreme heights, he will claim: 'I am superior to the great, the wealthy. I can afford to despise them.' And he will prove it then and there by heaving a brick through the window of a passing limousine."

Leslie said: "Now you are mocking not only me, but yourself. And you are wrong in one great essential. The pattern is never finished." And while she was saying it she could see her words sink beneath the surface of his gaze and fetch him back from the regions of abstract thought to which he had fled.

"You believe that," he answered her, "because you are young. Because you can still care terribly. When you're my age you will know. This is the way it happens." He caught her by the hand, strode to the far end of the studio, and stopped with her beside him under the great north window. It was made of a single tremendous sheet of plate glass and the rain cascading down it caught the faint light from within. You looked into it and there was only movement, swift, fathomless, without definition, beginning, or end. And out beyond this movement there was nothing.

Hollister said: "Look at that. What does it do to you? Wait, I'll tell you, because I can still remember. It picks you up and carries you out through it. It is mystery—romance. You can believe in Einstein while you stand here, because you can walk out through that into your life ten, twenty years away—just as you picture it. You do not know yet that today's vision can become next month's commonplace and next year's bore. Or that vision is the only reality—the only thing that you *feel,* and the only thing that is utterly priceless because you can escape from it."

"And you?"

"My dear," he answered, "I see the finished pattern, and I say: 'It's not the vision as I saw it twenty-five years ago, but it's warm and stout. It can keep me and mine cozy against the winter nights'; and, like a million other parents, I can say I'll give the children their chance. Felicia might have the spark—I don't know. If she does, I'll be saved."

Hollister looked down and saw that Leslie's eyes were wet. He lifted her chin and looked into her face. "There you are," he said. "You care. You are defenseless and at the same time unconquerable because your passion is unspent. You feel at this minute as though you could die for a dream, don't you? Be Jeanne d'Arc and love it?"

Leslie nodded.

"That's the thing. You can *feel* while I can only think. You can be moved to tears, while I can only gabble."

He turned and strode to the fire, and Leslie went back to her corner of the divan. The rain had stopped without their noticing it and the studio was very quiet. When Hollister turned back to Leslie again, she could see that his mood had changed. He thrust his hands into his pockets, took them out and examined them impersonally; at last he said: "I'm a poor hand at making plans. If Miriam were here she would attend to everything in a jiffy. But there's the camp in the hills. Nobody's using it, and you've got to take your mother up there for a month. It will do you both good after the long summer here. You must take some truck along and paint. It's a lovely country—rolling, you know, and there's a brook. I had entirely forgotten that you painted. You must take it up again. There'll be time. We'll make time. You must go tomorrow. You can load up the station wagon and I'll have Thomas drive you up. No, by Jove, I'll drive you up myself."

She smiled up at him wistfully. "You're an angel. You ought to throw me out on my ear for what I have said, and instead you hand me my castle in Spain."

"Well, how about it—are you moving in?"

She shook her head. "No, it can't be done. We're too far behind with the work. We've both been mooning too much this summer, I guess. Anyway, our stint isn't half done, and Mrs. Hollister

will be back in a month to take stock. We'll hold
out. Castles can wait, and besides, my usual Christmas fortnight is quite enough for one of the working class."

A knock sounded on the studio door. It was dis-
creet but it had about it the quality of haste. Hollister sprang to the door and opened it.

Thomas, the negro servant, stood on the threshold. He said: "I didn't know you was out here,
suh, till jus' now when I was goin' to bed an' saw
the light. Somebody telephoned about half hour ago
that Miss Leslie's ma was taken bad an' they was
lookin' everywhere for her."

Behind them Leslie's face went white. She
brushed the men aside and started down the path
at a run.

"Hold on," Hollister shouted. "I'll get the car."

By the time he had the garage open, she was at
his side. "Get into this," she ordered. "Your coat is
still wet, and it has cleared off cold."

He slipped into the old dressing gown that she
was holding for him, and that he used occasionally
as a sort of overall when the studio was chill.

"Thanks," he said, as the gears gnashed their
teeth under his inexpert hands. Then, like a nervous
horse, the roadster bounded clear of the garage, and
with agonized protest the clutch caught up its load
and hurled it forward.

CHAPTER 2

*D*RIVING with his usual watchful intensity, Hollister had no words for the silent little form that sat beside him. Once when they topped a hill and the full force of the chill night wind struck them, her thoughtfulness in remembering the robe in the midst of her own distress touched him through his preoccupation and, rather to his surprise, he dropped his hand from the wheel to cover hers for a fleeting instant.

Swiftly they dropped down the hill, the deserted street flowing smoothly up to meet them, and the rows of street lamps marching past on either side then stopping rigidly at attention as the roadster jerked to a standstill in front of the Gresham Arms.

Leslie's apartment was four floors up, at the top of the building. Light prisoned by four austere walls—confusion—a fat woman in a rocking chair—a medium-sized man standing—somebody leafing over a telephone directory—Leslie disappearing through a door across the room and closing it behind her as he reached it.

Hollister turned around. The people were vaguely familiar, their faces flashing up at him out of the past like portraits by some mediocre artist once seen in some forgotten gallery.

The man said: "Good evening, Mr. Hollister. I am glad they located Leslie at last. Mrs. Morgan was taken sick almost an hour ago."

The woman took it up then, in a resentful, monotonous voice: "We have the apartment across the hall. I heard somebody call out, then there was a sound like a fall, and I said to—"

Hollister gave up the effort to place the faces. They carried to his mind only some vague association with fish. They were probably unimportant, he thought. They were staring at him rather strangely. What he must do was to put their personalities aside and listen to what they were saying.

Then his gaze lifted and took in the opposite wall. It was windowless. At its center stood a small table with a light protected by a shield that illumined only a fan-shaped area of white plaster. In this field of illumination hung two portraits sketched in colored chalk on a dark ground. One he recognized instantly as himself, but himself as he had looked twenty years ago. The sketch was vibrant with life. It added to his feeling of unreality. He crossed the room and examined the other portrait. He had never seen Mrs. Morgan, but here she was. What was it that Leslie had said? "Small, and dark, and—brave." And the sketch was done with the same veracity and stark economy of means that had characterized her verbal portrait.

A purely detached emotion that had nothing to do with the tragedy that was housed in the little apartment and which, as a matter of fact, had gone out of his mind, contracted his throat and blurred his vision. He caressed a line with the tip of his narrow index finger as though it were something to which the sense of touch would respond. "By God," he said to himself, "she has it. She knows."

Leslie's voice cut through then, bringing him

to his senses, and swinging him back to face the room. She was standing in the doorway of the inner room, cool, and entirely self-possessed. "Has anyone called a doctor?" she enquired.

The occupants of the room gave off vague, negative sounds. Hollister sprang to the telephone, dislodging the body which was occupying the space before it and still ineffectually leafing through the telephone directory. The form dropped into the background without his even realizing its sex. He said: "I'll have my own doctor here at once." Then he called a number.

Dr. Pendleton was at home, fortunately, and he promised to run over immediately. Hollister went to the door to give Leslie the news, and she called to him to enter. With that fatal and indolent habit common with artists of classifying individuals as types, and picturing them in advance as belonging to this or that category, Hollister was unprepared for what he saw. "Infirm Mother" had meant—well, one of those very old women of Rembrandt's. Even Leslie's sketch had not forewarned him, because with that extraordinary gift of hers, she stressed neither youth or age, but essential personality. Now the form that he saw stretched on the white counterpane astonished him by its youth. He realized with a sense of shock that Mrs. Morgan was possibly younger than he. And she was beautiful, but of an almost transparent fragility. He took a bowl of water from Leslie, and held it while she wrung out compresses and held them gently to the white forehead.

There were sounds of arrival in the outer room, bodies shuffling up from chairs, and the doctor's professional briskness.

Leslie opened the door and invited the doctor to enter. Then Hollister heard her thanking and dismissing the people.

Dr. Pendleton entered, looked Hollister over in surprise, smiled slightly under his clipped mustache, said "Hello, Felix," and turned toward the bed.

The bedroom door closed, leaving Hollister alone in the living room. The relief from the anonymous presences that had been occupying it was enormous. His scattered faculties synthesized sharply and picked up the portraits, following the free inevitable drawing with an almost sensual delight. "But how could she do it?" he kept asking himself as he scrutinized his own face. "I haven't looked like that since—well, since the old days in Paris—since before I was married."

Dr. Pendleton entered, closed the bedroom door, and seated himself in the rocking chair. Then he went deliberately about the business of taking out a cigarette and tapping the tobacco down against his thumb-nail. His hands were fat and blunt, and at first glance appeared soiled, but upon closer observation the discoloration resolved itself into a thatch of black wiry hair that extended over the first joints of the fingers, and nails that were stained with chemicals. As the hands of a surgeon, you would have regarded them skeptically until you had seen them at work; then the slow pondered precision of each movement would have converted you. His large body seemed to rest in a perpetual lethargy within the limits of which he could exist indefinitely without sleep, and from which he lifted himself only upon rare occasions with a slow heavy-jowled smile, accompanied by a startling, almost fanatical, lighting of peculiarly opaque sloe-colored eyes.

Hollister, standing watching the doctor, his deliberate unfaltering manipulation of the cigarette, his flaccid bulk filling the ample chair, now sensed as he always did when alone with him another subtler insulation with which he surrounded himself—a sort of invisible, impenetrable aura from the protective screen of which Pendleton regarded him with dislike, suspicion, even, at times, hostility.

"Well, Bob," he enquired at length, "how is she? Nothing serious, I hope."

The doctor lit his cigarette, savoring his moment of suspense, and looking the other man over curiously, and with eyes that were frankly speculative. Then he snapped the match toward the empty grate and said: "Nothing serious. She'll come around. By the way, who's her doctor?"

Hollister did not know, and Pendleton supposed that he would have to get in touch with him at once and turn his patient over to him. The thought came to Hollister how alien Pendleton seemed against this background. At home, when Miriam was there, he dropped in often. His status was that not only of physician, but of intimate friend. It was an open secret that he had been in love with her before her marriage, and when she had brought Hollister home to live, she had brought her talents to bear upon the delicate task of reforming the disappointed admirer into the devoted friend. She had succeeded. She always did in her adjustment of human relationships. There were even times when under her persuasive charm the two men would meet for the moment in a free if uninspiring comradeship, which was dominated and directed always by Miriam. But this summer, with his wife away, he had seen little of the doctor.

Yet, strangely enough, this very night Pendleton had sought him out at the club. Hollister had been dining alone when he had arrived at his table and had stood massive and hesitant, looking down at him. He had refused an invitation to dine, but had accepted a highball, and had lowered himself to a seat. His protective aura was gone for the moment, and noting this, Hollister realized how indispensable it was to the man. With it he was almost oracular, the physician invested with ancient mysteries, an intimate of birth and death. Without it his mental processes were revealed with almost indecent nakedness, and they were the primitive and uncomplicated processes of a child.

Hollister, watching him, had experienced a sense of amused superiority, tempered by an involuntary pang of sympathy—almost of pity. He could see so plainly the struggle that had gone forward behind the pretentious façade, finally cracking it and leaving him exposed. His lumbering canine fidelity and devotion to Miriam, his eagerness for news of her, at grips with his aversion for Hollister, ending in final surrender and acceptance of the inevitable.

Saving him the embarrassment of enquiring, Hollister had plunged at once, volubly, into a recital of their travels, topping it off with excerpts from a letter which had just arrived from Felicia. He had been particularly pleased with her critical estimate of certain pieces of statuary that she had discovered in the Luxembourg, and reading it aloud to Pendleton he experienced one of his rare moments of almost overwhelming paternal pride. For a moment the contagion of an emotion warm and human had united them, and under its influence Pendleton had got heavily to his feet and dropped his hand on Hollister's shoulder. "Chip off the old block, eh!" he had said.

Hollister, looking now at the deliberately negatived bulk of the physician, could scarcely believe that their meeting had been less than two hours ago.

Pendleton said: "By the way, if you're personally interested in Mrs. Morgan you ought to see that she gets out of this heat for a while. She has almost no vitality, and these rooms up here under this flat roof must be terrific on hot days."

"That's quite a coincidence," Hollister replied. "I had just been planning to send them up to the camp for a month. How soon do you think they can go?"

Pendleton's look was one of veiled, inimical speculation; then he answered casually: "Oh, I should say in a day or two, as soon as she comes up from this turn. But you'll have to consult her own doctor, of course." He took out a prescription pad and a silver pencil, and after tapping his bared front teeth contemplatively for a moment, inscribed a line of hieroglyphics and signed it. "She should have this right away," he told Hollister as he handed him the slip.

"Good, the car's downstairs. I'll run uptown at once and get it."

He had his hand on the knob when Pendleton's words arrested him. "Hadn't you better change?" he asked dryly.

Hollister looked back and met the deliberately blanked-out gaze of the physician. Then he glanced down at himself, laughed, and said with sudden self-consciousness: "How absurd of me. You see, we were at the studio together, Leslie and I, and when the news came we rushed over just as we were, without stopping to change. I say," he laughed again, "wouldn't Miriam give me the devil if she knew?"

Pendleton did not give him an answering laugh. His eyes were still noncommittal, and Hollister's embarrassment increased. He said, defensively: "After all, this isn't so bad. It's an unconventional getup, but it does cover my nakedness."

Pendleton got up and held out his hand for the prescription. "I'll take that along and have it sent back, when I go. Now I'll go in for a final look at Mrs. Morgan, and you get home and into either a suit of clothes or bed." He opened the door and gave Hollister a slight shove through it, and into his heavy face came a look at once suspicious, resentful, and lewd. "You artists," he said. "You insist on being a law to yourselves, don't you?" Then he closed the door.

CHAPTER 3

WINGFIELDS had been built by Gabriel Aubery
in the mid-eighties. And Miriam always referred to
old Gabe as "the founder," preferring to identify
the family with postwar success and thrift rather
than, by probing the obscurity that lay beyond the
battle smoke of the 'sixties, to establish a dubious
claim to antebellum aristocracy.

And this was quite in character, for she was
possessed of that type of snobbishness quite common
in America—a type which finds its satisfaction in a
wide, democratic, and socially inferior acquaintance,
in contrast with which, while indulging in hearty,
even boisterous, intimacy, one takes on an added
luster. There was nothing that she liked better than
on market day to meet some grizzled and tobacco-
stained countryman and have him drawl, as he
reached his paw over the wagon wheel: "Proud to
see you, ma'am. Why, old Gabe lent me my first
money after the war. Sound and tough as a brogan,
too, he was." And she would stand and yarn with
him while Exeter whisked past in its late model
cars and admired her for the hearty and unaffected
democrat that she was.

When Gabe Aubery had returned to Carolina
in 'sixty-five, his entire worldly estate was represented by the bag of hide and bones which he be-
strode, and which had gasped and tottered its way
from Appomattox, a living witness to the magnanimity of a conquering but greathearted Union.

He fed his horse, starved himself, sweated and saved and, at the end of five years, he acquired a tract of land bordering on Hatton Road, two miles from the sleepily agricultural hamlet of Exeter.

Old Jeremiah Enfield, who was preparing the deed, was closeted with Gabe, trying to think of a name by which to record the tract, when the surveyor sent in the plat. It showed an accurate drawing of a chimney swallow, lying, wings extended as though in flight, north and south along the highway.

"Oh, hell," Gabe had said, folding back his mustache with two practiced fingers and smacking the spittoon with a brown liquid projectile. "Thar ye are—call her Wingfields."

In twenty years, three steps—farming, merchandising, banking, which accomplished the rehabilitation of many of the family fortunes after the war— had lifted Gabe to a position of wealth and importance in the thriving town of Exeter. Also, quite as a matter of course, he had married, trimmed his mustache, substituted a cigar for a cud, built the First Baptist Church, and begotten a son. But his real passion was Exeter, and his bank was the heart that pumped life through its singing arteries, until the town stood forth upon its five hills, raw, provincial, loud-mouthed and vital, bellowing for a material prosperity so vast that, devouring to satiety, it might at last forget war's long starvation.

When Gabe was fifty, he looked upon his handiwork and found it good. It was then that in a small shy way he began to take himself seriously as a founder. He summoned his wife, his son—then twenty-two, who was a none too promising employee of the bank,—and a bright young architect. The

result of this collaboration was a mansion in which a
founder might be expected to get seriously about the
business of founding. To Gabe it was indebted for
what simple virtues were to be found within its
walls—good square rooms, large fireplaces, gray native granite without, plain solid plaster within.
From the architect it received high gable windows
surmounted by iron grillwork, and a rather preposterous tower containing the grand stairway.

Mrs. Aubery had come off quite literally with
flying colors, and her stained-glass windows, which
climbed in a spiral with the stairs, even on a dull
morning left Exeter gasping in awed admiration.
But this was nothing to the effect produced on a
bright afternoon. Then the westering sun smote full
upon the windows, exploding the entire spectrum
inward, stunning the vision with multicolored
hurtling debris, and converting the huge perpen-
dicular cylinder of the tower into a child's kaleidoscope magnified to gigantic proportions.

It was quite typical that Gabriel Junior had
asked timidly for a poolroom, and had never played
in it. Pool at that period of Exeter development con-
noted the man-about-town. People should have
slapped him on the back and shouted, "Ah, ah, the
old pool sharper." But they didn't. They knew him
too well. He died at the age of forty-six without having ever attained to the saving virtue of a single
damning male vice.

But he did marry, and from his timid and
feeble loins sprang Miriam, to project beyond the
intervening generation all of old Gabe's driving
power, his singleness of purpose, his blind acquisi-
tive impulse toward material success.

CHAPTER 4

*A*ND here, forty-four years later, at a charming
Wingfields bowered in ivy and shorn by Miriam
of grillwork and stained glass, was Felix Hollister,
the man she had married.

He lay in bed on the sleeping porch that overhung the rear garden, and looked away through the
treetops to the gable of the studio rising sharp and
angular into the morning sky, and at the play of
young sunlight on the dew-drenched foliage. A cool,
intermittent breeze was blowing and it would let
the leaves fall into great masses of shadow and highlight, then suddenly blow the composition to pieces,
disintegrating the values and stippling the shade
with dazzling flecks of sun. In an adjacent maple he
caught the flash of a cardinal's wing, the first that
he had seen since June, and he remembered that it
was September, and that tomorrow Miriam and the
children would be home from their summer abroad.

Now the cardinal was at his matins, a shade less
passionately, Hollister thought with a smile, than he
had been when he had left for the honeymoon in
June. But his mate was emitting her invariable brief
admonitory response. She wasn't going to let him
forget that it was their business to nest, brood, mi-
grate, in an ever-recurring cycle, and furthermore,
that while music did well enough in its way art for
art's sake feathered no nests. The analogy to his own
married life caused Hollister to smile. Well, men

were foolish to expect honeymoons to last. Like
everything else, they were predestined incidents in
the inevitable cycle. He, at least, was to be con-
gratulated, for when that phase had passed, Miriam
had demonstrated her genius for homemaking, and
had integrated herself into his life as an absolutely
indispensable element.

She had always said that she would have two
children, first a boy and then a girl. And, doubtless
impressed by the almost uncanny combination of
luck and judgment that signalized her career, within
four years the capricious arbiter of such affairs had
met her specifications to the letter.

When Aubery had arrived, finances had still
been a vital problem, and they had taken him into
their room; the ivory crib standing between the twin
beds made a small, warm spot in the too-large, too-
chill house. They hadn't minded getting up at night,
their hands touching, their eyes meeting, over the
unaccustomed tasks. It drew them closer, fitted the
three of them together in a sweet, tacit, interde-
pendence.

But when Miriam returned from the hospital
with little Felicia, she had gone into the room in
which she had spent her childhood, and which
opened into the shining new nursery. That, of
course, had been natural enough. There were two
children to be cared for now. She was never one to
leave important details to another, and even the
experienced trained nurse who was placed in nom-
inal charge must be closely supervised.

Hollister understood this, of course, and looked
forward to the time when, the nurse having established herself in Miriam's confidence, she would re-

turn. Then the room which had grown so unaccountably large would contract again, drawing them to each other, folding them close in its warm deep privacy, and everything would be just as it had been before.

The realization that this would never happen came to him slowly, and, as with all of her plans, through the gradual emergence of the completed pattern by which she ordered her life.

There was not a single particular in which he could say that she had changed. Only now he gradually became aware that whereas, before, her emotion toward him had been tender and strongly personalized, now it had expanded to embrace the children as well as himself, and that while still tender it was primarily a primitive, almost fierce, protectiveness.

It was as though in her straight flight through life, in her adherence to an accepted and inexorable pattern, she had said of mating: "Now that is over. It has served its purpose." Then she had poured all of her undiminished energy, her inherited genius for organization and salesmanship, into the task of making their future secure.

Nothing could stop her. Within four years of her marriage she had carried her first two major objectives. She had established her family. She had taken a young unknown artist into a country where, as Chick Bedford had remarked, the vast majority of the inhabitants thought an etcher was someone who had been bitten by a flea, and had made him a going concern.

And so the months after Miriam's return had lengthened, and that brief moment was upon them which follows mating and childbearing when, with infinite tact, delicacy and understanding, a man and a woman must learn to be lovers again or lose from their lives forever a thing irreplaceable and infinitely precious. And Miriam had not recognized this moment. Overshadowed by the enormous designs that she contemplated, it had seemed of little importance, and it simply hadn't been in the pattern.

Hollister knew that down the hall there was a door. That he could go to it, each successive time with a growing sense of estrangement, and opening it without knocking, say "Hello, Miriam." But he knew, as she never seemed to know, that there is no such thing as an enduring passion by appointment, that a complete spiritual and physical love between a man and a woman is not a hardy perennial, but a series of brief, sudden and inexplicable flowerings, groping toward perfection through a cycle of a hundred births and deaths. Sown by the accidental touch of hands, the brushing of glances, each life rushing to full flower, to be seized instantly or to be lost utterly, and the cycle broken.

But while he sensed this changed attitude, which closed a definite epoch in their married life, Miriam projected him into the one which followed, with such velocity that at first he was only dimly conscious of the change. Once the nurse had proven herself capable of taking care of the children, and Miriam felt that it was safe to leave them, they spent a great deal of time away from Exeter. The pioneer in Miriam, only half submerged by a generation of easy living, prompted her to the purchase of a large touring car, and over the incredibly bad roads of the period and locality she hurled it with complete mastery but at an appalling speed.

Herself lacking an appreciation of the antique, she nevertheless, with her amazing flair for merchandising, appraised its value to others. Spring would find them encamped in Savannah, Charleston, St. Augustine. Or amid the glories of a Virginia autumn Hollister would be wafted north to Williamsburg, Richmond, or the fountainhead of Jeffersonian architecture at Charlottesville. Having arrived and settled themselves in convenient quarters, Miriam would canvass for subjects. Again that unique gift of hers for knowing instinctively the thing which would be of value to others would function, and without a real aesthetic sense of her own—indeed, holding it a little in contempt—she would return shortly with a list of subjects which would be unerringly right.

Hollister then would be put furiously to work on a wrought-iron gateway, a church spire, a court swarming with negro life, an architectural monument, and Miriam would pursue the curators of museums, directors of art galleries, and arrange for the exhibition of the etchings when completed.

It was not an unhappy time for Hollister. There was a stir and bustle that was exciting, and he was pleasurably infected by Miriam's certainty of an early and golden success. And after all he was translating beauty into a medium that he understood. He could sink himself into it until by some subtle process of absorption their identities would merge into a complete whole. Then when it was finished he would come up from it, enervated but uplifted, his body slack in a sort of voluptuous lassitude.

Of course, drawing had never given him the sense of passionate exaltation that he had got from modeling. He could remember himself back in those days in the Paris studio, standing before a figure, the clay still wet, and saying with the egotism of a god: "That's mine, and it is good because I made it." But still, drawing and the rigid exactions of the etcher's art had given him at least the illusion of a spiritual and physical satisfaction. And if anything was left to be desired it was, strangely enough under the circumstances, Miriam herself who furnished it. She was unusually handsome, with a figure that escaped the voluptuous only because of its extraordinary fitness. She attracted men. Even amid the assertive decencies of Exeter society, that prevented expression by word or deed, they lusted after her, and their lust expressed itself in an exaggerated courtesy that propelled her up steps by the elbow, helped her into the car, lingered over a casual handshake. And although Hollister knew that her spell was a physical delusion, he drew a vicarious and sensuous satisfaction from having her wanted. It gave him a sense of enviable possession, which is such a vital factor in any sex relationship.

And so their life together had proceeded, without deflection, upon the course that Miriam had mapped out. There was no waste. Everything that they had was utilized toward an end that was concerned only with tangibles, and so was visualized by her to the most minute detail.

Now, thinking back along the years, Hollister wondered if the pattern had not been started long before the children were born. Probably that day when they had stood before his first bronze in the little gallery on Montparnasse. Possibly even back in the days when they had been boy and girl together here in Exeter and, because she had been rich and he poor, she in complete adjustment with the crowd and he more or less of a lost dog, she had taken him under her wing and had fought his battles for him.

But that visit of hers to Paris had been definitely the conscious beginning. He had been twenty-two, and it was their first meeting since high school. His parents had died within a few months of each other, when he was seventeen, and he had taken his small insurance patrimony and gone to New York to study. He had always meant to study art, more specifically, to model. Then there had been three years in the North and two abroad.

Miriam had crossed with her mother after her graduation. Mrs. Aubery was at that time in mourning for her husband who had died shortly before the term closed. She was inconsolable at the loss of a partner whose mediocrity, moral rectitude, and spiritual vacuity all matched her own so completely that their union was one of those of which it was said in Exeter that they are made in heaven. And her genuine grief, reinforced by the conventional prohibitions of a bereaved wife as practiced at home, circumscribed her orbit sharply during the Paris sojourn.

It was unfortunate for Hollister that her visit should have come at that time, for it was one of those moments in his career when he should have been free to give himself without reservation to his work. It was the early summer of nineteen-eight, the year that, encouraged by Hans Purrmann and Mrs. Michael Stein, Henri Matisse had taken a few students into his atelier. Hollister's indubitable talent and his reputation as a hard worker had interested the artist, and he had admitted him on a sort of probation. It was an opportunity that made him the envy of his entire acquaintance in the Quarter, but they were soon speculating as to how long he would last with so many absences chalked up against him.

And so Hollister had devoted himself to Miriam. And it was characteristic of both of them that after the first week, with the exception of the time spent in the Quarter, it was Miriam who was arranging the itineraries instead of Hollister.

Miriam had been confused by the life of the Quarter. She had not been a prude, for a prude is consciously virtuous, and her conscious attitude had been deliberately, painstakingly, the reverse. Intellectually she had forced herself to accept the unconventionality of Hollister's friends, but under her apparently gay acceptance he had sensed the inescapable fact that she was continually and profoundly shocked.

But with her instinct for improving the shining hour, she manifested the greatest interest in the exhibits, private and public, to which Hollister conducted her. She would pause before a canvas and say: "Now, Holly, tell me exactly why this is good." And he, filled with that season's particular enthusiasms, would pour out his likes and dislikes, never in doubt, sure with the uncompromising egotism of youth.

Always she would stand listening with a frown

of intense concentration on her face, and later he would be surprised and flattered to hear her repeat his sentences word for word and with a most convincing effect at some studio gathering. "Monet!" she would exclaim. "He's old stuff."—and everyone in the group felt immediately that she belonged.

And then had come the great day when his first bronze was exhibited. Unable to restrain his eagerness, he had been on the doorstep with Miriam when the gallery was opened. The figure was a small one, not over eighteen inches in height. The nude, slender form of a woman gave the effect of hanging wearily forward with the arms extended and agonized as though nailed to an invisible cross. The face was twisted with pain, but the lips were curved in a triumphant smile. Upon the base was a small plate bearing the word: "Maternity."

Standing before it, with Miriam beside him, Hollister was so moved that he did not realize that she was puzzled, disturbed. At last she said: "Tell me yourself, Holly. How do you feel about it?" And he had answered: "How can I? It's me—that's all."

Then standing there, he had told himself the things that he couldn't say aloud, even to Miriam. He thought: "It's crude. God, I've got a lot to learn! But there's something there. There's worship. There in that figure that I made with my hands is a flicker of the worship of beauty that I felt that first day when my model took the pose."

That night, sitting together at a little sidewalk table, with the night life of the boulevard streaming past, loitering, laughing, drifting, she had said: "You don't mind if I ask you some practical questions,

do you, Holly?" And he had smiled and told her to
go ahead.

In an incredibly short time she had her facts
catalogued and was counting them off one by one
on her fingers. He had been working for five years,
and "Maternity" was the first concrete result. He
felt that he was still only a beginner. It had cost
him eighty-five dollars to have the casting made.
Its sale was such a remote possibility that the idea
might as well be dismissed at once. His funds were
practically exhausted. He had a natural talent for
drawing, but it didn't interest him particularly. He
didn't know why, only a pencil felt dead in his
hands, while a lump of clay that you could grasp
was something that lived. "Why, you can hold it
in your hands," he had told her, "and you can feel
its heart beat." Then he told her that he didn't
know what he was going to do next. That was the
thing that she found it hardest to believe. She had
always known exactly where she was going, what
she wanted, and where to get it. Finally she raised
her face to his and looked candidly into his eyes.
"I just can't get you, Holly. Not knowing what you
want—what you're going to do next."

He had sat for a moment looking into her eyes,
and suddenly he had known that he needed her
terribly. That even in these few weeks her grasp of
practical matters that to him were formidable, at
times almost terrifying, had given him a sense of
security; that she would be leaving in a week, and
that the thought of parting was more than he could
bear. "But," he had told her huskily, "I do know
what I want, and I know what I am going to do

next." Then he had taken her in his arms at the
little sidewalk table, and kissed her.

After a moment she had asked shyly: "Was that
a Latin Quarter kiss?" And he had told her that it
was a good old-fashioned Exeter kiss, the kind that
compromised a woman beyond redemption except
by marriage, and that he stood ready to make good
as soon as he could raise the price of a ring.

They had got up together. He had stopped
to buy some cigarettes, with Miriam by his side.
Then he had heard her gasp, and had turned to find
a large, bearded man in a velveteen coat grasping
the lobe of one of her ears between a thumb and
index finger, while with his other hand he lifted
her hair away very gently.

The picture came back to him so vividly that
he laughed aloud. Miriam looking into the intent,
bearded face with an expression of horror—the
man's surprise, then overwhelming embarrassment,
and his stammered: "Mais, c'est un compliment,
mademoiselle,"—then, with dawning understanding,
"Pardon, you do not live in the Quarter, no? Ah,
you must be an American. But you have the most
beautiful ear in the world."

Miriam had turned her back to the man. She
felt that she had been outraged. Hollister's eyes and
those of the man had met, and the look of understanding, almost of apology for her, that Hollister's
had flashed had been intercepted by Miriam. It was
the only time Hollister could remember ever having seen her in the grip of a cold, deadly fury. The
man had terminated the trying scene. He had patted
Hollister intimately on the shoulder and said:
"Take the lady home, son, back to America, and

tell her that in France all men are brutes." Then he had sauntered away to a nearby table. All about them at the little tables people were looking at them and laughing.

On the way home they had stopped on a park bench to have it out. It was then for the first time that Hollister had suspected that Miriam's sense of humor had a blind spot. She always had such good stories. She could keep the crowd laughing for hours at a time, back in Exeter. She ought to see how funny this situation had been. But, instead, she kept right on arranging the words bestial, disgusting, vulgar, into various combinations, and vowing that the creature had deliberately made her ridiculous, and that she'd never get over the humiliation.

It was a long time before she was sure whether she would forgive Hollister, but her passion for making plans came to his rescue, and she had finally taken refuge in practical details. She would have to go home and figure it all out. Her self-confidence was superb. Hollister was to go on working until he heard definitely from her. And he needn't worry himself to death over ways and means. She would take charge of practical matters from now on.

Then Miriam had left for home, taking some of his sketches and charcoal drawings with her. He had wanted her to include at least one of his plaster figures, but, somehow, she hadn't seemed interested.

Presently things had commenced to happen. Miriam was never one for love letters in the usual romantic sense. Her emotions expressed themselves in action, and her absorption in their mutual future resulted in a series of brief, concise records of her progress.

She had stopped for a month in New York, on her way back to Exeter, and had studied art in its economic aspects. She had exhibited Hollister's drawings to dealers and they had been received with flattering attention. She had met a certain dealer— a good one, who was enthusiastic and wanted to take Hollister on when he returned. This dealer had even offered to stake Hollister, but a short intensive investigation of this phase of the business had convinced her that it was not worth considering. It was very important in that it meant a sincere belief in the artist's ability. If the dealer was actually willing to put money on his judgment, he meant what he said. But they had a way, she had ascertained, of making a cash advance against future work, then they would think that they owned the artist body and soul. No, sir! This was her proposition, hers and Hollister's, and she intended to get off to a clean start.

Then, with that decided, she and the dealer had got down to brass tacks. They had canvassed the field and he had demonstrated the advantages of etchings as the shortest cut to a really substantial success. He had pointed out that in paintings you could put weeks into a single picture, then it would have to fetch a large price to make it pay for the time and labor involved. And there were comparatively few people who could afford a good picture. But with etchings it was different. You made your plate, then printed dozens of copies. And there were hundreds of customers for good etchings at prices ranging from twenty-five to fifty dollars. Hollister must concentrate on that medium. He was destined to become one of America's foremost etchers. Later, of course, he'd have money enough to do exactly as he pleased.

Then in the spring, Destiny had collaborated with Miriam, and events that would normally have resisted even her determined manipulation transpired in Exeter and completed her pattern to the smallest detail. When the administrators of her father's estate finished their labors, it was found that reverses had dissipated his fortune, and that there remained only Wingfields and ten thousand dollars insurance. Then Mrs. Aubery had died, and the estate had become Miriam's.

"Can't you see how it is going to work out, Holly?" she had written. "We'll settle here. The place will give us a background, and the money will stake us in style in Exeter for two years. The South is becoming suddenly prosperous, and we can count on local loyalty. We simply *can't* miss. You are coming back after years of foreign study. You are a real hundred-percenter, and you are coming back to interpret your own region instead of going expatriate like so many other Americans. They'll love it, and they will back you here to the limit. Cable if you need money for the trip, and plan to come at once. I am crazy to see you and talk it all over. Love, Miriam."

It all seemed incredibly long ago to Hollister as he lay listening to the birds, and watching the warm light climb down the trunks of the sycamores as the sun mounted over the roof. He raised his hand and pressed a call-button. In exactly twenty minutes, Thomas would appear with breakfast. Just time enough for shower and shave.

But instead of getting up, Hollister let his mind

drift back to the early days. It seemed a far cry from
the bread and tea of the Paris breakfast, the damp
chill little room, the loneliness. It would be good
to see Miriam again; to feel the house quicken to
her vital presence. ˜And he would have three days
with the children before they left for college. He
found himself wondering a little wistfully what they
would be like now. What with college, summer
camps, house parties, they had grown to be almost
strangers during the past few years.

He thought that he could get a fairly accurate
picture of Aubery. The boy had sprung from his
loins, but he was Miriam's creation. Smart, hard,
and sound as a silver dollar. He was taking business
administration at Yale, and last Christmas only the
boy's charming manners—a little too charming perhaps, a little too obviously "Southern"—had dis-
guised the fact that he had definitely patronized his
artist father. Hollister had not even been consulted
about that boost in his allowance, and had been told
about it quite casually after the holidays were over.
Miriam was very proud of Aubery. He had given
her pointers on certain income tax allowances, and
together they had shaved the returns so thin that
Hollister had been alarmed and, with the artist's
ignorance and fear of law, had half expected a call
from an investigator of the collector's office.

But with Felicia it was different. There was
something of Hollister in her, that lay beneath the
pliant exterior and that stubbornly refused the conventional mold. Curiously the picture of her that
was most easily evoked in his memory was that of
a slight, tiny figure trotting about the studio after
him, and holding up a pencil and paper with the

insistent demand for a picture. Subsequent impressions from kindergarten, grammar school, high school periods lay over this early one, but could not efface it. When she had gone to Vassar she had elected the arts, music, drawing. Miriam had heartily approved. Art was a good thing provided there was a business head in the family.

A knock sounded on the door. Thomas stepped out on the porch, and, grinning at Hollister, said: "Good mornin', suh. You mus' be oversleep. It's pas' eight o'clock, an' Miss Leslie been in the studio half hour." He went about the business of setting up the folding table and placing the breakfast tray. He looked speculatively at Hollister, and his grin widened. "We better be gettin' in practice, you know, suh. Miss Miriam comin' home tomorrow."

$\mathcal{I}$N THE studio Leslie had everything ready for the day's work. She looked small and tired, Hollister thought, standing beside the big press with the dampened sheets, the ink and plates all placed ready for the heavy labor of the day.

"Your holiday isn't going to do you much good," he said, "slaving away like this as soon as you get home. You should have stayed the full month as we planned. I was really getting along famously without you."

She gave him a faintly indulgent smile. "I've just been taking stock," she said. "I wonder how many days you actually put in at the studio."

Hollister looked up, his brow wrinkled from the enormous effort of calculation. At last he said lamely: "Well, you see I was only a part-time printer. My real job was chauffeur and janitor to a rich old lady and her daughter who were playing at camping out in the hills."

"Exactly, and if they hadn't stopped playing and laid off the help at the end of three weeks, there would have been a sad dearth of art in our fair Southland for a full twelvemonth—"

"I trow," Hollister finished for her.

"Not at all. I ween."

"That," concluded Hollister, "is always a woman's privilege. For my part I think it more manly to trow. Therefore I trow."

46

The thought came to him how foolish Miriam would think them, and he wondered how she would take this new relationship that had grown up between Leslie and himself during the past month. It would, of course, strike her as trivial and a little undignified. She would quite understand their telling each other amusing stories, and she would accept that. With her own reputation as a storyteller, she could look upon Leslie's efforts as a professional might upon the performance of an amateur, and her sense of superiority would preclude the possibility of jealousy.

But this pointless fooling, as she would call it, would be different. It was nothing that you could set your teeth in and carry away to bury like a good bone against the next dinner-party conversation, or talk fest at the club. And if you tried to repeat it afterwards, it was simply moronic drivel. And moronic drivel was of no value under the sun.

This line of thought brought Hollister back to the portrait of Miriam that, down in some deep stratum of his subconscious mind, he had been revising during her absence, and he sketched in a new and revealing line. Miriam didn't have a ray of authentic humor. But she had such an excellent substitute that it had taken him all of these years to be certain. And her counterfeit coin was her amazing sense of values. She could appraise a story, a situation, instantly, by its effect upon others. If it produced laughter in the discerning, it was effective and it went into her repertoire. Situations would arise from time to time that would touch the combination and, automatically, from the storehouse of her infallible memory would come the appropriate

joke or story. It would be greeted by genuine laughter, and since she had told it and had provoked the
response she was perfectly sincere in her belief that
she possessed an unusually keen sense of humor.

"Oh, hell," Hollister said to himself, "Miriam
is the grandest girl in the world. She is true as steel,
and I am jolly lucky to have her to look out for me."

CHAPTER 6

Two days after the home-coming, there occurred a situation in the studio. Not a crisis, for crises never developed in the Hollister household. This particular situation had sprung full-bodied from Hollister's negligence during Miriam's absence, and his guilty realization of that, coupled with his inherent inability to mobilize his forces of resistance, put him at a disadvantage. Then, too, upon Miriam's return she had been simply splendid about everything. When he had confessed to the vacation in the hills, she had said: "That was swell of you, Holly. I am glad you managed to get down out of the clouds and do something about it." Then she had hastened on with plans for "taking up" Mrs. Morgan. And it must be admitted that it was with some slight misgivings that Hollister saw her becoming a "case" and receiving an assignment somewhere between the projected Exeter Maternity Hospital and the Junior League milk fund. He had said then: "You'll have to step lightly, you know. She's not a charity." And Miriam had shelved the subject with: "Don't be ridiculous, Holly." Then Leslie had returned from lunch, and Felicia had dropped in, making a fourth for the situation.

Miriam had been doing some calculating. Now she said, casually: "We have just about half enough prints for the season, but I've thought of a way to take care of that. We will pull the proofs and a dozen prints from each plate. Those will take care of the dealers and the fall and winter shows. Then we'll ship the plates to New York and have Lontier print lots of twenty-five as we need them."

Hollister saw the idea growing in Miriam's mind, building and elaborating itself rapidly as her plans always did. She went on: "As a matter of fact that's a swell idea, because when we are out with them in the South, if we run out of a certain popular subject, we can wire for more instead of waiting till next summer to run them here."

Hollister asked, "Do you mean have someone else make my prints?"

"Of course. They'll do perfectly well for the Southern shops and local exhibits. Only a connoisseur could tell the difference, and it would save you a lot of time that you could put in on new plates."

Hollister was instantly conscious of the mental attitudes of the several occupants of the room. The proposition that Miriam had made had destroyed the group unity, and now each drew in upon herself and waited. Leslie, who had taken a chair near them but not actually in the circle, got quietly to her feet and busied herself at the sink with some acid she had been mixing. Her back was an uncompromising silhouette against white enamel. Felicia sat forward, looking into his face with a penetrating, almost impersonal, scrutiny. She might have been watching a subject in a laboratory experiment. Miriam, engrossed with her plan, sat thinking straight ahead into the economics of her new policy, weighing the cost of the New York printing against Hollister's time and energy. Her face cleared. She said with finality: "It will work out splendidly, Holly. It's really an inspiration."

He was acutely uncomfortable and he wished that she had selected a time when they were alone to discuss the matter. Felicia's gaze was particularly disconcerting. He wished that she would give some sign as to her own feeling instead of watching him in that detached appraisal. His look asked her sympathy. But her answer was a slight ironic smile that framed and accentuated rather than softened her scrutiny. Behind him he could feel Leslie's gathering scorn. He thought miserably: "They both live off of me; even Leslie keeps going from what I have to earn, and they'll take it, then sit in judgment." He wanted to cry out to Miriam that he would feel like an artistic fake. That the only thing that made an etching was its completion under his hands. That was the only thing that he still clung to, and as long as he did that he was keeping faith with himself.

Instead he said, in a note almost of apology: "Of course, they'll be actually different. I work as hard at a print as I do on a plate. I know some of the other fellows have printing done. It's ethical and no doubt it's good business, but somehow I've always felt that when you signed your print and hadn't done every bit of it yourself, you weren't quite playing the game."

Aubery entered then, and stood leaning in the doorway, surveying them with an Olympian detachment. He had been playing tennis, and was wearing a sweat shirt and flannels. Fresh from his tremendous physical labors, his bronzed height and pulsing vitality made his father feel singularly pallid by comparison. Hollister had the conviction that if he spoke then his voice would pipe just a little in spite of all that he could do for it.

"What's it all about, Mater?" Aubery asked; then, seeing that Hollister was on the defensive: "Dad holding out on you?" The absurdity of this possibility appealed to his sense of humor, and he grinned good-naturedly down at his father. "How 'bout it, Dad," he said, "—need any help?"

Miriam deferred to him immediately, as though he were the man of the family, explaining her point of view; then turned back to Hollister, taking up the argument where Aubery's entrance had broken in on it. "Why, Holly," she said in her humoring voice, "can't you see you're talking nonsense? When you're selling a customer an etching, no matter who prints it you aren't selling a pig in a poke. They see the picture when they buy it, don't they?"

"Yes," said Hollister. "Yes, of course."

"And what's more," she went on, with triumphant logic, "does a sculptor cast his own bronzes? Of course he doesn't, and what's the difference?" She came over and tousled his hair with her comely, masculine hands. "You're an old darling," she told him, "and you'd just love to be temperamental, wouldn't you?" Then she looked at her wrist watch. "There," she said, "that's settled, and I'm late for my meeting."

At the door she turned. "You'll not be so pushed now, Holly, with this new arrangement. Why don't you close the studio for the afternoon and take Felicia over to the club or something? She'll be going in the morning and you ought to play around together for a while."

With a courtly bow, Aubery drew aside to let

her pass, then brought his racket twanging down
upon her flat firm buttocks. She countered with a
resounding slap, and they went roaring out and
across the garden together.

Hollister turned to Leslie with a rather embarrassed smile. "School's out," he said. "You can
run along home."

She thanked him with unnecessary formality,
and with a face that had been deliberately emptied
of all expression. Then she pulled her little hat
down over her ears and bade them a prim good
evening. But on her way to the door Felicia stopped
her, reaching out a long arm and plucking her by
the sleeve. Leslie turned back and, ignoring Hollister, they conversed in an idiom that was new in
his experience.

Holding the other girl by the sleeve Felicia
looked up and said: "I like you, Leslie, and I bet
you're fun. Let's see something of each other sometime."

Leslie laughed down at her, surprised but
pleased. "I've always liked you too," she admitted.
Then she asked casually, "Do you ever get tight?"

"Only occasionally, but when I do I'm said to
be something of a success."

"What about tonight then? I'll be in all evening. Drop over if you can break away."

"Swell," Felicia agreed.

"And by the way, I've got the makings," Leslie
threw over her shoulder as she closed the door.

Hollister smilingly asked: "Is that the way
women make friends nowadays?"

"Sure," Felicia answered unconcernedly. "Life
is too short for beating about the bush. You like a

person's looks and you say so. You stage a little party, take enough drinks to blast out the inhibitions, and when you come up out of it you are either going to be friends or you are not, and no time lost. It's not a bad system."

They laughed together, holding the lighter mood against a shyness that hovered between them.

Alone with his daughter, Hollister found himself strangely at a loss for words. Their relationship, which should have developed through the years into a gay comradery, had taken a wrong turning somewhere and had left them only a strangeness and a formality through which to reach toward each other. The long separations, followed by her brief, crowded visits home, gave them only occasional moments alone and these were spent in making conversation rather than in any spontaneous interchange of ideas. And under the surface of objective chatter he was always conscious of a reaching out of each to the other that somehow failed of contact, like hands that strive to meet and clasp in the dark. Always, over the trivial talk of school and play, he felt the hovering presence of something tremendous and elusive, something that if captured only once and put into words would suddenly prove the open-sesame to a complete intimacy. But he knew that this was not a thing to be taken by force, to be snatched and imprisoned between a day and another day. And tomorrow Felicia would be gone again, and the enigma of her essential self would have deepened, the distance between them widened, when the next hectic vacation should bring her home again.

And he speculated upon the tragedy of parenthood, the dismayed surprise of a father when his child is born, to find that he is less than nothing in its life, the sweet and gradual growth of dependence. Then the inevitable loosening of the bonds, the drifting, the far horizon—emptiness.

Now he looked up and met her gaze still fixed upon him in cool appraisal, and he said, "Well, Licia, shall we get on over to the club?"

She reached over and picked up a cigarette from the table, tapped the tobacco down, lighted it, and blew a funnel of smoke toward the Gothic shadows of the ceiling. Then she smiled across at him. "That your idea of a good time, Dad?"

Suddenly all of Hollister's preconceptions went into the discard. The cigarette—he didn't know that she smoked. The almost mocking tone of the question. The proffered friendship behind the smile. She wasn't a child any longer. She was a woman, and they were starting out all over again at scratch.

He laughed aloud. "God forbid! But—"

"But Mother told you to, and like a good, long-suffering papa you are willing to dress little Felicia up and take her to the circus. Well, you'll never have to do that again, Dad. I've grown up. No," she said, getting decisively to her feet, "we'll stay here and talk. I've been itching to know what you've been doing. Come and give me a look-see."

Hollister was excited as he stepped with her to the cabinet where he filed his prints. He knew from the letters that she had written from Europe that her point of view was fresh and her criticism surprisingly competent. And he felt instinctively that she would be honest. He handed her an etching of an old Charleston gateway, watching her face eagerly for her verdict.

She studied it for a moment, then said: "Your draftsmanship is practically flawless and so is your mastery of the medium, and the range of values is extraordinary. How in the world did you get this brilliance of effect?"

"That print," he said, beginning to expand under her approval, "is more than half dry point. I heightened my values by cutting directly into the plate after I'd finished biting it out with acid. I'm glad you like it."

"I don't say I like it," she said, meeting his eyes squarely. "I say it's a good job."

"Oh!" he said, taken aback. Then, defensively: "What's the matter with it?"

"It's hard to define. There's a sort of stale taste about it. I seem to remember your doing the same subject before. Didn't you?"

Hollister admitted that he had. Then went on to explain: "You see, it's a very popular subject, so when the plate wore down I made a new one."

"From the subject?"

"Why, no. I was too busy to get back down there then, so I copied the original."

"I see," she said slowly. "Do you do that often?"

"Why, yes," he answered. "There is a steady demand for what Miriam calls my standard subjects. Recently she found that a firm up north had perfected a steel surfacing process which makes a plate practically indestructible. So now as my old copper ones wear down I do them over and have them surfaced. Naturally it doesn't give me much time for browsing around and sketching."

Felicia put the print down and let her eyes wander over the studio with its ample spaces, its sumptuous furnishings; then she brought her gaze back to Hollister's face, and met his eyes fixed eagerly upon her. "Am I to tell you what I really feel about all of this, Dad,—the studio, this case of prints, Mamma's high-pressure management? Or am I to know my place?"

"Most criticism is tripe anyway," Hollister answered. "The best we can hope for is that it is at least honest. Go ahead."

"All right," she said. "Here goes. When we were in France we did one of the Citroën plants. I get the same feeling here: that I am doing a simply magnificent factory."

Hollister's face paled, then flushed. His suffering was so acute that instinctively he hit back. "Miriam tells me that it costs over three thousand a year to keep you in college. The trip this summer cost over two thousand. It takes fifteen thousand a year for us to live. Where'd you think it came from —art in an attic?"

Impulsively Felicia threw her arms about Hollister's neck and kissed him. Then with her face held against his she said: "I'm a cad. Just a common, dirty cad. Won't you forget that I said that?"

Hollister released himself and leaned back against the cabinet. "Let's talk this out," he said.

"No, Dad. Please don't. I'd rather not."

"I insist," Hollister said in a hard level voice. "A little while ago you told me you were a woman now and not a child, and I thought: 'Fine. Now we are going to start out on the level, talk things out, understand each other.' But now I see that you are

not willing to play the game. You avail yourself of
youth's privilege to blurt out unpleasant truths,
then seize a woman's right to change the subject
when it threatens your own peace of mind.

"But I won't have that. Let's face the situation.
Let's get somewhere. You have your own ideas, your
own opinions. That's right. I want you to think for
yourself. And I want you to hit from the shoulder.
You think that I am a hack. Very well, let's concede
that. It takes time to break new ground and a new
departure may end in failure. It is not the sort of
thing that a man can do alone. He has to have the
backing of his family. What would your mother
have to say about it? And Aubery—you would expect him to understand, I suppose. Then there's
you. I suppose you would be prepared to chuck your
studies and settle down in Exeter?"

Felicia's eyes dropped and a heavy flush darkened her face. She turned half away from Hollister
and fixed her eyes on the masses of green framed
by the great north window. And Hollister was thinking: "Now this at any rate is real. She is my daughter, or she's Miriam's. She will have to show her
hand now." And suddenly the problem itself became of little importance in his mind, a mere academic abstraction. The big thing was how Felicia
was going to respond. If she really believed in him,
she might take the chance; if she did not, her answer
would give her away. She remained silent, looking
from him out the window. And his courage began
to fail. He could see now the position in which he
had put her, and instantly the father took the place
of the artist. No, definitely, it wasn't fair. Or was
he merely getting frightened? Here they were, just

starting out afresh. And, not content to let well enough alone, he was gambling for all or nothing. He was about to speak, to ease the tension. He was going to say, "Come, Licia, let's forget it," when she turned back to him and he knew it was too late. That his moment had passed.

She met his eyes squarely and said with studied casualness: "Of course, that wouldn't work, would it? At least you couldn't just up and smash everything to pieces like that."

"No," Hollister answered. "No, of course not. It was silly of me."

"You see," she continued, while her voice took on color and warmth, "I'm terribly in earnest about my career. No, not career—I hate that word. It has got to mean playing around with frock shops and tea barns. But I mean my work. I haven't talked to you about it yet, but after college I want to go to the League. I know I've got what it takes if I only get the chance. You can understand that, Dad, can't you?"

"Of course, I can. You have a right to your chance. I had mine."

"But you see, Dad," she hurried on, "it really means the quickest way out. Up there with the best teachers, the right atmosphere, I'll really arrive. I'll be off your hands some day. If I came back here I couldn't buck Exeter. I'd—I'd—"

"—end up like me," Hollister finished for her.

A deep painful red suffused her face. But she was not to be diverted. That was the Miriam in her, Hollister thought: she knew what she wanted and she was willing to suffer, to make others suffer if necessary, but she was going to win through. She said: "There's nothing in the world that can't be managed, Dad, if we just get down to it. And we've got to pull together. And there's this to be said for things as they are. You are well fixed, you can get ahead fast now. Financially, I mean, and soon you can quit and do what you want to—a couple of years—"

"Those were almost the exact words that Miriam used. That was our starting point twenty-two years ago."

She hesitated a moment, then kissed him lightly on the cheek. "I know," she said, in a suddenly flattened voice. "It's a mess, isn't it?" She turned from him with a gesture that dismissed the subject and crossed the room to the divan. She had the long beautifully shaped body of her mother's youth, but there was an indefinable difference, a co-ordination so perfect that movement with her was like the rise, the sweep, and the lapse of a wave. Physically she was Miriam but pitched in a higher key.

Hollister followed her with the trained artist's eye that traced the lines of her figure through the masking fabric of her dress. His brief moment of revolt had passed, and now its bitterness gave place to a purely aesthetic delight in her beauty that stirred memories of a time when such an emotion as this was immediately translated, however inadequately, into form. He said impulsively: "By Jove, Licia, I'd like to model you. You make me wish I were still messing with clay."

From the divan she looked at him over her shoulder. "Why don't you?" she said. "I think that would be great fun. We'll put that down for the Christmas holidays."

He said, "But I meant—" and stopped in sudden embarrassment.

"In the nude," she finished for him. "I don't think I'd mind—you. You see, I've done a little posing. I'm rather used to it."

"But, my dear!"

"Oh, I don't mean before mixed classes," she laughed. "Just privately, for some of the girls. And you needn't look so frightened about me. My morals are sound. There's something about having been born and raised in Exeter, you know. By the time you leave, it has established itself as the custodian of your morals. You can become as modern as you please in your convictions. You can paralyze the good old conscience—then when you're all set to go on the loose, there sits Exeter watching you from a dark corner. And you rather hate yourself, but you've got to behave."

They laughed together, both glad to be on the surface again. And Hollister asked about her work at college, and had she brought some sketches for him to see.

But Felicia brushed his question aside. She reached over to the table and picked up a folder of red Morocco leather that she had brought to the studio with her. Then she drew something from it and held it concealed in her lap. "Guess what," she commanded.

Hollister entered into the spirit of their old childish game. "I know," he said; "there's a corner sticking out. It's a photograph. And since you've been doing Europe with a tour, it's probably either the Leaning Tower of Pisa or the Mona Lisa."

"You are getting warm. It is a photograph, and

it is a work of art, but it is not on the Cook's itin-
erary."

"Then," answered Hollister, "I give up."

"It's principally an explanation," Felicia said,
becoming suddenly serious. "If you help it along
with your imagination, you'll know why I was such
a cad a while ago. And you'll know why I offered
to pose for you." She held the cardboard up facing
Hollister and added: "I'd be proud to pose for the
artist who did that."

Hollister sat and looked at the picture. The
studio was filled with heavy silence, across which
sounded an occasional bird call and the drowsy hum
of a distant lawn mower. At last Hollister raised his
eyes to Felicia's face. "Where did you get that?" he
asked.

"It's in the private collection of Louis Lane.
Does that name mean anything to you?"

"Louis Lane—why, yes. Lane was studying in
Paris when I was there. But this can't be the same
man. Poor old Louis never collected anything but
his own outlandish canvases. He was small, and
rather comic, and only half there most of the time."

"Well, he's very much there now, and if you had
kept up with modern trends you would know exactly how important he is, and what being in his
collection means. My roommate at college had a letter to him, and she wangled us a bid to tea. The
minute Mamma entered the room she saw your
bronze, gave a scream and rushed over to it. Lane
was awfully excited. He had picked it up years ago.
Said that you had showed more promise than any
man in his crowd, and that he had been watching
the American sculpture awards for years, sure that

you'd arrive. He said that he had about concluded that you must have died or you would certainly have been heard from."

Hollister reached over and took the photograph with a hand that shook slightly, then holding it at arm's length, he squinted at it through half-closed eyes. From time to time he would change its position. Then, when it became too familiar, he crossed the studio and held it before a mirror to get it in reverse. At last, in a voice that was dry and bitter, he said: "Concluded that Hollister was dead, eh? Well, I don't suppose Miriam would have let it go at that."

"Well, you know Mamma, Dad. She was just like Barrie's old lady with the medals. She buttonholed Lane and started chanting over your various societies and awards. Then she had some kodak snaps of the house and studio in her bag, and she couldn't help giving him an earful about that."

"You couldn't stop her?"

"I did after a while, and got her out. You see I had a feeling somehow, the way you'd feel about it. Then later I got Lane to let me send a photographer to get this for you. So that's how it was." Hollister was silent. After a moment Felicia concluded: "You mustn't blame Mamma. You know, she's really a dear and she's enormously proud of you."

"She ought to be," he answered. "She made me." He handed the picture to Felicia and said: "Here, you take this. It was sweet of you getting it for me and all, but—maybe you'll understand. Somehow I'd rather not have it underfoot."

"Yes," she said slowly. "I understand. And of

course I want it. It will give me something to live up to."

There was a moment of embarrassed silence which Hollister broke abruptly with: "Let's have a drink. I've only whisky here. All right?"

"Good stuff?" she asked.

"Five years in the wood."

"Neat," she said.

"Adult now, eh?"

"Adult, and hard."

Hollister filled two whisky glasses, handed her one, then raised the other. "To the dead," he said.

"No, Dad, I won't drink to that. Here's to the living."

"To both," Hollister amended, "to the quick and the dead."

They touched glasses and drank.

ℋOLLISTER sat at a small metal table on the veranda of the Exeter Country Club, drinking a highball with Jerry Enfield and waiting for Miriam to come down and drive him home. How long he would have to wait he had no idea, for a talk fest was in progress and Miriam was in her element. Jarvis Maxton was there and he and Miriam had started matching stories. They were both in perfect form, and presently the others had become merely a cheering gallery while the two principals continued in lively competition. Maxton had told an absent-minded-professor story about a legendary uncle who had taught chemistry at the state university. When he had finished Miriam had stepped in before the laughter had subsided and, with the smile of affectionate indulgence that always prefaced one of her stories at Hollister's expense, had said: "That was almost as bad as Holly. Did I ever tell you about the time he almost got away with an old woman's suitcase in the Grand Central—"

Hollister hadn't in the least minded her telling the story. But the thought of sitting there for the next ten minutes, wearing the fixed grin that he always adopted upon such occasions to convince Miriam's auditors that he was taking it in good part, suddenly became more than he could bear. They were not interested in himself anyway, he reasoned, but in his highly farced replica that Miriam was

65

putting through its paces. That his reasoning was correct was presently substantiated when he slipped quietly away without, he was sure, anybody having noticed his going.

It was pleasant sitting on the broad veranda with the sharp, arresting noises of club night life stepped down by intervening walls to a composite buzz, companionable and unobtrusive. And it was good to let his glance leap untrammeled across half a mile of dew-drenched turf to a moon rising beyond distant hills, and talk or not as he pleased, Jerry being that sort of companion.

It was extraordinary, he thought, what the inevitable and involuntary process of living did to people. Take for example the six of them who at the moment were sheltered under this roof, and who had been schoolmates at the old Exeter High. Jerry, Jarvis Maxton, Mame Maxton, Pendleton, Miriam, and himself.

Jarvis was, of course, their most conspicuous success. But in the distinguished financier there was not discernible a trace of the bumptious, quick-tempered, hard-hitting, undeniably tough youngster whom he remembered. He was completely civilized. He had learned long ago that the sweetest and most profitable revenge for a blow taken is not a swift one in return, but a strategic attack through the realm of finance, whereby the victim pays long and painfully through the nose to the practical advantage of the victor. Early in his career he had realized that a man could best attain stature by devouring his fellows, and this he had done, systematically and with relish. Like all men of his type who have battered their way ruthlessly from the bottom to the top, he was thoroughly liked, thoroughly hated, and thoroughly feared.

That was, Hollister thought, possibly the bond of kinship between him and Miriam. She, too, had learned that anger spent wisely can be made to pay. Or perhaps this had been instinctive—the woman in her. But there was that other side of her, too. Her essential kindness, her genuine, if a trifle obvious, good-nature, her unswerving loyalty.

And Pendleton—poor old Bob. He wondered what part Miriam, who touched all life so vitally, had played in his. Calf love becoming a lifelong obsession, knowing her to be possessed by another man, bringing her children into the world, abandoning hope, but still fatally bound by that dumb, pathetic steadfastness of the unimaginative. Yielding at last physically, and with what self-loathing, to the appetites of a gross body, while all that was decent and boyish in his love followed after her, looking out at her now and then from behind his impenetrable screen.

Mame Maxton—no longer an entity—just Jarvis' wife. Trying to remember back, he could not even find her own name.

Hollister came back to Enfield and, sipping his highball, lifted his glance across the table. Jerry looked up, their eyes met, and they smiled. Then, tacitly accepting the silence, both looked away across the links. Good old Jerry, Hollister thought. He at least was always the same. At school, a large, slow, ruddy boy possessed of the physical power and social position to make him the dictator of the class. And his judgments had always been fair, his protective interest in the smaller boys unfailing.

This portrait out of the past Hollister set against the one across the table, noting with the sure eye of the artist the lines that the years had etched. In the subdued light of the veranda, he saw an athlete gone somewhat to flesh. Massive, but not soft, rather just a little slack, and the beat of healthy color under the tan of face and neck would have been more convincing had it not been for the discounting effect of a slight puffiness about the eyes, and a recent grossness of jaw that caused the brow to seem disproportionately narrow, shifting the accent of the face definitely from the mental to the physical. But the face was not unattractive. The years had blurred but not effaced its boyish charm, and its unmistakable selfishness was offset by a slow-burning but invariably triumphant good-nature. It was a face that life had done its best to spoil by too much kindness. In spite of the slight pouches under the eyes and the crow's-feet at their corners it was still adolescent, still untried. In the man's bulk there was no suggestion of inertia, the impression that it threw off being rather that of an enormous reserve of muscular energy awaiting release by some powerful physical stimulus. Twenty-nine years between the two portraits.

After Enfield had graduated from high school, he had left Exeter with his family, and it was not until the fall of 'nineteen, after the Armistice, that he had returned. Hollister had seen him then, he remembered, at a Victory Loan rally. He had been a glamorous figure in khaki, with his wings and service ribbons, two years of flying behind him and three enemy planes to his credit. Even the disillusionment of war had not, it seemed, freed him of his sense of personal responsibility, his feeling that a game had to be played to a finish. And when he had been "drafted" by the local committee for this "last offensive," in his native town, he had obediently reported for duty. Enfield could not speak in public, and he had hated being lionized, but he devised a simple and direct system for unloading his quota of bonds. To each man who signed up with him he gave a verbal agreement to take the securities up personally at par at any time during the ensuing five years.

Exeter saw him no more until the slump of the early 'twenties, then he returned for two days. In his pocket he carried a dog-eared memo book with the name and address of every purchaser of his Victory Loan quota. The bonds were then selling at 85. When Enfield left, after forty-eight busy hours, he had quietly possessed himself of over a hundred thousand dollars' worth of the securities at par. Hollister had always thought it a pretty sad commentary on Exeter that so many of its citizens had allowed him to do it, but with markets falling and war profits vanishing, it was every man for himself. Enfield out of khaki was just a rich eccentric with a quixotic sense of honor. So they shrugged their shoulders and took his money. Pendleton, Hollister remembered, in spite of the fact that he was in a financial position to pocket the loss and not miss it, had been one of them. Miriam kept her bonds, of course.

Well, it was odd what life did to people as the years kept rolling up. Again their eyes met, and this time Enfield spoke. He was wearing flannel trousers and a tweed coat, and as he sat forward to address himself to Hollister the movement of muscle under the fabrics gave them sudden character and came to full expression in the fist that was closed about the fragile highball glass.

"I'm pulling out," he said. "I've had a bellyful of Exeter."

Hollister regarded him with a quizzical smile. "The wonder is that you've stayed this long. You must have wound up your uncle's estate a couple of months ago. There's nothing here but these accursed parties and golf. You don't care for either and—you're free."

"Oh, I don't know. It hasn't been bad," Enfield conceded. "It was what I needed to get me tuned up for the air races." He broke off abruptly and held out his hand with the fingers open and rigid. "Look," he said, "not a tremor. After last year's meet I couldn't light a cigarette with one hand for almost a week. It had me scared blue. But I'm sound again." His voice lifted to a note that was almost one of defiance: "Sound, I tell you. Sound as a dollar."

From sudden emphasis he sank back into silence, staring moodily out at Hollister. Then he asked abruptly: "How old are you?"

"Forty-six. Why?"

"Just wondering. I'm forty-five. It's time for stock-taking. Time to go to the bookie and find what we've got to spend on the rest of our lives. You'll be sitting pretty. You have everything: smartest wife in town, children, a reputation, an interest that will see you through. You've got what we all need at the turn of the tide—security."

Hollister's figure tensed and his face hardened. He flinched visibly under the word that Enfield had spoken. "Good God!" he flung out, "if you could only know how I loathe that word. You've always had money. You can't understand what a shibboleth security can become to those who started out at scratch; how you can build it up stone by stone until it has you walled in so jolly tight you daren't even step outside for a holiday."

He picked up a flask from the table and poured himself a drink, registering the fact that it was his fourth, and that he was already feeling the alcohol in a throbbing need to drive ahead, tell Enfield all about it, trample on old reticences, to hell with it! His movements were exact, disciplined, yet charged with a nervous tension. He gulped his drink and hurried on with: "But that's not the worst of it. There is a certain thing that it does to you over and over until it changes you inside. It gets you believing what everybody says, that a man's done at forty-five, that unless he's crazy he'll sit tight on what his youth has bought him. That the pattern is finished and only a damn fool would smash it."

His excitement heightened. Under its spur, and with the strange dualizing power of alcohol at work within him, he looked at himself from without, and impulsively he launched upon a self-portrait. On a note of scorn he exclaimed: "And that's exactly where I stand tonight. I know which side my bread is buttered on. I am considered a good etcher. I am academic, comprehensible. A competent critic can pick up an unsigned print of mine and say, 'That's a Hollister.' And because I have a wife, children, home, all the paraphernalia of success; and because there are hundreds of people who want to know exactly what a picture is about, and can afford to pay for a Hollister, I'll keep on making them over and over until the end of the chapter."

He broke off abruptly and motioned with his empty glass toward an adjacent table where one of two men was making erratic circles on the marble with his glass and forming words slowly and with infinite care as he labored through an incoherent story. "There's Kenly," he said. "Look at him. That's his escape. But that isn't escape, really. In five years they'll be saying that he went to pieces when he had everything to live for. How ridiculous! He's already dead and he won't accept it. He has broken out of the utter tedium that he has built out of life and is hell-bent upon recapturing a flash of his spent youth. But he'll never make it. It's all buried downtown in his stodgy bank with a row of figures for its grave and a dollar mark for its headstone."

Hollister met Enfield's eyes and their stare of slight surprise brought him a sobering moment. Immediately there fell between them the embarrassed silence of diffident men who have touched suddenly upon naked emotion. Hollister muttered something about being a realist, and busied himself with cigarette and lighter. It was the Scotch, he supposed. That or Enfield's complacent assumption that because he was anchored for life God was in his heaven and all was well with the world.

Anyway, now that he came to think of it, it had provoked him to overstatement. It wasn't quite fair to Miriam to leave it at that. He gave a short, deprecatory laugh. "Forgive me for letting you in for all that. It was silly of me, and it must have given you a false impression. But I suppose we all like to shoot off our heads now and then. Of course, I'm jolly well fixed. Miriam is a wonder, and even if I had a chance of stepping out of it all here, I wouldn't. I couldn't possibly get along without her, for one thing. Then there are the children, and ridiculously enough my good name. Both of our families have always lived here, you know, and even if Exeter has become a city, when it comes to the conventions we are still incorrigibly small-town."

But now Enfield was speaking, and Hollister got the impression as he raised his eyes that his companion had not been listening to his retraction, but had been engrossed with his own thoughts. Looking out over Hollister's shoulder into the night, he was saying: "Contrasts always help us to get values. I suppose I look pretty lucky to you."

And Hollister thought: "Now he'll claim his inning, and we'll be all mired up again. Why couldn't he let well enough alone!"

But Enfield was not noticing him. He kept right on talking over Hollister's shoulder into the misty moonlight that lay over the links.

"One by one I have realized most of my ambitions. All-American fullback, you'll remember—that is, if you follow your sports page; a record in hammer throwing, an intercollegiate boxing belt—all of the truck that the heavyweight beeves go in for. Then after college they said I was done. The old heart had sprung a leak and it wouldn't mend. Not that it was really bad, only it meant a limitation. But I had money—too much, maybe—so I took up driving and lined up a shelf of racing cups. There's something about speed that gets a fellow. I'm not good at expressing myself, but I think it must be the coupling up of what you've got in you with the power of machinery that makes you feel bigger. Anyway, at anything over seventy-five an hour I always used to get the old kick back again—still do, for that matter. Then the war, and in spite of my old murmur I got my wings. By 'seventeen the British weren't so damn particular and they let me by."

Enfield paused and sipped his glass. His eyes, as he looked out into the moonlit sky, were wistful. "Flying had cards and spades over driving," he went on. "Not that you get the same sense of speed, but there was the novelty of it and, of course, the thrill of fighting. And remember, I was gambling two ways. At anything over twelve thousand the old heart started missing, and at fifteen each breath was like a bayonet through the chest. But I got three enemy planes before the Armistice pulled me down."

For a moment he paused, sunk in retrospection. "Great days, those. I suppose I ought to be satisfied to have had them. Those months on the front were the peak for me. There'll never be anything like them again." He became cognizant of Hollister, and said hastily: "Don't think I am bragging, please. I don't do that. Only I am telling you what happened. What the doctors would call a case history. You understand."

Hollister said: "Certainly; go ahead." And he was thinking how incredibly young Enfield was emotionally. Life had been a live wire to seize and hold as long as one dared. Always there had been a higher voltage to try. Nerve, muscle. How far could they carry one, he wondered.

"Then," Enfield was saying, "after the war, along came air racing. That was easy, because I could always hang along under ten thousand. And there was a better chance here in America than anywhere in the world to hang up a record. We built the safest ships here then, but we hadn't gotten around to speed, and Europe could fly circles around us. It looked easy at first. I had money to spend. I said I'd be the first American to make the Schneider races. That didn't look impossible. I finally got up to two hundred and fifty. But right at that figure my jinx was waiting for me. Then last year I slid back. I said it was the plane, and the press believed me. I thought so myself until I got off the field. Then suddenly, just like that, I knew. I suppose war flying had something to do with it. I suppose you burn out faster that way. It was when I tried to light a cigarette that I knew the jitters had me.

"You see, it's like this: When you're fit and take your seat you and the plane are one single thing. You can't figure out where you stop and the plane begins. You think, and like that the controls react. It's as though your nerves went all over the ship, and if something breaks it actually hurts you. When your wheels touch in a landing you feel it as if you had slapped the ground with your hand.

"But that day when I had got off to myself I had a curious feeling that the plane all through the race had been something separate from me. That it had a will of its own, and that I had had to fight it for what I got. And right then I went to pieces. I didn't go up for three months. It was after I got here, you may remember, that I went back North and got them started on the new ship. She's a swell job, Hollister. You must go out to the port some time with me and see her. I believe she's got the speed in her, and if I can hold together for this meet, I can at least quit with a record."

On the table Enfield's fist tensed on the high-ball glass, and Hollister watched fascinated, half expecting to see its fragile transparency fly into nothingness under the pressure. Then he raised his eyes to Enfield's, and saw with shocked incredulity that they were wet. He was at a loss for words. The crisis was too real for the trite "Cheer up—I'm sure you'll make it" that automatically popped into his mind. "Incredible," he thought, "—getting tragic over a sport at his age, my age." Then suddenly the vague feeling that he had had about Enfield crystallized into certainty. He had never grown up. Speed had caught the boy up, and had projected him through life with never a moment to stop and touch what he was passing. And now, having finished with him, it was about to hurl him off to gasp his days out in a vacuum. Now he saw clearly why the man had envied him.

Hollister leaned forward. "Isn't there a woman —haven't you ever had a woman in your life?"

"Too many. None that counted. I always thought they tied a fellow down so."

There was nothing for Hollister to say. The silence which fell between them was invaded by sounds from the club. A syrupy waltz poured out of a New York studio along a thousand miles of ether into the lounge behind them. The steady brushing of light feet over the hard wood. The refrain picked up in the window by a clear young soprano that in a moment danced away with it into the gay composite of music, laughter, movement.

$\mathcal{B}$EHIND Hollister a party stepped out of the wide doorway onto the veranda. In the second before Miriam spoke he knew that she was there. He was always sensible of her presence through an instinctive reaction within himself, a sort of muscular and nervous awareness that prepared him for the drive of her dynamic personality. In the only purely original thing that he could remember her saying, she had put it with humiliating accuracy. "Felix," she had told an appreciative dinner table, "is good for sixty miles an hour when he gets going. But he can sit around for hours waiting for me to come and throw him into gear."

"Oh, there you are, Felix," she called in her vital contralto. And Hollister got spryly to his feet and turned to meet her.

She was bringing Jarvis Maxton along and Hollister could not help thinking what a well-matched pair they were. Maxton was his own age, but he was going stronger than ever with his big tobacco merger shaping up, and his mind already busy with next season, next year. In spite of his assured place in his own field, Hollister never felt quite at ease with Maxton. It was his fatal faculty of sensing the other man's estimate of him and taking instant color from it, rather than standing up confidently in his own shoes. Maxton made him feel somehow that as an artist he was set slightly apart from the world of affairs and was, accordingly, inferior. This feeling produced an unfortunate result as, in his eagerness to do Miriam credit and appear to be one of the crowd, he would find himself almost without his own volition greeting her friend with: "Glad to see you, Jarvis. How's the market going today?" Or if the season happened to be late summer and the crop was being offered: "What's the leaf doing these days?"

Instantly, having spoken, Hollister would regret the asinine pretense. None the less so because it was always politely brushed aside by Maxton. But he knew that this would not save him the next time. He could curse himself, but he could not mend his ways.

Once after one of these experiences he had gone home and rehearsed his next meeting with the magnate. He would say quickly, while his nerve lasted: "By the way, Jarvis, what do you know about etchings? Did you ever hear of Meryon, Haden, Whistler? Would you recognize Benson's ducks if you saw them, or Hutty's trees, or Rosenberg's Ghetto types?" He would give Maxton a long minute, then he would break the embarrassed silence: "Really, you must forgive me. I forgot for the moment that as a general rule American businessmen know or care very little about art."

But, of course, that conversation had come to a stillbirth. When Maxton and Miriam had stood looking at him he had simply lost his nerve and found himself asking about the market again.

He could see now that Miriam was excited. Excitement did not act upon her as it did upon most women, rising to the surface and dissipating itself in bright talk and laughter. It seemed always to move beneath, under perfect control and with definite direction. Instead of lifting her suddenly into a higher key, it seemed to Hollister to be diverted into the current of her normal energy, a power to be utilized and not wasted. Under its drive she gave off, he had sometimes imagined, a grave, almost ominous note, like a perfectly functioning motor that has picked up its load.

Now he wondered what she wanted from Maxton. She had so many irons in the fire. Perhaps he was going to build her that maternity hospital. Or maybe he'd escape with only her coveted swimming pool for the club. Whatever it was, he decided cynically, Maxton would take his medicine and like it. But when Maxton spoke he was surprised at the cordiality of his manner, and the look, almost of respect, with which he greeted him.

"I've been having my first lesson in art appreciation," he said, "and it has been tremendously interesting. Miriam has been telling me all about your work. I've always liked your pictures, but I had no idea that we were harboring such a celebrity in Exeter."

Out of his embarrassment and surprise Hollister said: "When a man's press agent happens to be his wife, you ought to be forewarned and have your pinch of salt ready. Really, I'm not—"

Miriam was giving him a look that he knew. It always accompanied her pet injunction, "Don't meech." He left the end of his sentence fluttering in air.

Enfield had got up and joined them. And Miriam said: "I suppose you two old gossips have been

having a great time at our expense, all by yourselves out here."

"Oh, I don't know," Enfield answered with his
slow good-humored smile. "We've been rather busy
with our own soiled laundry. It's a relief sometimes,
you know."

Maxton offered cigarettes. Hollister and Miriam
accepted, but Enfield shook his head and fumbled
an evil pipe up from a baggy side pocket. "I used to
smoke 'em," he said, "but the manufacturers cured
me."

In a horrible, intuitive flash Hollister saw what
was coming. He had heard this before, and he knew
that Enfield rather fancied himself saying it, and that
there'd be no sidetracking him before he had finished. He was standing there, demanding attention
by reason of his very size. One could not pretend
that two hundred pounds of self-expressing bulk was
nonexistent.

"The manufacturers?" Maxton enquired politely. His indulgent smile anticipated a friendly
joke.

"Yes," Enfield went on. "My artistic sensibilities are about nil, I guess, so I managed to weather
those revolting, obese silhouettes that leered at me
from the magazines and billboards. But I have a
sense of humor, and when one concern spent a million dollars to tell me that their fags were better
because they were toasted, and another matched it
with a million to announce that theirs were best because they were not toasted, I gave up the mental
struggle and laughed myself out of the cigarette
market. Now I smoke a pipe with an English tobacco
that doesn't advertise in America. And when it does,

being English, it will have the good taste to leave my avoirdupois, my Adam's apple, and my kissableness to me and my God."

His lighter flashed, and for a moment he stood inhaling the heavy, aromatic smoke. Then his glance met that of Maxton and he paused while his lighter flamed and died in a sudden breeze.

"Oh, my God!" he exclaimed, "I'd forgotten. You make the damn things, don't you?"

Everybody laughed, and Maxton said: "Make them, and what's more, sell them. But for heaven's sake don't take my advertising as a measure of my artistic taste. Some day when you are ready to be completely disillusioned in your fellow man, drop in and I'll give you a private lecture on the psychology of advertising." His glance took in the circle of faces and lingered on Miriam's. "But what's this, anyway?" he asked. "Now that I come to think of it, I begin to suspect a conspiracy."

Miriam said: "It's an odd coincidence, but Jarvis and I have been talking about that very thing. I've been giving him some of my views on the subject."

"And quite as effectively, if a little less brutally," Maxton laughed.

"The velvet glove," Miriam warned him. Then, turning to Hollister, she said: "Come, Felix. It's time to be going."

That was one thing Hollister admired about his wife. Her departures were always definite and final. She knew when a situation or a conversation was over, and she never hung about playing with its frayed edges. Like everything else about her, her good-byes were decisive. She said that she was going, and she went, leaving behind her the full and un-impaired impress of her vigorous personality.

When Miriam was along, Hollister never drove, and now as she swung the long roadster around the circle and launched it in swift sure flight down the avenue, he settled himself and wondered wearily, and with a vague sense of personal menace, what was up.

They were on the highway to town before she spoke. Hollister felt that charged, humming quality in her strongly now, and her beautiful alto speaking voice was lower, richer, more vibrant. "This is the biggest idea yet, Holly," she told him. "If we land this, we're fixed for life. We're more than fixed. We're rich. I got the idea when I was in England this summer, and I've been working it out ever since I got back."

Sensing his mood, withdrawn and watchful, she gave him an abstracted smile. "I should have con-sulted you first, dear," she apologized, "and I meant to, even if there was only one way of look-ing at it, but when the chance of a good talk with Jarvis came up tonight, I got one of my hunches. Something told me to crash in and I couldn't miss, and—" she dropped a hand from the wheel to grasp Hollister's thigh in an almost masculine grip—"I believe he's sold."

"Maxton?" he queried vaguely. "You're not go-ing to make a collector out of him?"

"They're right. You do need me," she an-nounced with conviction. "You can't think bigger than a print collector. Boy, I tell you this is tre-mendous. I worked it out this way: The South is an awful lot like England in some ways. We have a tradition. Why, even here in a place as up and coming as Exeter it isn't the Maxton Building that we take people to see for all its twenty stories. It's the old Telfair place. Take Williamsburg, Savannah, Mobile, New Orleans. It's Colonial, early American that interests people. We're history conscious. Why, take the way your exhibits in those places have gone. Well, they've made you, that's all. Not that you're not a good etcher. You're top-notch. But you must admit that at least half of a picture's value is in its subject appeal."

She gave him a moment to digest that critical pronouncement, her eyes challenging him from under the narrow brim of her modish hat. But Hollister let it pass. He must not waste himself upon abstractions. He must save everything he had for the impending conflict.

When she was satisfied that he would not take issue upon that point, she plunged ahead to her next objective. "You have specialized in architectural and historical landmarks, and it has not only given us a good living when other artists have been starving to death, but it has made you a reputation. I don't suppose you realize it, but your name has a very large publicity value."

Publicity value. Sitting beside her in the hurtling darkness, Hollister flinched. This was going to be terrible. Probably even worse than the annual round of exhibits that he always started after Christmas and during which he moved through a confusion of resort hotels, teas, lectures—half gigolo, half salesman, transferring the summer's output from the studio in Exeter to the oblivion of innumerable cultured drawing rooms.

His resentment rose. He told himself that the exhibits were the last expedient beyond which he would not go. Whatever it was that Miriam had in her mind, he was going to resist. He must decide upon that now, with nothing to back his judgment but *feeling*. She would go on with her plan and her unanswerable logic. She would prove herself right. She was always right. She knew it and so did Exeter. She would point to the success they had made of their lives, to Felicia at Vassar, Aubery at Yale, his place in society, his large popular reputation. He would listen to her, and she would be unanswerable, because to all she had to propose he could offer no concrete alternative. That had always been the trouble. He had known from the beginning that there was something that he needed desperately to do, to say. Something that must be first conceived, then, when his hands became knowing, given form, meaning. It had all been vague, amorphous, utterly selfish he supposed, now that he came to think of it, but at any rate an integral part of himself. He had been groping for it when Miriam had found him. Of course he had been unhappy in those days, at times desperately. But there had been compensating moments of intoxicating elation.

Since his marriage things had been different. He had left the peaks and chasms for a plateau across which Miriam had directed him with an unswerving hand. Of course, he had been unhappy at times, but it had not been the old boyish agony compounded of hope and frustration, and it had responded to the sedatives of home, children, approval, security; and lately—well, say for the past ten years—he had ceased to question. Life, after all, was something to be met with as little conflict as possible. It could always strike back harder than you could. Miriam had a genius for whistling it to heel. He hadn't. But tonight he was upset. There had been that strange outburst of his to Enfield. And now this reckless determination to resist.

They were in the streets of Exeter now, and the Saturday night throng of countryfolk and mill people was swarming along the pavements, adhering like flies to the shopwindows, and streaming aimlessly across the thoroughfares when the lights flashed red on the traffic. Miriam was in her element when she was driving in traffic. It always exhilarated her to take what to others might be chances, but to her were new and successful demonstrations of her driving judgment. Under her hand the long, powerful roadster would soar through the tangle of scuttling and dilapidated Fords that invaded the streets of a Saturday night, like an eagle among barnyard fowl.

Hollister, with nothing to do but sit beside Miriam and wait for the drive to end, and with his sensibilities sharpened against the impending conflict, was exposed to the full impact of the town. The incandescent hideousness of Main Street. The tawdry and forlorn attempt at holiday gaiety. Extinguished faces of mill operatives, countryfolk, dull and mildly curious, drifting without motivation, clotting momentarily into little groups that dissolved and formed again, staring with weakly covetous eyes at the flamboyant overstuffed parlor suites, corseted dummies, rayon frocks. The raucous crash of mechanical music from a cinema palace. And, under him, like the hand of some evil genius, the alternate swoop and rest of the car as the lights clicked automatically from red to green.

Instinctively he closed his eyes, and instantly he was out of it all, back in the Exeter of his boyhood. The Exeter where the wagons came in the early morning by hundreds to fill the big hitching lots. Main Street with its double row of trees and its pavements of crumbling bricks that had weathered to a lovely variegated pattern, purple in the shadows, warm reds and browns where the sun struck through the trees. And the faces, different somehow. Still holding something of the peasant quality, a peace and a dignity imparted to them by the earth which gave them life, and which had not yet become primarily a feeder for the mills, the shops, the kitchens of the townsfolk. A wave of nostalgia engulfed Hollister. To what fate was he hurtling forward out of the old certainties? Could he ever be a part of this new Exeter, he wondered, or was he destined always to be an alien in spirit while his body kept repeating the conventional gestures that he had learned by rote, and that were his only protection in the swift, ruthless progression?

So deep was Hollister in his reverie that he did not at once come to the surface when, free of the traffic, Miriam again plunged headlong into her campaign. When he did turn toward her he realized with a feeling of panic that, behind his carefully schooled air of eager attention, his thoughts had wandered and his forces of resistance were scattered. Persistently the pictures of the old Exeter kept recurring, flashing across the details of her plan and dislocating his line of defense.

Miriam was saying: "It's amazing that they

haven't seen all of this before. Why, it's as plain as the nose on your face. Except, of course, it is a part of our national blindness, the determination of the powers that be to believe that because we are one country the people are all just alike. What I said to Jarvis was, 'Go ahead and give the North and West the usual thing. That may be their stuff and you say it pays. But in the South play up to *class* and not *mass*. We have an aristocratic tradition here, and where you have that you have social snobbery. Get the class market in your pocket, and everything else will follow.' " She turned to Hollister. "What do you think of that, Holly? That was brass tacks, wasn't it?"

Brass tacks! God! What had brass tacks to do with a dream that had got lost in a fog?

Then—peace.

Paris. A bench in the Luxembourg Gardens in the drowsy summer noon. Had all that changed, too? Hollister wondered. They said that since the war everything was different. No, there was never any going back. Life was always a hastening stream with the tide set one way. If you were strong, you might be able to breast it for a moment, turn, breathe deeply, look about you, even reach a hand back to clasp one that you had pressed yesterday and lost during the night. But if you had not mastered the rhythm, if you had been born out of your generation maybe, you were jolly lucky if you had someone who could get you through—

Miriam, for instance.

"By that time I had him sitting on the edge of his chair, I can tell you. Then I boiled it down to the fewest possible words and gave it to him straight.

I said: 'This is the big idea. Holly's name means something to the cultured class. As a matter of fact, there are hundreds of people who couldn't stand a test on the great masters, but who have a Hollister etching in the front parlor. And it is a darned good etching, too. His name stands for something. He's one of their own boys who has made good in a big way. And what's more, he hasn't been giving them Venice by moonlight, but something in their own home town, something they knew already and loved. Now,' I said, 'here's the big idea: Clean up on all of that association of ideas. Run a series of good, line reproductions of signed Hollister etchings, his standard Southern subjects, and somewhere, placed prominently but not knocking your eye out, a dignified ad linking the subject up with the cigarette.' ''

Even with all of the warning that she had given him, he hadn't thought of this. It was too utterly preposterous. His face kept on looking at her, eager, attentive. But in his mouth there were no words, only a dryness and a taste like brass.

They were in the suburban belt now. It seemed strangely deserted. Everyone, apparently, either went uptown or to sleep. Life or oblivion. No halfway measures for Exeter. The houses were thinning out, lawns widening. Out of a row of bungalows the Gresham Arms jutted into the sky, its four stories by comparison with the ranked one-story structures giving it a ridiculous and disproportionate height. An emotion half envy, half resentment, assailed Hollister. It was the way nowadays that he always felt when he thought of Leslie. She would be sleeping now in the austere little cubicle next to her mother's room that he had seen when Mrs. Morgan was ill.

His envy sprung from the fact that she had managed to live so utterly apart from Exeter. She had held her own tempo in spite of what was taking place about her. In the little flat at the top of the building those two women managed to be as completely alone as though upon a desert island. And he resented his own exclusion from that tiny world.

Once Leslie had said with unexpectedly mature wisdom: "We think of life as something having continuity. We say that we must get the most out of life, because it is passing. Somehow I can't see it that way. I think we each live a number of small existences, and each one of these runs its course, then is finished. Each has its own obligations, its own little code of morals. And each one that we enter should be a fresh adventure. Today this is my life. It is a full life because I have Mother. Some day it will be over, finished. I will never know anything like it again and I want to live it to the full now. That's why nothing, nobody else matters. But when it is done I am not going to spend my time looking back. That's foolish. I am going to be traveling too light to pack any regrets along with me. And I am not going to be like you, talking about finished patterns, and all that rot. Not while there is a new incarnation waiting outside of every closed door."

Now the ugly apartment house had dropped behind them, sliding back into a tangle of street lights until it was suddenly obliterated by the crest of a gentle hill. But Hollister hung to the thought of Leslie. There was about it something bright, hard, unyielding, that held his attention and kept him from the painful imminence of Miriam's plans. "Some day," he thought to himself, "Leslie will come through. And she will come through because she's a miser. She is hoarding everything she's got against her big moment, and under the velvet she is tempered steel. They'll never break her."

On the stretch of open road that took them to their gate, the car hitting sixty, Miriam gave a low, rather self-conscious laugh. "I've a good mind to tell you what he said when I finished, but you mustn't think me conceited to repeat it. He said: 'By God, Miriam, Hollister's a lucky fellow.' Then I came back with: 'Thank you, Jarvis. If that's a personal compliment, I didn't hear you. But if it means that you're sold, shake!' I held out my hand, and after a moment he laughed and took it."

The car slowed down. The headlights swung an arc and centered on the high granite posts, the elaborate ironwork of the gates that stood ajar to receive them. Miriam's laugh sounded again, low, rich, vital. "Swell, wasn't it! I must write Aubery all about it tomorrow. He'll certainly be proud of the old woman."

And Hollister was thinking: "I can't let this thing go through. And I could never make Miriam understand why. She would never realize how I'd feel about it, how my old crowd would see it. And even if she did, she'd laugh us off. 'Of course they'd sneer,' she would say. 'They have failed. Most of them are nobodies, and you have succeeded. What if you have built up a reputation, then made legitimate capital of it. That's business, isn't it?' " No, it would be no use to argue. But there was one last, desperate expedient. It would not be a contract until it was signed. Maxton was a businessman, and he'd insist upon a contract before he put any money out. And why fight with Miriam over it now? Why not avoid conflict as long as possible? Then, if it actually came to a contract, just sit tight and refuse to sign. That surely was the sensible thing to do. Just wait, sit tight, and hope.

$\mathcal{S}$UNDAY had always been a bad day for Hollister. In the tenth year of their marriage, Miriam, having already thrown overboard the iron grillwork and stained glass of the earlier Wingfields, decided to jettison old Gabe's Baptist church as well, and build herself an Episcopal chapel. It was the third milestone in her progress toward cultural and religious enlightenment, and she was content to stand upon that.

The church was called St. Mark's, which did well enough for a name, but it was the personal possession of Miriam Hollister, and upon that score she left no doubt in the minds of the growing number who followed her into the wider freedom of Episcopalianism.

Hollister noticed, at first with amusement, then annoyance, this proprietary attitude. And there were times when, swept forward by some plan for modernization or expansion into the social rather than the religious field, her manner conveyed the impression that God, while still secure in his social position, had been reduced so far as her church was concerned to the status of a tenant whose occupancy was strictly contingent upon good behavior.

She was, of course, a regular attendant upon Sunday service, and during the first year Hollister had accepted what she had demonstrated to be the inevitable and had accompanied her, balking only at a proffered seat on the vestry.

But one day during a particularly dogmatic sermon Miriam had detected him in the act of scribbling a bit of doggerel on the back of a collection envelope. She had reached over and possessed herself of it, folded it up and placed it in her bag. Then she had given him a look of stern disapproval before returning her gaze to the pulpit.

When they reached home after the service, Hollister had asked her for the paper, and in answer to her questions had replied: "Why, it's my confession of faith. It's what I believe about God. But I don't think you'd like it, so you had better give it back to me."

"That's something I have always wondered about," she told him. "If you have any religion at all, I'd like to know what it is."

"Go ahead," he had said then, "but if it strikes you as flippant, remember you asked for it."

Miriam had taken the crumpled envelope from her bag and smoothed it carefully out over her knee. On it in Hollister's angular but legible hand was written:

> "I built a little chapel once
>   As pretty as you please.
> I put a clergyman inside
>   And fell upon my knees.
> But God lay on the mountainside
>   In purple B.V.D.'s."

Miriam had torn the paper across and thrown it in the fire. Then she had said: "Holly, that is the most sacrilegious thing I ever saw. I don't see how you can dare to go to church when you can deliberately ridicule the Deity."

"That's exactly what I have been thinking," he had answered. "Perhaps I had better not risk it. You see, he's not my God, and never can be. Mine is out on the mountainside just as I said. And it would be just like him to be caught in his B.V.D.'s while he lay looking up at the sky. And even if he was, I don't think he'd care a good honest damn."

Then, while Miriam regarded him in frozen silence, he had made her a proposition. "I'll tell you what. Let's split on it. You are happy in St. Mark's —suppose you keep right on there, while I put in a couple of hours every Sunday morning taking a tramp with my particular deity. It really might be an excellent idea, you know. It gives the family two chances instead of one. You have a business term for it, haven't you—hedging, diversity of investment?"

And that had closed the subject. It was the only essential point of their exterior lives upon which they remained definitely apart. But as the years had passed, the fields, the woods, had gradually lost their spell. The Sunday tramps had become fewer. The old ecstasy of finding himself alone under the ample sky that had carried him oblivious and untiring along the miles commenced to fail. There were recurring moments, but they came only under some strong and specific stimulus. Autumn in its dramatic rush across the hills. Spring yellowing the bare branches with its first adventuring leaves. The first snow whirling down out of a slate-blue north, then lying cold and virginal under a glittering winter sky. These moments still called him afield of a Sunday morning. But for the most part he kept

orange—exciting, unprecedented. Form, lifting like a fountain, seen for a teasing, elusive moment, then gone in flying spray. But *abstract*. You had to have something to tie it to on the canvas. If he would concentrate with every atom of mental and physical power that he possessed, he was sure that he could turn the trick and seize this maddening, elusive abstraction, render it concrete, mold it into something new—something that was of the very essence of himself.

Then while his conscious mind seized, discarded, held what seemed to offer promise, all with desperate haste, a deeper sense would eye the clock and whisper: "One hour gone. What's the use of getting head-under in a mood just to have it smashed. Just to get nothing out of it but that kicked-in-the-stomach feeling when, lost in it, you hear the car. The garage door closing. Miriam rushing in on her way to the house to tousle your hair and tell you what a dear old bear you are. The children. The neighbors. The rector for dinner. Cocktails. Those famous little canapés of Miriam's. The club for supper. Bed." Then seductively: "Better wait and get a fresh start next Sunday. Click right into it and get going the minute the car leaves."

Then the brushes going back into the cupboard, the fresh, plump little tubes of paint back on their shelf to lie there, prim, virginal, rejected, the canvas back into its corner where it could not provoke the inevitable questions. Another cigarette. Then the studio taking shape, looking huge and overdecorated, and, suddenly, lonely without Leslie. Too late now to go out walking. Really too late to do anything. A little early for an appetizer, but anyway, just a spot. Another cigarette. A spot. Then the car. The garage door. Miriam in the flesh. The house, the garden, the studio, all suddenly on the alert, whirring busily along into another week. Oh, well, who was he anyway to complain—jolly lucky —Miriam—the children—everything. All set, to use his favorite phrase, until the end of the chapter.

$\mathcal{A}$ ND the Sunday following Miriam's proposition to Maxton differed very little in its essentials from its predecessors. But still it was not the same, and its dissimilarity lay in its *tone*. Hollister was conscious of this with his awakening. The sense of impending conflict lay at the back of his mind like the sultry haze that presages a hurricane, dimming the sun, deepening the shadows, and giving the day an air of oppression and unreality. So that, when the car rasped its single note and swung into the highway, he failed to experience the usual sense of instant release.

He thought of going for a walk, for the air was brisk and the autumn colors were commencing to come up on the hills. There would be sumac in the fence corners, and the sourwoods would have turned. But at the gate the highway lay before him absolutely deserted. His gaze followed the band of concrete as it climbed a long, low hill, then sprang out beyond it into an empty sky. The prospect seemed utterly barren, and plodding one's way through it a desperately lonely thing for a man to do. He turned and retraced his steps to the studio, but the usual sense of pleasurable anticipation, almost of adventure, that was characteristic of his Sunday mornings, was lacking. He thought: "Now, I must make the most of these hours." But this thought had itself become a custom, and behind it this morning there was no actual compulsion toward anything in particular.

He seated himself in the big leather chair with his elbows on its arms and his fingers together, and made a deliberate effort to sink into one of his reveries. Paris. The old atelier on the Boulevard Montparnasse. He tried these with a sort of dogged persistence, as an angler will cast his fly again and again in the hope of a rise. No response. Above him the studio roof seemed to lift higher, the walls to recede, leaving him more and more alone. Suddenly, Leslie.

Instantly, with that extraordinary power of visualization which was at once his strength and his weakness, he had conjured her there before him, sitting in the corner of the divan with the air of utter weariness that she had worn that night when her mother was stricken. It was strange that, having been thrown so closely together in their work for a number of years, any thought of her that came to him now started with that night. What lay back of that seemed vague and of little interest as though it concerned some stranger met casually, and now gone upon her way. For a moment he let himself go, conscious only of the release from his overwhelming sense of loneliness. Sunk in his contemplation of her, he felt about him the atmosphere of the room slowly changing, warming, assuming the normal. He yielded to it. Everything would be all right now. With a sigh, he relaxed in the big chair and closed his eyes.

He followed the events of that night swiftly. Leslie's arraignment of him. The shock of Mrs. Morgan's illness. Pendleton. The man was an ass.

Then preparations for the journey to the camp. The ride out in the early morning through a world purged clean by a night shower and glittering like a jeweler's window in a flood of young, level sunlight. He had offered them Thomas for the duration of the stay, but Leslie had laughed the idea off. "What, go to heaven for a month, and then be watched all the time by a servant! No, sir, we'll have none of it."

But there had been wood to cut and fetch, water to be pumped into the tank by hand. There had been supplies to be bought and transported. And the result was that Hollister found himself spending more nights with them than he did in town.

His interest in the affair was enormous, and he entered into the spirit of it with the unspoiled enthusiasm of a boy. To begin with, it was the first altruistic impulse that he had experienced since his marriage that he had carried by his own hand to a successful conclusion. Of a strongly sympathetic and emotional nature, his response to such appeals as penetrated his preoccupation was immediate. But he had always been tortured by a fear that he would fumble details, that his manner of giving would offend. "Damn it all, Miriam," he had said once during that first year in Exeter, "it isn't that I don't want to help. But I can't give a nickel to a beggar without feeling as though I were reaching down from a monument in the public square."

Then he had gone on: "Now, there are Mrs. Hawkins and the three children across the tracks. I walked by there today, and I don't believe there has been a dollar in the house since the freight killed Hawkins a month ago."

It was then that Miriam had employed the phrase that had become so characteristic of her. "I'll take care of that," she had said at once. Times had been fairly tight then. No one had heard of Felix Hollister, and they did not know how long their stake would have to last. But Miriam had taken charge of the destitute and demoralized little household, supporting it from economies practiced in her own housekeeping. She had engaged a lawyer and collected damages from the railroad. She had put the tired slatternly little woman into her own laundry, and within a month had converted her into a tidy and not uncomely woman who turned out family linen that was the envy of Miriam's friends. The two Hawkins girls were married now. The boy, who Miriam had decided should become an automobile mechanic, was running his own little shop. Mrs. Hawkins was still in the Hollister laundry. Not because she had to work for a living, but because she was sure that no one else could give the proper degree of satisfaction to her mistress.

The success of this demonstration had amazed Hollister. It gave him a basis of comparison, and in the light of it he was overwhelmed by a sense of his own inadequacy. And so, since then, by tacit agreement, it had always been Miriam who had done the giving. She knew how. Hollister didn't.

But the visit of the Morgans to the hill camp was in a way his own creation. The idea had been conceived, the plans formulated and executed by himself. There was something almost intoxicating about the pleasure that he got out of it.

Chugging up the last steep incline in the station wagon, after his day in town, he could scarcely control his eagerness until the moment when he would pull up before the veranda where Mrs. Morgan, a faint color in her cheeks now, would be watching the sunset, and Leslie with sleeves rolled back from sun-browned arms would be waiting to help him unload.

Then would come work. Half an hour at the woodpile that at first blistered his hands and caused his shoulders and arms to ache so acutely that he lay awake at night cursing his softness. Then after the wood came the force pump that filled the little tank in the loft. He had rather liked on previous visits to sit on the veranda in the cool evenings, and listen to the rhythmic thump and suck as Thomas bent his broad back to the task. He had never dreamed what work it was. At first it caught him just over the kidneys, and had him wondering whether he was approaching that inevitable dead line at which Pendleton would shake his head with malicious pleasure and advise him to slow up a bit on alcohol. "A Sunday cocktail, perhaps, but not the regular evening highball."

But by the end of the first week the pains were gone, and for the first time in years Hollister had known what it was to feel the blood race, the heart pound, and sweat start under the stimulus of hard physical exercise. It gave him a sensation that he had never guessed existed—an almost animal delight in his own body. And one evening this caused him to do an unprecedented thing. The thought of a plunge in the bathroom of the cabin seemed suddenly tame and uninviting. Seizing a towel, he had raced down the hill, stripped in the lush growth that overhung the brook, and flung himself on the bright pebbles with the cool, swift water racing over his body. And there he had lain staring up at the strip of sky which gradually darkened until at last it had winked down at him with its first pale star.

Always after the plunge there would be a dainty supper prepared by Leslie, at which the three of them would sit saying very little and being enormously content. Later there would be a walk with Leslie. Or he would look over her sketches (for she was continually at work during the days). And finally sleep, swift and obliterating, the moment his head touched the pillow.

In looking back there was only one thing that baffled him, and that was Leslie's attitude toward himself. He would not have believed it possible, after that night when she had spoken her mind with such passionate conviction, for them to revert without the slightest self-consciousness to their original status. But Leslie had managed to do just that. She made, he thought with some irritation, almost a fetish of their employer-employee relationship. Even at the camp it had cropped up again and again, interrupting with its sudden chill a mood of spontaneous gaiety or a conversation that had taken an intimate turn. And, too, she made it obvious that she had no desire to attract him, deliberately invalidating, it seemed to him, her charm as a woman. In spite of her pallor she never used make-up and while at the camp she always dressed in a smock that, while neat and appropriate enough, reduced her figure to complete anonymity. With his height-

ened physical sentience this at first annoyed then
intrigued Hollister, and he would watch her leaning
at times against the dry, strong hill wind, and trace
the lines of her young body through the clumsy
disguise.

Now, sitting alone in the studio, that was the
picture of her that came to him. The young, confi-
dent body leaning outward against the weight of the
wind, and beyond, distant hills, very blue, tossing
away toward the horizon with an effect startlingly
like that of the sea. And he thought that once on
the little island of Samothrace, a sculptor must have
seen her prototype standing so, facing the broad
winds of the Aegean, and that drunk with the picture he had fallen upon his marble and made it
yield him the Winged Victory.

And sitting there, gazing upon this image, not
with the eyes but with the painfully intense and
isolating scrutiny of the mind, dwelling upon it,
and for the moment possessing it, he was conscious
of a strange transformation that was taking place
in some deep stratum of his being. Now it symbol-
ized for him neither Leslie nor the cold immortal
beauty of stone, but youth—high breasted, seduc-
tive, and incalculably desirable. And all that was
still young in him, that should have been poured
into living and heedless loving, but that had lain
forgotten and ignored under this frugal roof, rose
mightily for a blinding moment and tricked him
with the illusion of fulfillment.

Then the spell snapped, and he knew that he
had been duped and derided, and that his tragedy
was not that of youth that has been squandered, but
the far greater one of a youth that has outlived its

time, that has become a tarnished coin which is suspect in the bright market places of all the world,
and for which even the zest of spending has given
place to a fear that lies upon the borderland of
panic.

The physical reaction was terrific. He felt it in
his viscera like a quaking jelly. His kneecaps trem-
bled, and when he staggered to his feet tears for
which he despised himself blinded his eyes.

He knew later that he was standing before the
divan, and was looking down at the end of it where
Leslie had sat that night of the storm. He tried to
recapture her image, but his mind, fighting a great
lassitude, failed to find her. But she was an emotion
burning somewhere far off, warm, faint, and weakening in its effect on him. He wondered dully if he
was in love with her. Into his face came an expression of disbelief, followed by one of fear. "But that's
impossible. I can't let that happen," he said aloud.
He turned away toward the fireplace, and stood with
arms crossed on the mantelpiece, forehead resting
on them, and eyes fixed on the ashes of an old
fire. Then, abruptly, passionately, he exclaimed:
"Christ!" And with one of his characteristic gestures,
angular, gauche, and filled with a restrained violence, he seemed to free himself from invisible
bonds, and plunged into purposeful activity.

Swiftly he assembled paints and canvas, and,
looking about the room, his eyes picked up a decanter and glasses that stood on a Chinese taboret.
He commenced to paint them with feverish haste,
squeezing the tubes recklessly onto the stainless
mahogany of a new palette until its border was
decorated with splashes of raw color. But he had

scarcely got the picture started before, with an impatient oath, he seized his palette knife and scraped it from the canvas. But in a moment he was at work again, painting now from memory. From a mass suggesting masonry that grew at the left of his canvas the jutting figure of a gargoyle began to take shape. Here was none of Hollister's careful draftsmanship. He was working too rapidly for that, but there was already the taut, attenuated grotesquery that the medieval craftsman knew so well how to express in stone. But again the impulse failed. The brush paused and considered, hovering over the canvas, then drew a long, careful stroke that threw the head into sharp definition. "Tripe," Hollister muttered, "damn tripe." Again he attacked the canvas with the palette knife.

The supple blade cut behind the heavy pigment, carrying it away in clots and streamers that curled back from the canvas leaving it at last clean enough for a fresh start. At the far end of the studio the clock commenced to strike interminably. And that watchful exterior part of Hollister's mind started to whisper: "Noon already. Only one hour longer." In a frenzy of haste he seized palette and brushes and attacked the canvas.

Chaos. Red, yellow, purple, green, streaming across each other and changing with the rapidity of a kaleidoscope. Form emerging, then receding. Hands that worked faster and faster, finally discarding brushes and palette, squeezing paints directly on the canvas, mixing and spreading them with thumb or palette knife. And Hollister behaving like a man quite drunk, muttering curses at the canvas, lost utterly to time and place.

Outside in the sunny garden the drone of
heavy tires on gravel, the garage door traveling its
oiled track, then closing with a soft bump, footsteps
receding toward the kitchen wing; and, approaching
from the house, voices. Miriam's rich contralto: "I
wonder what's become of Holly. He's usually at the
house to greet us when we come from church."
Then, lifting in a call: "Holly! Oh, Holly!" A male
voice with a resonant boom: "He's probably com-
muning with nature. And I must say I can't blame
him with grounds like these to wander in." A female
voice that lilted: "My guess is that he is in the studio
lost in an artistic reverie." Miriam again, nearer
now, laughingly: "Mooning, I call it. We'd better
go and drag him out."

The door of the studio swung open and Miriam
ushered her guests in, two women and a man. Hollister was standing at the far end of the studio facing
his easel, with his back toward them. Miriam called:
"Oh, there you are, Holly," and started forward.
But from the figure at the easel came no sign of
having heard. He was leaning forward tensely jab-
bing at the canvas with the ball of his thumb.
Miriam's voice sharpened with irritation: "Holly,
where are your manners? I've brought Dr. and Mrs.
Sampson to dinner." Still there was no response, and
Miriam turned toward her guests with an apologetic
laugh and a gesture that said, "But what can one
do with an artist husband?" Then she crossed the
room swiftly. At Hollister's side she came to a full
stop.

The others had trailed after her and now they
stood in a semicircle behind the oblivious painter.
Miriam's gasp was distinctly audible in the silence

of the room. Then she caught her husband by the arm and swung him forcibly away from the easel. "Holly!" she exclaimed, her voice edged with alarm and anger. "What on earth's the matter with you? Have you gone crazy!"

At first all that she got was the impact of color: red, purple, magenta, in violent conflict. Then slowly a pattern that, once found like a key to a puzzle, suddenly flung the picture into focus. There was a bed across the foreground, upon it the exaggerated breasts and long white limbs of a woman. Hanging over the figure, with rudimentary hands that held back heavy purple draperies, was a form, obese, lewd. There was the rondure of a pendulous belly, above it twin half moons that suggested flabby male breasts, and out of the purple shadows a spheroid that hung inward over the supine figure, with a great beak of a nose showing in perspective. Most certainly no one could say that the thing was human, but of one thing there could be no doubt: it was lust incarnate, unleashed and gloating over its prey. It made Miriam suddenly horribly ashamed that she should be standing looking at it in the presence of a man. But more than that, and for the moment overshadowing it, was the feeling that it gave her toward Hollister: that there was something sinister, enigmatic about him, and that in all these years she had never guessed it. With a swift, instinctive gesture she seized the canvas, reversed it on the easel and dropped it as though it burned her.

Almost instantly she recovered her poise, and exclaimed with a fine air of ingenuousness: "I'm awfully sorry, Holly. We had no right to intrude in the midst of your work. But it's Sunday and I thought you'd be loafing."

She flashed Hollister an appeal for help, but she saw at once that this was useless. He looked like a sleepwalker who has been rudely awakened, and he stood there dumb and uncomprehending. She turned to the others and hurried on. "Ough, wasn't that horrible! Positively I feel like a peeping Tom. It's really revolting what pictures are like in their embryonic state. You must all come back when Holly has finished this and try to forget what it looks like now."

Hollister heard her voice going steadily on, giving him time to collect his faculties, and he made an enormous effort to pull himself together. The man's clerical collar caught and held his attention; then he had it—Sunday—dinnertime. Guests. The Sampsons, of course, and a small plump partridge of a woman who was busy looking spiritual. Then Miriam's voice stopped and the others caught up the sound and carried it forward. Dr. Sampson boomed something and dropped a hand affectionately on his shoulder. The small plump person lilted a remark about fellow artists understanding each other. Laughter followed in which he found himself joining automatically. Then he was back on terra firma and being presented to the woman. She was a sister of Mrs. Sampson, he gathered, a Mrs. Trent—a poetess. She had composed the words to a number of religious songs, and one of these had been sung during the offertory. He shouldn't have missed it. Of course he shouldn't. If he only had known. But perhaps he might still have an opportunity of hearing some of her poems. He certainly would. As a matter of fact, Miriam had asked a group to meet at the studio at four o'clock and they would be treated to a few of her favorites.

Laughter again, and Hollister realized that he had shaken hands with the woman with his paint-stained hand, and that now she looked as if she had participated in a murder. But what a godsend laughter was! To its noisy accompaniment Hollister conducted his victim to the sink and applied turpentine; and when they returned Miriam said: "Isn't he perfectly terrible! Just suppose you had to live with him. But there's one thing that he can do. And it's high time he got about it. He can mix a swell cocktail."

CHAPTER 11

$\mathcal{T}$HE afternoon was warm and Miriam herself was wearing white, and so, in spite of the lateness of the season, she had insisted that Hollister don his white flannel suit. He had got it the year before for an Exeter summer wedding, and he loathed it. But with the studio episode fresh in his mind, he was in a docile mood, and without a word had done as he was told. Now as he sat in the group of thirty or forty people listening to the reading of the poems, he noticed with a sort of vicious satisfaction that, when he had moved the press to make room for the chairs, he had inked the suit hideously and quite beyond the cleaner's powers of restoration. Looking at the great stains on leg and sleeve, he felt more at ease on the uncomfortable folding chair. He hoped the stains would be seen. They were a sort of voiceless protest against what was taking place in his studio, an advertisement of the fact that he was not of it but was there under compulsion and solely in the capacity of host.

In a far corner of the studio he could see his easel with the canvas turned face to the wall. In thinking back, he had only a vague idea of what the picture was like. It was strange, he thought, that he could not summon it up as he could all of his other work. Usually he had only to recall one of his etchings and there it was before him complete in every detail, just as it had left his hand. But this was different. He had not said, "Now I will do a Colonial gateway," then gone consciously about the process of reproduction. He had first been aware of an intense excitement that had impelled him to paint without the least idea what would come of it, and his mood had been malicious, destructive. It had possessed him to the exclusion of everything else. And as he had worked he had experienced a new and fierce elation, a sense of physical and mental awareness that transcended anything in his past experience.

Even now, with the spell broken, this mood persisted. Whatever it was that he had done, it had been so real that by comparison the group of well-dressed people who now filled the studio seemed to lack actuality. With their concerted bursts of well-bred applause spaced by intervals of polite attentiveness, they seemed little more than automata controlled by the plump woman standing before the fireplace. He remembered with a sense of malicious satisfaction the effect that the painting had produced on the group that had surprised him at work. And he had to conquer an almost uncontrollable impulse to step forward, reverse the picture, and watch the effect that it would have upon the audience. But of course he couldn't. This was Miriam's party and she had a right to her own tastes. He forced his mind back to externals and looked about him.

There were only three or four men present besides himself, and he noticed that very few of the women were of the country club crowd. Apparently poetry, even devotional poetry, could not compete with Sunday golf. Then he realized that this was the other side of Miriam's life. She was being the patron saint of St. Mark's, and these were her fellow parishioners. And he marveled suddenly at the multiplicity of her interests and the fresh and naïve enjoyment that she derived from an occasion of this sort. She had particularly liked herself when presenting the reader to the gathering: "So few opportunities here in the South . . . one who can bring us a message . . . follower of beauty." Hollister knew all the phrases by heart.

He turned his attention to the reader. It was only by a conscious effort that he could hold his thoughts on her performance. The singsong of her rhymed metrics produced a sort of hypnosis that deadened the mind to her subject matter. But once he had got his attention fastened on the poems he was at first surprised and then indignant at what he heard. She had apparently decided that the Psalms of David, while adequate as to content, were not, taken as poems, all that they might have been. She had accordingly arranged a number of them into tidy little verses composed in rhymed couplets. Hollister caught the words:

"The Lord is my shepherd: I shall not need.
Beside the still waters my feet shall He lead."

Now, the Twenty-third Psalm had always seemed to him the most beautiful and moving poem in the world, and the need of prayer which had persisted in him long after he had severed all connection with the Church, had found its satisfaction in the serene and flawless beauty of its lines. And so in times of stress he had always turned to it and been comforted.

The voice continued, lilting its words out into the quiet of the room:

"Yea, though through the valley of death shall I flee,
I will fear no evil for Thou art with me."

And suddenly Hollister found himself hating the absurd little figure standing there on the hearth-rug. She was no longer merely an insipid little rhymester, a purveyor of execrable art, but a profane egotist. And his hatred extended to the audience, and even to the studio for the part it was playing; and he knew that he was not of them, nor ever could be, that if he stayed and listened he would become physically sick, and that his only salvation lay in flight. He got to his feet and was instantly conscious of Miriam's eyes telling him sternly to sit down and behave himself. But it was too late now. He was some little distance from the door, which made it worse, for he had to press his body between those of the sitters, and someone whose chair was directly in the doorway had to move to let him pass. But at last he was out, with the clear afternoon sky overhead, and behind him the rhymed couplets tinkling away into silence on a note of pained surprise.

Bareheaded and without giving a thought to how he must appear in the stained white suit, he strode to the gate and turned into the highway. For a while he stormed furiously along, conscious only of the feeling of relief that increased in direct ratio to the distance traveled from the studio. And he did not care what Miriam was going to say when he got home. In fact, he could not help believing that when she saw the thing in its proper perspective, she would sympathize with him in his revolt. That absurd little person improving on the Psalms of David. Suddenly the humor of it came home to him, and he laughed aloud.

Later he realized that he was passing the Gresham Arms, and his pace slackened. Then, yielding to impulse, he entered and started to climb the stairs to the Morgan apartment. Since he had seen the funny side of the incident his mood had changed to one of gaiety, and now he could scarcely wait to tell Leslie about it. She could be depended upon to see just how funny it was. She would understand. And he knew that if she had been at the reading that afternoon she would have walked out, too, and it lessened his sense of isolation, of having been for a long time among a people who spoke an alien tongue.

He knocked, not knowing how she would take his coming. And when she opened the door she saw this in his face, with its expression of an audacious small boy. And she saw in his eyes the mood of irrepressible gaiety. She laughed frankly up at him as she held out her hand.

"This looks like a jail break," she said. "Are the bloodhounds after you?"

"At least a hundred," he assured her. "The swamps are alive with them, and there's a posse armed to the teeth. You see, I've committed a heinous crime. May I come in and claim sanctuary?"

She stepped aside and he entered. "Shall I lock the door?" she asked.

"They would never think of coming here," he said. "They'll go howling off to the Country Club and sniff around my table on the veranda. In Exeter on Sunday one either flees to church and is saved, or to the club and is lost. No possible third choice has ever entered their heads, and they know me as one of the lost. So you see we are safe."

They were in the room now, and Hollister let himself go into the depths of an easy chair and heaved a sigh of relief.

"We'll have to be quiet," Leslie said. "Mother's resting. She's been rather low lately and I have had to keep her quiet. Make yourself happy and I'll be back in a minute to take your confession."

Presently she returned with ice, a small silver pitcher of water, and a bottle of cognac.

Hollister was restless. He got up and moved jerkily about the room. Pausing before the sketch of himself, he asked: "How did you know I'd ever looked like that?"

"You do still," she answered, "behind the new façade. All I had to do was to watch my chances and take a peek through the windows when nobody was about."

"Of course you know that's dangerous, and I'm not sure it's decent. I must remember at least to keep a dressing gown handy."

She was measuring liquor into two slim glasses, adding cubes of ice. She laughed up at him. "Please don't. I like you so much better in the nude."

He crossed the room and sat in the open window looking down at her, his long legs braced against the floor and fists in his pockets. "You're free enough with my windows," he told her. "But what about yours? You've got a façade, too, but you never leave the blinds open."

"Oh, but I do. I've done it again and again, but you've never taken the trouble to look inside." She held out his glass to him. "Speaking of façades," she said in a matter-of-fact voice, "don't you think that the Gresham Arms would be less interesting to the neighborhood without your unmistakable back in one of its front windows?"

He accepted the glass and her suggestion, and occupied the easy chair.

"You haven't told me yet what you've been up to," she prompted him. "Go ahead. I'm all attention."

He told her about the gathering in the studio. She listened with her head thrown back against her interlaced fingers, the column of her young throat rising from the V of her blouse to the determined little chin, and her eyes watching him down the perspective of her face from beneath lowered lids. When he had finished she laughed, then was immediately serious.

"That was funny," she said. "But it was splendid, too. I am proud of you."

"But I can't make myself out," he said, with a puzzled frown. "A month ago I'd have taken it lying down."

"The façade's cracking. That's what. I knew it wouldn't hold forever. You had better have that dressing gown handy. Some day there's going to be an earthquake." She raised her glass. "Here's to it."

Hollister sipped his highball, then looked up in surprise. He said: "Where on earth did you get hold of this?"

"You needn't be afraid of it," she assured him.

"It's authentic. I brought it South with me and have been keeping it against a special occasion."

"You flatter me."

"Oh, not at all. When the boss comes to call—"

Hollister interrupted her. "Look here, I am getting awfully tired of having that flung in my teeth. I think of you as the only other living soul in Exeter whose gods are my gods. To me you are always first my friend, and I love the thought of that. Then you are my artistic conscience, and sometimes, naturally, I hate you. And lastly you do the work of a couple of good, strong men, and I value that enormously, but because it brings you to the studio every morning, not because I get better than value received for my money. Yet the last is the thing that you always remember. I wish you would tell me why."

Immediately there was an air of constraint between them, and he wished that he had let her remark pass. They could have carried on for a while longer, laughed, forgotten the studio episode, Miriam's people, the loneliness.

Leslie sat sipping her glass. Her eyes were pensive and a little wondering. At last she set the glass down and leaned forward. "Hasn't the answer ever occurred to you?" she asked.

"Yes," he said, almost angrily. "It's plain enough, I suppose. You don't approve of me. You think that I have compromised with life. Sold out. And you are not old enough to realize that the basis of all friendship is compromise. We must take people as they are. Not as we would like to make them."

"I was afraid you would think that," she told him somberly, "but you are wrong. We have to carry on here, both of us, and we must understand each other. This isn't Paris. It isn't even New York. Here it's like—well, living in a shopwindow, and there's only one possible relationship for us. You think that I am critical of you. Well, I'm not. I haven't the right to be. But—forgive me for seeming rather brutal—I've got to save my own hide. If there should be talk you'd scarcely know it. Sometimes I wonder if you would even care a lot. Mrs. Hollister would make a flying trip to New York and come back with a new secretary, and I'd be out."

Hollister uttered a quick denial.

"Oh, I know you'd protest. I could count on you for that. But can't you see that the very fact of your taking my part would be used against us? No, you'd have to keep out of it, and I, of course, would have to go."

She leaned forward impulsively and took his hand in both of hers. "Don't you see we can't let that happen? As long as Mother lives nothing, nobody, else matters. You've got to help me. I haven't got anybody else."

Hollister got to his feet. "So that's it," he thought. "What an egotistical ass I am!" His laugh was short, sardonic.

"It won't be long," she hurried on. "Not as years go. And you have been so wonderful already. Some day when I am free—when we're both free—you'll look back and you'll be glad you helped."

Hollister smiled down at her. He was no longer bitter. He said: "You win, first, last, and always. Shall I go home now?"

Without raising her eyes, she nodded an affirmative, and he turned toward the door. But when he had reached it he heard her call "Felix," in a voice that was sharp with pain. The sound of his given name in her voice moved him strangely, and he stopped with his hand on the knob and waited.

She crossed the room swiftly and stood looking up into his face. He met her eyes and knew what she was telling him to do. It was incredible, but there could be no doubt about it. For a moment he was passionately alive. Then in the act of taking her into his arms for the kiss she was offering, he felt the tension break, his passion chill. A kiss was nothing. It was only the impulse behind it that gave it any meaning. And what had prompted Leslie? Did she wish perhaps to impose an obligation? No, he couldn't think that, not of Leslie. But he must be careful—Miriam—the children—Leslie herself. Hadn't she asked him to help her; to see her through for her mother's sake? If she had risen to his momentary upflare of passion it might have been different. But she had offered herself impassively, almost impersonally. And about her now, like an aura, hung that air of childish purity that was so characteristic of her, and that, while he hesitated, made even a kiss seem to him like a violation.

He took her rather solemn little face between his hands. Then smiling ruefully down upon her, he kissed her lightly upon the forehead. And instantly he knew that he had blundered, that he had been tricked by his fatal habit of compromise, that, having recognized her gesture, he should have carried it through with at least a show of gallantry, and that in rejecting her he had been at best patronizing, at worst insulting.

Slowly, incredulously, she drew herself away

from him, and stood tense and white waiting for him to go.

He fumbled behind him for the knob, opened the door, and let himself out into the hall. Then, as he turned toward the stairs with his mind still centered on Leslie, knowing that he had hurt her, and cursing himself bitterly, he was arrested by a loud peremptory voice. Turning instinctively toward the sound, he found himself looking through the open door of the apartment across the hall from the one occupied by the Morgans.

He could not at once collect his faculties, nor could he identify the group of people who sat within his field of vision. But he saw at once that he was recognized and that he was faced by the necessity of performing the appropriate social gesture. Miriam was always after him for not knowing people, not being sociable and playing up to her in her efforts to have him known and liked. People could either help or hurt you, and they must be placated. His feeling about it was similar to that of the primitive who blindly chanted his incantations to propitiate his hostile gods. He knew that he had seen this group before, and he suspected that he had had more than a casual acquaintance with them. There was certainly something very familiar about the fat woman who rocked unflaggingly back and forth, the short consequential-looking man, and the third figure that by its very failure to register upon the senses of the observer piqued the memory into a forlorn and hopeless quest.

The voice that had stopped him was still talking, and although he had not identified it, and in his confusion had no definite idea as to what it was

saying, it imposed upon him some obscure obligation of politeness to wait for a break in its mono-
logue and at least exchange a "good evening" before
passing on. And in the meantime the group sat looking at him in a sort of abstracted recognition, as
though they, too, were waiting for the voice to cease.
It was one of those situations unreal and yet familiar,
and as difficult of termination as though all the
participants were actors in a dream.

Hollister made a final desperate effort to place
them, to fit names to faces. This was the sort of
family that you knew with certainty that you had
met, and should know, yet when you tried to identify
it, it eluded you and slid off again into the mass.
There was something frightening about its anonymity. It was not merely Mr. and Mrs. This or That,
but Exeter, ubiquitous, watchful, biding its time,
waiting until your guard was down, ready to strike
from the dark. The voice reiterated some statement
with emphasis. The situation was becoming ridiculous. Suddenly, almost angrily, he wished for
Miriam. She always linked names to faces, and she
always had the password ready. She knew which
faces would light up at "I hope the baby is better,"
which would respond to a word about that last
campaign that she had captained. She could reduce
the general to the particular. And when you had
done that, you had disarmed the enemy. Well, he
did not have Miriam. The situation was preposterous and must be brought to a close. He must plunge,
then as quickly as possible get away.

He stepped to the threshold and made a discovery. The voice proceeded from a radio, and hang-

ing above the instrument, framed atrociously in heavy gilt, was one of his own etchings.

Smiling his frank, disarming smile, he stepped into the room and said, "Good evening."

With robotlike precision the three figures bowed in acknowledgment.

Now that he was inside the small overcrowded room, he got the full impact of the voice. It filled the space with a loud, mellifluous sound: "And, my friends, Saul of Tarsus was not the only traveler whom God has blinded with a great light that he might see."

Pitching his voice above that of the machine and nodding toward his picture, Hollister said: "That's familiar. It's like meeting an old friend to come across one of my etchings."

Silence. Then: "For Faith is a blindness, but a blessed blindness that closes the eyes to the wickedness—"

Backing away, Hollister said desperately: "I must be going. I only wanted to say that I am complimented that you like my work, that I am represented in your home."

The man reached over and clicked off the machine. In the sudden silence, he said: "We have been attending evening service at St. Paul's. The door was left ajar so that Mrs. Redding, who occupies the next apartment and who is bedridden, could worship with us."

"Oh!" exclaimed Hollister, aghast. "I beg you a thousand pardons. I'll go at once. I only—"

It was the idea of going that precipitated the final blunder, tricking him by its inevitable association of ideas. "My hat," he said, looking about him helplessly, "—did I bring it in here?"

The voice that answered him was sharp, vindictive, and so unexpected that it startled him. It came from the chair whose occupant had failed somehow to register even a transient impression, and who, evidently sensing this, was savoring her moment of reprisal. She was leaning forward and looking at him with narrow close-set eyes that glinted spitefully out of a youngish, homely face. She said: "Doubtless you left it in Miss Morgan's room, and I expect you'll be glad enough to go back and get it."

The words stung his memory to life. Of course! These were the people who had been in Leslie's sitting room that night when Mrs. Morgan had been taken ill. He had had his mind full of other matters, and he had rather ignored them, he supposed. They probably hated him. He got into the hall, and then he remembered that he had come bareheaded. He said, "Please forgive my intrusion."

At last, oh, blessed relief! he was on the stairs. Behind him the voice clicked on and blurted a loud "Amen." Then the swelling music of an organ flooded the stairwell, washed Hollister's retreating figure along before it, and finally, with an almost human crescendo of triumph, landed him in solitary ignominy upon the pavement.

CHAPTER 12

IT was nine o'clock when Hollister reached home. The hall lamp was burning, and there was light in the dining room. Abovestairs there was darkness, and everywhere complete silence. He braced himself instinctively and entered the dining room. The table had been cleared with the exception of the cover at his place. On the slab of dark mahogany the linen looked too immaculate, the ordered array of silver too bright. It was as though through long association with their mistress they had acquired the power of absorbing, then transmitting, her thoughts. They made Hollister aware of his soiled and dusty suit, the lateness of his arrival for the meal, his shocking rudeness of the afternoon.

And the fact that Miriam was not present was ominous. She was never one for procrastinating, and he had expected to find her waiting for him with the scolding that he knew he deserved. He could have sworn to the turn that conversation would take. She would first have given him a profound conviction of sin. Then she would have forgiven him freely, wholeheartedly. And while he was feeling grateful, she would have touched on the Maxton proposition and offered him the opportunity of capitulating and rewarding her for her own magnanimity. This was the situation that he had prepared himself to meet, and he was sorry that it was going to be postponed with the likelihood of surprising him at some moment when he would be unprepared to resist.

He crossed the room and opened the door of the butler's pantry, and discovered Thomas puzzling out the headlines of the morning paper. He was sitting forward with a pair of large horn-rimmed spectacles on his nose, and so engrossed was he that Hollister had to speak before he was noticed. He looked up then, graying wool, glasses, and profound absorption giving place to startled recognition.

Hollister said: "Why, hello, Thomas. What are you doing here? This is church night, isn't it?"

Thomas was getting into his white butler's coat. He said with dignity: "Miss Miriam told me to wait an' give you supper. She said to tell you she's gone to bed with a headache."

In silence the man brought him his supper—a salad, several slices from a Smithfield ham, hot buttered rolls.

Hollister remarked on a conversational note: "I can't remember the last time Miss Miriam had a headache. Can you, Thomas?"

"No, suh, I can't rightly say I does."

"Ahem—she didn't seem cross, by any chance?"

"She was very quiet, suh, an' she didn't eat no supper."

Between bites Hollister commented: "That looks bad, doesn't it, Thomas?" He cut his eye humorously at the man. But there was no answering gleam.

Between them there had always existed that relationship, common enough in the South between master and servant, of an intimacy which sensed in-

stinctively the barrier in each beyond which trans-
gression meant a presumption. It admitted of an
extraordinarily free interchange without the least
sacrifice of dignity on the part of either master or
man. But now Hollister sensed a withdrawal.
Thomas did not want to be questioned. He was
going to stand on his dignity as a servant, and refuse
to be interviewed. And this in itself was ominous.

Hollister took out his billfold and abstracted
two dollar bills. "You needn't wait," he said, "I'll
carry these things out when I have finished. You're
already late for church, but if you hurry you'll be
there for the collection. Take these along and give
them to the Lord."

The man hesitated, and Hollister added on a
note of irritation: "Don't be ridiculous, Thomas.
I'm not tipping you. That's my penance for being
late. Now get along."

The negro took the money, folded it with a
meticulous care that stressed his association with it
as that of a mere agent, and put it in his pocket.
Then he said: "Thank you, suh." And from the
door: "Good night, suh."

An idea occurred to Hollister and he asked
sharply: "Nobody been here tonight, I suppose,
Thomas?"

"Nobody but Dr. Pendleton, suh."

After a moment Hollister asked: "Did Miss
Miriam call him on account of her headache?"

"No, suh, it was after he gone she said she didn't
want supper. Then she gone upstairs."

Hollister sat staring vacantly before him, and
after a moment Thomas scraped his foot on the
floor. Then the master looked up. "Oh, yes," he

said, "you're still there, aren't you? That's all. Good night."

Later, Hollister, lying in bed on the sleeping porch, wondered what was happening to his nerves. From time to time conscious thought would skid softly into the sheer fantasy of a dream, but in the very moment of escape he would be jerked back sharply to lie broad awake, cursing his restlessness, and speculating upon the object of Pendleton's visit.

Now that he came to think of it, the doctor's attitude toward him had undergone a change during the past several months. There had been times at the club when he had actually seemed to avoid him. There had been that time just after Mrs. Morgan's illness when he had attempted to discuss the case with him. Pendleton had been positively uncivil, and had told him shortly that he had better consult "the woman's" own physician. "The woman"—what had he meant by that, spoken with the particular accent that he had used? Good God, he couldn't think that he and Leslie— But that was too ridiculous for words. No one could question his devotion to Miriam, his complete loyalty.

Yet that was an idea, preposterous as it might seem. There had of course been that night when appearances might have given rise to a false impression. But Miriam had been away, and there had been no one else to stand by the Morgans in their emergency. At any rate, he had told Miriam all about it when she had got back from her trip, and she had thoroughly approved his action. She was the sort of person who could understand. And she knew him from the ground up. He had to smile at the idea that any situation could arise that would not immediately be cleared up by her in her usual forthright manner.

The thought of her steadied him as it always did. After all, Pendleton was used to dropping in on her for a talk. They had played together as children. He had brought both of her children into the world. What more natural than that Miriam should feel that in view of his own behavior this afternoon, he needed disciplining; doubtless her early retirement carried no deeper significance than that.

The shrilling of the telephone bell snapped his train of thought, and had him out of bed and on his way to the instrument before conscious direction had supplanted instinctive action. In the darkened hall he took down the receiver, and Leslie's voice, high pitched and frightened, was at his ear: "Mother's dead. Can you hear me? Mother is dead."

"Yes," he interrupted sharply. "I hear you. Don't keep on saying it."

The extension in Miriam's room clicked open. "Yes," said her deep, cool voice, "this is Mrs. Hollister. What is it?"

There was a slight gasp, then: "I was talking to Mr. Hollister. Are you there?"

Hollister said: "It's Leslie, Miriam. She says Mrs. Morgan is dead."

"Oh, how terrible! You poor, dear child. But are you sure?"

On a note of hysteria the voice came back. "Of course I'm sure. She's my own mother. She isn't here any more. She's dead."

Hollister cried: "For God's sake, don't keep repeating that. Quiet down."

Miriam cut in compellingly. "Hush, both of

you. You're both getting hysterical. Now listen, Leslie. Have you called a doctor?"

A faint negative came over the wire.

"Well, do so at once. I'll be with you in fifteen minutes."

Hollister heard her hang up, then from Leslie: "Felix, you're still there, aren't you?" and, in answer to his affirmative: "It's you I need. You're coming, aren't you? I'm frightened."

Miriam's door opened and she looked out. "Don't stand there talking, Holly. Get into your clothes and bring the roadster around as quickly as possible."

He said into the receiver, "Of course I'm coming." He groped blindly for the word that would transmit his feeling to her, that would express the sudden sharp ache for her that was so acute as to render him physically weak. But there was no word. There never was. Words were for thoughts, but a feeling could be unlocked only by sight, touch. He blurted: "You must buck up, Leslie. And take something—some ammonia."

Out on the highway, with Miriam at the wheel. The car splitting a cold autumnal wind that sang in the telephone wires and burnished the stars until they glittered—hard, metallic, and infinitely remote above the sleeping earth. In the distance the street lights of Exeter, a chaotic tangle that, as they topped the hill, fell suddenly into their familiar grouping. The highway becoming a street, and volleying its globes of light up toward them to hurtle past on either side as they approached the houses.

Miriam saying: "The poor child. Of course we must do everything, Holly. I suppose Mrs. Morgan will be buried here. As far as I know they have no family, no roots anywhere."

Hollister thinking of Leslie. What was it that she had said about life? That it was not continuous. That it was a succession of small cycles, each complete, each unrelated to its predecessor. What were theories worth now, in the presence of death! Her voice over the telephone had not been that of a philosopher, but of a frightened child not knowing where to turn.

And that was the impression that she gave him when they entered the room. The door was off the latch, and Miriam opened it and entered without knocking. Leslie was standing at the open window with her back to them, and when Miriam crossed and took her in her arms, she turned like one in a dream, and looked, not at her, but at Hollister.

Miriam was saying in her brisk, authoritative way: "Now, you're not to worry about anything. I've been through this with a number of my friends, and I know exactly what to do. I'm a born manager, you know."

Hollister watched the two women standing without movement in the postures that they had assumed upon Miriam's entrance. His wife with her arms about the girl and her head held sideways so that she could look her sympathy into the averted face. Leslie stunned, submissive, apparently incapable of resistance within the masterful embrace. They made him think of a scene played clumsily by amateur actors, in which parts were spoken, gestures made, by obvious prearrangement—a scene in the sincerity of which nobody could possibly believe.

But of this Miriam was evidently unconscious.

She said: "And you mustn't worry over the expense. At a time like this it is so hard to have to consider finances. You can leave that to us." Over her shoulder she cast a glance at Hollister. "Can't she, Holly?"

Hollister saw pain sweep Leslie's face and burn whitely. He had the sudden odd impression that she had left her flesh prisoned in Miriam's arms and that her spirit had sought sanctuary beyond the closed door of her mother's room.

He cried: "For God's sake, Miriam, let her go. She knows what we'd do. She doesn't have to be told."

She turned to him in surprise, and Leslie, in the moment of release, seemed to draw herself together, body and spirit, and face them, composed and resolute.

She said, with formal politeness: "Thank you for coming, Mrs. Hollister. But there's nothing that you can do. I am over the first shock now. The doctor will be here presently. Not that she needs him now, or you, or me, or anybody. But I suppose he'll have to come."

"But, my dear child," Miriam cried, "there'll be things to do. You'll have to have a woman with you."

With sudden intensity Leslie said: "Nobody else could touch her. We've always been alone. We're used to it. She wouldn't have anybody but me." She paused for a moment, then she came close to Miriam and said gently, "We want to be alone now, please."

Miriam, taken aback, stared for a moment; then, accepting her dismissal, said crisply: "Certainly, we'll go at once. At a time like this your feelings must come first." She consulted her wrist watch. "It's three o'clock. I don't suppose there's anything to be done until after breakfast. You'll call us up, won't you, when you need us?"

Hollister went impulsively to Leslie, and took both of her hands in his. "Won't you let me stay?" he begged.

They stood for a moment looking into each other's faces. Then Leslie turned to Miriam: "Will you let him stay? You see, he knew her. He understands."

Miriam stood looking from one to the other. Hollister could see that she was perplexed, disturbed, and that the slow, irresistible, but disciplined tide of her anger was mounting. He remembered then her strange behavior of the evening before, and the fact that Pendleton had called. He had a sudden conviction that his relations with Leslie had been discussed, and that they were under suspicion.

From the street came the noise of a motor that stopped before the building. A car door slammed, and hasty steps sounded on the stairs. Miriam's face set in its familiar mold of determination. "Of course," she said tartly, "he can do as he pleases. But this is evidently the doctor, and I shall wait until he goes. Even at a time like this appearances must be considered."

Dr. Brice was a nervous little man, shabbily dressed, with tired eyes and an anguished face. He should never have taken up medicine, for his sympathies were so acute that no amount of exposure to suffering could effect in him that callousing process so necessary to those whose duties habitually expose their emotions to the shocks of illness and death. He was the antithesis of Pendleton. Acutely aware that in every struggle with his inexorable foe he was destined to ultimate defeat, he carried with him an air of baffled futility, which, with his shabby tweed suit and habitually apologetic manner, was sadly prejudicial to his practice.

Miriam knew him, of course, and she greeted him at the door. "Come in, Doctor. Felix and I have just come, and we haven't been in yet." She turned to Leslie. "Do you want to go in with him, dear," she asked, "or would you rather wait here with Felix and me?"

The doctor's eyes picked up Hollister and he bowed vaguely, then looked inquiringly to Leslie. Without a word she crossed the room, opened the door for him to enter, then followed him into the bedroom.

Miriam turned at once to Hollister. He was dismayed to see that she was very angry. She said: "Leslie has deliberately used this situation to put me at a disadvantage, and you might as well know now that I resent it."

"But, Miriam!" Hollister exclaimed.

"No, don't interrupt. There is something that I must tell you. I am sorry to have to go into it now, but she has forced my hand, and I must warn you before I go and leave you in this equivocal position, virtually spending the night with her—"

"But, good God, Miriam, it isn't a social call. The child's mother is dead."

"Oh, you'll stay, of course. It would make me ridiculous if I insisted on taking you with me. She's probably clever enough to know that, and I wouldn't give her the satisfaction." She stood for a moment, her lower lip held beneath her large, perfect teeth. Then she crossed to Hollister and gripped him by the arm.

"Listen to me," she commanded. "Bob Pendleton came to see me early in the night on a very unpleasant mission. It was the sort of thing that only a real friend would have done. He told me that it is all over town that you are carrying on with Leslie. That you have been seen calling here at all hours, and that he, himself, has seen you here in very unconventional attire."

In her anger she started shaking him as though he were a naughty child. "Now, I won't have it," she announced. "I am not going to have my life upset by a silly scandal. I'd rather not send her away, because that would look to outsiders as if I believed it. But I warn you, if it keeps up I'll fire her back to New York. You'll be without a secretary and she'll be without a job. Do you understand?"

Bewildered by the unexpectedness of the attack, Hollister said: "But I can't believe that. It's a damned lie—about us, I mean."

"We won't go into that," she said, with one of her characteristic dismissals. "What I want you to get into your head now, before we are interrupted, is that we expect to go on living here for the rest of our lives; we belong to the children; we owe them a clean name. Keep your eyes open and don't do things that will give people something to talk about."

Beyond the door sounded steps, and the doctor's voice raised in some trite but sincere expression of grief, the intonation conveying the content as clearly as though the words were audible.

She shook Hollister again. "Do you understand me?" she demanded, and he was shocked to see how furiously angry she was. But almost instantly he sensed a change in her violence, giving place to that peculiar quality of hers of commuting emotion into irresistible energy and directing it upon any obstruction that stood between herself and her objective.

He felt himself bending under it, moved as he always was not only by its compulsive force but by an habitual attitude of dependence upon it, the remembrance that in every situation that had arisen between them she had proved to be unanswerably right.

She must have seen this in his face, for as the door opened her expression changed to one of relief, and she released his arm and stepped away.

Dr. Brice entered, leaving Leslie in the bedroom. His face was tragic, and Hollister saw that his forehead was damp with sweat. "She has been dead for hours," he said, and the way he said it gave the impression that he was thinking aloud rather than addressing his remarks to the Hollisters. "And now I shall keep wondering what I might have done for her, if anything could have prolonged life. I suppose I shall report the cause as heart failure." He produced a soiled handkerchief and dabbed it at his forehead, regarded it abstractedly, and went on. "Of course there was nothing to do. She was simply spent. That was all. Almost no blood pressure for months. Digitalis, strychnine, and lately adrenalin. But there's a limit and she must have reached it this afternoon." He looked up at Hollister. "I suppose

I am as good as most doctors you'd find in a town this size. At least I have had a large experience. But it's terrible how little any of us really know." He looked up and met Miriam's eyes—surprised and disapproving—and said with an apologetic smile: "But I shouldn't be telling you that. You must have faith in us. That, at least, is something."

He held out a hand that was small and delicate as a woman's. "Good-bye," he said. "I'm glad you're here. Leslie is the pluckiest girl I ever met, but she will need friends now."

They stood together after he had gone, listening to his receding footfalls, the roar of his ancient motor swelling up in the silence, then throbbing away into the night.

Tacitly they dismissed Leslie from their talk. Miriam, herself again, cool, poised, assured, stood waiting.

Hollister broke the silence. "I like Brice. He's got no swank, and he's honest."

"Yes," she answered, "he's honest, and kind. I'll hand him that. But he gets precious little out of it. They say he never sends out a bill, and if you want to pay him you have to hunt him up and literally force it on him. Naturally he's being worked to death."

"And yet," Hollister replied, "I fancy he finds the game worth the candle. I don't believe he has much sympathy left to spend on himself."

But Miriam had now dismissed Dr. Brice from her thoughts. Picking up her gloves and bag, she turned to Hollister. "I suppose I had better go," she said. "Call me if you want me, and remember what I told you."

He went with her to the door, and as he opened it she turned and looked long and searchingly into his face, then he felt her lips on his, not tender, but unyielding and possessive. The door closed after her, and he heard her light sure tread upon the stairs.

Alone in the room that expressed Leslie so completely, Hollister's thoughts returned to her. But now, since the talk with Miriam, everything was different. Their relationship had been thrown rudely into the open. It was no longer a subject for abstract speculation, but had to be faced realistically.

Striding back and forth across the little room, with hands jammed into his trouser pockets, he put himself through a relentless catechism. Was it possible, he asked himself, that he was actually in love with the child? Certainly not, he decided, in the sense of a passionate desire for possession. He was forced to admit that since their vacation in the hills she had been constantly in his thoughts. But the Leslie of his reveries was somehow a very different person from the practical and deliberately impersonal Leslie with whom he was thrown into constant association in the studio. The disparity between these two, the imagined and the actual, their way of meeting at times for a fleeting moment, almost merging, then separating and mocking him, stirred him to sudden anger, and he cursed the profound secretiveness with which even a woman whose shibboleth is honesty moves in all of her relationships with men.

He thought with wounded pride of how he had come to her that afternoon, instinctively, scarcely realizing where he was going until he had found himself in her apartment. She had told him then that her motives for staying on in Exeter were concerned only with her mother. Then, seeing that she had hurt him, she had offered him a kiss as impersonal as a handshake, and had sent him away with the same old sense of frustration, the feeling that he had, somehow, failed to measure up to expectation.

What would she do now? he wondered. And at the thought, his anger gave place to a sense of impending loss so acute as to be almost frightening. She had made it plain that, freed from the necessity of caring for her mother, there would be nothing to hold her in Exeter. Yes, she would follow her star now, and he could no more detain her than he could prison one of the stars that was swinging its orbit beyond the windowpanes. She was going out to conquer, strong in the divine ignorance of youth.

He was staying. He was maturity, its lesson learned, carefully hoarding its gains. But in her going he knew that he was losing something that would be irreplaceable. Paradoxically, here in Exeter where he was looked upon as an outstanding success, she alone knew how abysmally he had failed. And yet, her persistent belief in him, her anger at his philosophy of acceptance, had been the factors that had stirred him to occasional rebellion, and had saved him from utter capitulation.

He had believed that with her moral backing he could resist Miriam in the Maxton matter. He had counted on that. Now, if she left—well, he didn't know. Miriam, Maxton, and behind both of them Exeter, all knowing that he was wrong, hammering it into him until the final opportune moment when his defenses were down, and he would be beaten.

His thoughts flinched away from that, and he became aware of the room. Its atmosphere had undergone a subtle change. Physically it was exactly as he remembered it. The cushions on the divan still held the imprint of Leslie's body where she had sat that afternoon, but her spirit had withdrawn before the grim, pervasive, almost palpable presence of death.

Behind the door of the bedroom there lay a heavy tombed silence, broken from time to time by some small usual sound, a footfall, the movement of a chair, amplified now to startling proportions by reason of their tragic significance. And from beneath the bedroom door Hollister fancied that a chill air issued to lie in a lifeless stratum about his feet.

He got up, crossed to the window and threw up the sash. In robust negation of death the cold night wind blew past him, stirred a picture on the wall and leafed over the pages of a magazine that lay upon the table. He drew a deep, invigorating breath and leaned out into the night.

Overhead the sky was changing. Borne down upon the north wind, dense masses of cloud rolled like breakers across the sky, giving only fleeting glimpses of stars that had become soft and humid in their wake. A quick cold spatter swept Hollister's face. Then up from the roofs of the bungalows that flanked the apartment house arose a soft drumming.

He lowered the window and with a conscious effort faced about. Now the room was definitely cold and sent a chill through the light suit that had been the first to his hand when he got Leslie's message.

The radiator beneath the window was chill under his touch. But there was a small grate, he noticed, and in it a fire was laid, ready for the match.

He had just started a blaze when he heard the door behind him open. He conquered the impulse to turn, and presently he heard a light footfall, and Leslie was beside him looking down into the flames. She stood taut, motionless, with her eyes lowered and upon her face an expression of outward composure. But this was given the lie by her breathing, which sounded in faint shuddering exhalations against the silence of the room.

Moved by a need for expression that transcended speech, Hollister slipped his arm about her, and drew her to him. She yielded passively and he held her close, feeling the faint rhythmic shudders that swept her whole body.

After a while he said gently: "You must sit here by the fire and warm up, while I get you something to drink."

He drew the divan close before the grate, and she let him seat her upon it and place a cushion behind her head.

Brandy and glasses stood upon the taboret where they had left them the afternoon before, and he poured a drink and brought it to her.

She raised her face and he saw her eyes for the first time since she had entered the room. Their utter desolation shocked him, and he found himself exclaiming brokenly: "Good God, Leslie, don't look like that. Your life's not over, you know."

Ignoring that, she said in a flat, colorless voice: "Put that down, please. I can't touch it. Then come and sit by me. It's you I need."

He seated himself beside her and took one of her hands in both of his, feeling between his palms the light swift pacing of her pulse.

She shifted her position until her head lay against his shoulder, and rested there with her eyes closed. He could feel the tension going, her weight gradually settling until it conformed to the curve of his own body, bearing lightly against it from knee to shoulder.

The cloud of her hair was shot with firelight, forming a nimbus about her head, and looking down over it, Hollister saw her extravagantly long lashes, black against violet shadows that lay beneath the closed eyes. It surprised him that, with her lying quiescent in his arms, he felt no passion, only a soft, enervating tenderness, at once sweet and bitter, and disarming, a need to protect, instead of an urge to take. He drew her closer and brushed her temple with a kiss.

She opened her eyes and smiled up at him in shadowy questioning. Then she lowered them again, and presently spoke gravely, almost wonderingly:

"When we were sitting here this afternoon, laughing and drinking our brandy, she had gone. I thought she was still here, and I sat over there making plans for her, and at that very minute she was somewhere else. She had gone without my knowing it. You wouldn't think that could happen, would you?"

She looked up into Hollister's face, and he shook his head, not trusting his voice.

"And after you had gone, I got her supper ready. I was so glad that she was resting, and I was singing in the kitchen. Something from *The Mikado*." There was a slight pause. "She always loved Gilbert and Sullivan. Then when I brought her supper, she was still lying just as I had left her, so I put the tray beside her, very gently so as not to wake her, and came in here to wait. Then I dropped asleep on the divan, and when I woke up, the room was cold, and I knew that something had happened. I got up and ran to the door, and while my hand was on the knob I knew that she had gone, that when I entered I'd find the room empty."

Her voice faltered, then went on gravely questioning. "What do you suppose tells us things like that if there isn't a God? There was something that knew and told me. Don't you suppose that means anything?"

"Yes," he answered.

"Being a pagan is so easy until you lose someone you love, and then—well, you wonder, that's all." She broke suddenly. In the curve of his arm Hollister felt her shaken by paroxysms, rhythmic and devastating, like a woman in travail. But she made no sound, and he waited, holding her close, for her grief to spend itself.

At last he said sharply: "Don't think about that now. You're tearing yourself to pieces. You've got to carry on."

The spasms abated, and finally she said: "Thank you. That's over, now. I won't do it again."

There was silence for a moment. Hollister said: "You promised me once that when your time came to step out of this life in Exeter into the next cycle, there'd be no regrets. You said that you'd be traveling too light to pack even memories. Remember?"

She smiled wanly. "That's right," she said. "That still goes—but it isn't as easy as it sounded."

He hastened on. "There'll be your work now. A clear road ahead, and everything to live for, waiting around the next turn."

"Yes, I know," she answered. "I thought myself so clever when I said that. Only there was one thing I didn't count on. Even if I win now, it won't matter without anyone to share it. Nothing matters where you are alone."

"But you are not alone," Hollister said.

She turned in his arms and looked long and searchingly into his eyes. "You would care?"

"I could never make you understand quite how much I am going to miss you," he said.

She disengaged herself and crossed the room to the window, leaving with him again that sense of anticlimax, as though he had in some way failed her.

Standing in blurred silhouette against a sky that was turning from black to a yellowish gray, she spoke out into the faintly luminous murk: "Well, the first night is over. If you can live through that I suppose you can keep on going. I'll never stop being grateful to you for helping me through."

He crossed and stood beside her. "No thanks between us, ever, Leslie," he said. "And besides, there's today to be lived through. What do you want me to do?"

She turned and looked up into his face, her own in the gathering light invested with a new and strange maturity. "You can do everything, can't you?" she begged. "And you won't mind if we leave Mrs. Hollister out of this?" Her voice became urgent, words pressing one upon another, as though she feared that he would protest if given an opportunity to speak. "You see, it isn't a place for strangers. *She* would have wanted just you and Dr. Brice—just the three of us, and there'll be so little to do. You won't mind that, will you? Please, please say you won't mind."

"Of course I don't mind," he said emphatically. "And neither will Miriam. She's sure to understand. And I'll confer with Brice at once. You can leave everything to us."

She looked up at him gratefully. "She would want everything quiet and simple. She said that often. You'll have to arrange for a little place for her, and she would want a minister, but not in church, only at the last. You understand, don't you?"

"Yes, I know," he said gently. "You needn't worry." Then he saw that she was shaking again; not crying, for her eyes were quite dry, but that the nervous spasms of the early morning had returned. He took both of her hands, and looked into her face which, calm, almost stern, tried to give the lie to her traitorous body. "You can't stay here alone," he told her firmly. "I'll call Brice to be with you while I'm gone."

But she urged him toward the door. "No," she commanded. "Go now and leave us. There's nothing that either of you can do here."

Hollister hesitated, trying to decide what would be best. But she thrust him suddenly away, her composure gone, and in a voice that was edged with hysteria cried: "Oh, please go, now, quickly. Can't you understand? We want to be alone."

*H*OLLISTER had made Thomas build a fire in the studio and prepare the couch for his use that night, and a tray of cold supper stood waiting on a low table beside the hearth.

He had gone there immediately upon his return from the funeral and had locked himself in. He had not slept for thirty-six hours, and except for a hasty breakfast at Brice's bungalow that morning had eaten nothing since the day before.

Under the weight of that lassitude which follows extreme emotional and physical exhaustion, he lay sprawled in a big chair before the fire, conscious only of his imperative need to be alone, to think his way through the situation that now presented itself to him. Before he saw Miriam again, he would have to reconstruct his entire conception of her. Not an easy matter, after all these years during which she had been the pivot about which his life had revolved. It was not her behavior about Leslie at the Gresham Arms that morning—or was it last night? he wondered dimly. It was in character for her to take a thoroughly conventional attitude when Pendleton had gone running to her with his story. He had always known that beneath the generous impulses and ready sympathies of the woman he had married there was a stratum that could be as hard and unyielding as iron. And he had known that when you imperiled her own future or that of the children you touched that stratum.

But her behavior at the cemetery that afternoon had left him completely mystified. It could not have been reprisal. That would have been stupid and Miriam was too clever for that. Everything she did was motivated. And he had never known her to inflict pain willingly on anyone. But why had she done it?

Casting back in his mind for some clue, he went over the events of the day from the time he left Leslie in the gray and dispiriting dawn. Starting with a light, cold drizzle, the rain had increased steadily as he splashed his way to Brice's bungalow. Then while they made the simple arrangements, chugging about town in the doctor's little car, it followed them in a cold relentless acceleration until it finally settled into a loud, undeviating monotone. It affected the nerves like a single note of music played interminably and from which there was no escape. It was so actual, so pervasive, that the drama which was played out against it showed in retrospect as shadowy and unreal by comparison. That is, until the moment when Miriam arrived at the ceremony. That was actual enough.

It had been arranged as Leslie had wished. Hollister had run out to the house and explained to Miriam just why it was impossible for her to attend. He had made it plain that this was not a funeral in the conventional sense, but a final, pre-arranged, intimate parting between Leslie and her mother. And Miriam had told him that she understood perfectly.

At the grave were only Dr. Brice and Hollister,

Dr. Sampson and Leslie, with the undertaker's men in the background, and the casket set on battens over the grave. The awning made a small island for them in the waste of yellow mud. The lot was at the edge of the cemetery, separated from the highway by a woven wire fence, and from time to time a car would swish past breaking the rain and road puddles into spray that shrouded it as it hurtled on into the murk. The hour was four-thirty, yet the visibility was so poor, he remembered, that many of the cars were burning their headlights.

Leslie was standing beside the grave with Hollister and Brice on either hand. Stationed at the head, Dr. Sampson was just beginning to read the committal service when Miriam arrived. Hollister had been looking toward the highway but, with his thoughts upon Leslie, he had not recognized the car when it stopped beyond the fence. He had been conscious only of a dim resentment at some stranger who could be led by idle curiosity to intrude at such a time. Then, doubting the evidence of his senses, he had seen Miriam alight, raise her umbrella, enter the cemetery and proceed toward them. She was wearing the new burberry that she had got in London, with a modish hat fashioned from the same material. One hand was engaged with the small umbrella, and in the other she carried her ivory and silver prayer book.

Leslie, who was standing between Hollister and Brice, was oblivious of her approach until Dr. Sampson's silence caused her to look, questioning, toward him, then she followed his gaze and saw Miriam arrive and take her place on the other side of Hollister. It was as though some powerful centrifugal force had been hurled into the little group. Hollister, looking at Leslie, got the same impression that he had had when Miriam had taken the girl in her arms that morning: that she had departed and left in her place only a frozen effigy. Brice sensed it immediately, and Hollister saw him take Leslie's hand and press it between both of his. Dr. Sampson had been quite oblivious. He had stood waiting in a state of reverent suspension, the book held open against his surpliced stomach. Then when Miriam had taken her place, they exchanged brave, sad, funeral smiles, and in his resonant voice he had launched into the beautiful impersonal ritual. Miriam was the only one who had brought a prayer book, and when the time came for responses, she made them. They were both letter perfect, and their voices rising now singly, now in unison, seemed to Hollister to exclude Leslie, Brice, and himself from all participation in the obsequies. It was as though, vested with some mysterious authority from beyond the grave, they had already come between mother and child and that even the falling earth could not make the separation more irrevocable.

When it was over, and they had left the grave to be filled by the waiting men, Miriam had turned, without saying anything to Leslie, had entered her car, and with a nod and a smile to Hollister had driven away.

Dr. Sampson had bid them farewell. Then the three of them had driven to town, saying nothing, listening to the steady drumming of the rain, watching it sluice gray and obliterating over the windows of the undertaker's sedan.

They dropped the doctor at his bungalow. In

the open door for a second they saw a little girl rush into his arms and his anguished face break suddenly into a smile. Then the door closed and they drove on to the Gresham Arms.

At Leslie's door they stood for a moment looking silently at each other. Then Leslie held out her hand. "Good-bye," she said. "You look ill. Go home and get to bed. Don't let's talk. Don't let's even think until tomorrow."

But Hollister said: "I've got to tell you one thing. I hadn't anything to do with Miriam's coming. That's something I just can't understand."

Leslie's face changed. The still, frozen look had gone. She asked tensely, as though it were a matter of transcendent importance: "You told her not to come? That I didn't want her?"

"Yes," he said. "That makes it so inexplicable—"

"I'm glad," she interrupted, and her tone was almost one of triumph. "Now that it's over, I'm glad." She stepped back into the room, leaving the threshold between them. The tombed loneliness of the apartment closed about her, and Hollister felt it chill upon his face.

He said: "Leslie, you mustn't—" and stepped impulsively forward. But she closed the door firmly upon him.

CHAPTER 15

MAXTON's private office was situated at the top of the building which bore his name. The floor was laid in red Spanish tiles, and there was a rosy tint in the rough stucco of the walls. And these two shades glimmered in the rich depths of Bokhara rugs that were scattered with studied casualness about the floor. The furniture was of blackened, massive oak which even to the discerning might have passed for antique had it not been for the fact that the wormholes had been overdone, and had patterned themselves rather more self-consciously than one would have attributed to so low a form of animal life. There was a refectory table, surrounded by comfortable leather-cushioned chairs, at one end of the extensive apartment, and across one corner stood a great desk with a red leather chair behind it. Upon the desk an elaborately carved cabinet of black oak carried on the illusion of the antique, an illusion which was shattered by a row of call buttons along the side facing the chair. A telephone on a flexible arm was housed in the base of the cabinet, beneath the buttons.

About the refectory table were seated four people. Maxton occupied the chair at one end, and facing him sat his advertising manager, a lean, suave, cogent man in the mid-thirties, who had very little to say, but who when he spoke was instantly accorded Maxton's flattering attention. His name, flung into the confusion of their arrival, had sounded to Hollister like Frelander, but already he was unsure, and if it became necessary to address him, he decided he would turn and speak directly, avoiding the use of the name.

Opposite Hollister sat Miriam, her head and shoulders showing in sharp outline against the light of a deep casement window, and her face animated and amazingly youthful in the glow that was flung upward from behind cornices and deflected into the room by the rosy stucco of the ceiling.

Maxton was saying: "I suppose it is bad business to express myself enthusiastically on the eve of a trade, but, after all, this is a sort of family affair here in Exeter. Frankly, Felix, we want to use your etchings, and," he turned toward Miriam, "your idea." He paused and produced his cigarette case and lighter. In silence they went through the ritual of taking and lighting. Then the closing click of the case, sharp, metallic, seemed to switch Maxton's trend from the personal to the business aspect. "However," he went on smoothly, "that is as far as I can go. It has always been the policy of our corporation not to interfere with the administration of the various departments by those who are held responsible for their management. I have brought Mr. Frelander from New York to talk the proposition over with you. I deliver you to him with my blessings. I can only add that with conditions such as they are, he will have to watch his advertising budget very carefully."

Miriam flicked the ash from her cigarette and regarded Maxton with her shrewd, calculating smile. "I'm sorry to hear that you are losing your nerve, Jarvis," she said lightly. "I remember that last year in the face of the depression you boosted your advertising. I thought it had worked. At least I believed in it myself to the extent of two hundred shares of your common, and I noticed that, with everything else slipping, you paid your regular quarterly dividend last month. Am I to understand definitely that you are cutting down this year?"

Maxton looked at her ruefully for a moment, then he laughed with frank admiration. "Oh, hell, Miriam!" he exclaimed, "haven't you any respect for business procedure? I am what is technically called bargaining, and you should at least let me think I'm getting away with it." He looked the length of the table and said: "Go ahead, Frelander. You see what you're up against. You've heard of these dreamy artists who let you steal their shirts. Well, here you are: Go to it."

Miriam said: "It takes two to make an artist, just as it does a quarrel. Felix does the dreaming, but you may take my word for it, I keep an eye on his shirt."

From the two ends of the table came male laughter, shorter now, and sharper. Hollister grinned across at Miriam, and she smiled back confidently into his eyes. Then Maxton and Frelander turned toward her, presenting their shoulders to Hollister and dismissing him as completely as though he had left the room.

The sense of not belonging, of being different, hence inferior, which he always felt with Maxton, was now heightened by the opulent and oppressive atmosphere of the room. Obviously the work of a decorator, and devoid of the smallest personal accent, it was nevertheless symbolic of the man himself, for it demonstrated the power of wealth to acquire what it wanted, even its own complacently accepted and stereotyped standard of beauty, by a single patronizing gesture.

He realized dully that his coming had been a mistake. It would make his final stand more difficult. He wondered why he had not foreseen that. Then he remembered. He had been only half conscious when Miriam's summons had come. The incidents that had crowded one upon another—Leslie's frantic call, Miriam's inexplicable behavior at the grave, and finally Leslie's letter of resignation which she had brought to the studio that morning—had been constantly in his mind. He had just succumbed to exhaustion and had achieved complete oblivion when Thomas had knocked on the studio door with a tray of late lunch and Miriam's note. It had said: "Darling, don't sulk. Remember your engagement with Jarvis at five." Then he had remembered vaguely that before it had all started to happen, Miriam had warned him of the impending interview and had pledged him to attend.

Again aware of the room, and the three intent faces, he heard Frelander say: "I suppose you understand, Mrs. Hollister, that this is in the nature of an experiment—"

Beyond the window which framed Miriam's silhouette the light was changing. A moment ago the bright square had showed a foreground of treetops, with here and there a gable or a spire, the whole dominated, almost crushed, by a vast blue hemisphere of sky. Now the values had shifted. The late sun, already below the range of distant hills, had plunged the foreground into shadow and was drenching the upper air with yellow light. From a fold in the rolling country where the factories lay, a dark smudge commenced to take form, drawing itself out in a thin line of deep violet, then flowing downward to mingle with the shadows, and blurring the horizon until sky and earth seemed to melt into each other.

Moved irresistibly by the sudden and unexpected revelation of beauty, Hollister rose and walked to the window, and stood there with his back to the others, his head bowed, and his hands in his pockets, looking out into the gathering twilight. Now seen from his lofty perch, the sky had become a vast hollow sphere with night rising like a slow tide to fill it. And he saw Exeter far below him, looking small and lonely, flinging out her first lights against the encroaching darkness.

An emotion somber yet exquisite invaded him, a sort of nostalgia for a home that might have been his yet which somehow he had missed. Exeter, even this new strident Exeter, was beautiful, and he had never guessed it. But it should be painted like this, lying subdued and quiescent beneath an immeasurable sky. From the ground he had seen it only in harsh but powerful outline, pre-empting the heavens with the arrogance of a Pennell drawing. Pennell's stuff, he thought, but not mine.

He became conscious of the voices of the others, Miriam's in a tone of amused incredulity, Maxton's plodding, argumentative. Excited by his discovery, he spun around and called:

"I say, Jarvis, this is magnificent. I had no idea you had anything so beautiful up here. Don't mind if I come up some time and take a shot at it, do you?"

They all turned and regarded him with eyes that were preoccupied, angry, hoping that they could dispose of him without shattering the spell which they had woven around the table and from which each hoped to emerge victorious.

Maxton snapped: "Certainly, any time you want." And Miriam said crossly: "Please sit down and keep quiet, Felix. You seem to forget that you are attending an important conference."

Now, fragile as a bubble, it was shattered, gone. Obediently he took his seat, and tried to focus his attention upon them, while they expunged him from their consciousness.

Maxton resumed in a tone of patient argument: "But can't you understand, Miriam—it's in the nature of a gamble, and it isn't fair to expect us to take all the chances. As far as we are concerned, it's not a matter of price on each release—we can adjust that—but of committing ourselves to a whole series before we see the reaction we get from the trade."

Bewildered, lost, Hollister looked across at Miriam. Her eyes were bright, and she was speaking in the low, controlled voice that he knew so well, and under the even flow of which he sensed that grave, humming note of a motor that has picked up its load. Watching her, and himself caught by the spell of her dominating personality, he even lost for the moment the realization of his own part in the transaction, the knowledge that it was himself who was the article of barter, and that if Miriam scored now, while he sat by in silent acquiescence, his ultimate withdrawal would be all the more difficult.

Then, sitting there, admiring her in spite of himself, he was groping again for an explanation of her behavior to Leslie. His first theory had been that she was prompted by the same motives that had made her stay in the room and meet Dr. Brice, instead of leaving at once as Leslie evidently wished— a determination to make the whole thing a family affair in the hope of avoiding gossip. But Leslie, he was sure, had read far more than that into it. She had returned to the studio on Tuesday morning, and had handed him a letter which was addressed to Mrs. Felix Hollister, and unsealed. "You may read it," she had told him, "but I want her to get it today." He had opened the letter and found it to be a formal resignation to take effect in a fortnight.

"But why write to her about this?" Hollister had asked with a sinking heart. "Why not discuss it with me?"

"You forget," she had answered, "that it was Mrs. Hollister who engaged me. And besides, she will be expecting it. She and I understand each other."

Guessing what she meant, but still not believing it of Miriam, Hollister had asked: "Do you mean that she did it deliberately, to make you hate her, to force you out!"

"To force me out!" she had exclaimed with a short reckless laugh. "Well, that's probably how she would put it. I'd rather say 'to set me free.' "

Then, telling him that she would return to work on Wednesday, she had left.

Again Miriam's voice, implying finality. She was looking past Hollister and saying coolly: "Well, I suppose there's no chance of getting together. Your proposal is really ridiculous, Mr. Frelander. You can't think seriously that I would consent to having a couple of releases made, then the whole thing thrown over, with my idea turned loose for anybody to pick up and make away with. I came first to Mr. Maxton because he is a personal friend, but we're going to trade on the whole series or nothing, and that's final."

She glanced at her wrist watch and got to her feet. "Come on, Holly," she said, "the party is over. Jarvis, hold my coat, will you?"

When she had slipped into her coat and buttoned the collar high about her throat, she turned to the two men: "Suppose we say next Monday afternoon at four for your final limit. That gives you six days to think it over. And don't get the idea we're running after you on it. I know we have a good proposition, and that there's always a buyer for something good. If I don't hear from you on Monday, I'll copyright the idea and the series, and send it on to an agent in New York to sell. So there you are, gentlemen. You may take it or leave it."

Abruptly her manner changed, and she extended her hand graciously to Frelander. "I'm happy to have met you," she said. "When this is all over, no matter which way it breaks, you must make Jarvis bring you over for one of Holly's cocktails." She turned and nodded brightly: "Mustn't he, Holly?"

Then, while Hollister was shaking hands and seconding the invitation, she went up to Maxton and took him by the lapel of his coat, smiling mischievously up at him. "And by the way, Jarvis," she said, "when you are making out the check, it would be a good time to go right ahead and let me have the one for the hospital. It will be so easy to get it all off your chest at once."

Maxton laughed aloud. "My God, Miriam," he exclaimed, "you're marvelous, simply marvelous." He turned to his advertising manager. "Did you get that, Frelander? It's monumental, it's epic. She not only wants next year's profits for her pictures, but I am to endow a hospital to boot."

Plunging earthward in the express elevator, Miriam gave Hollister's arm a triumphant squeeze. "They'll buy," she said. "They're simply crazy for them. Don't ask me how I know it. I just do. And I'll get Jarvis' check for the hospital, too. You just wait and see."

CHAPTER 16

$\mathcal{S}$ATURDAY night. It was Miriam's birthday, her coming of middle age as she called it, and Pendleton had tendered her a dinner at the club. It had been distinguished from other club dinners in that they had "dressed," champagne had been served, and beside the place of each guest there was either a corsage or a boutonniere.

The party had consisted of Jarvis and Mame Maxton, Enfield, Pendleton, and the Hollisters. It had therefore taken on the nature of a reunion of their old high school group, and since Enfield was leaving for the races on the following morning, a send-off for the flier as well.

It had not differed superficially from other meetings of the group in either its grave or its gay moments. There had been the usual obvious banter that served as dinner conversation, supplemented by toasts to Miriam and Enfield. Then they had retired to the cardroom for the several hours of bridge which had become a Saturday night institution.

But for Hollister the time between cocktails and coffee had seemed interminable, and as course followed course the nervous strain had become definitely an ordeal. He was acutely conscious of the fact that Pendleton's chronic resentment of him, which years of habituation had taught him to ignore, had increased to a thinly veiled hatred—a hatred which only their mutual dependence upon

Miriam kept from open expression. And sitting beside Mame, with Miriam and Jarvis across the table from him, he was embarrassed by the knowledge that the advertising deal was still pending. He felt that while, as the property about which the bargaining was proceeding, he had assumed a new importance, this importance attached in no way to himself as an individual, and that his own personality was diminished in their eyes thereby. Toward the end of the dinner his nerves had played tricks upon him and he had begun to read into the clumsy badinage a tacit conspiracy subtly to belittle him, even forgetting for the moment that subtlety was beyond the range of his dinner companions. When at last they pushed back their chairs his relief was enormous.

As neither Hollister nor Enfield played bridge they had drifted off together, and, since the night was unusually mild for October, they had finally settled in two easy chairs on the veranda.

Over a highball, Hollister said: "We'll miss you, Jerry. You're the only one of the old crowd whose relationships with the others are not complicated. We're just an average lot, what you would call the run of the mill, I suppose. But down inside, we've all gone off at tangents. We need you now and then to pull us together. You ought to come oftener."

Enfield filled and lighted his pipe. "As a matter of fact," he said, "I'm very apt to. I've been thinking a lot about it since I've been here. And now that the old place has come down to me, it has been put up to me squarely. I find that I can't bring myself to sell it. A fellow ought to have headquarters somewhere, and I'm thinking of opening it up, putting a housekeeper in charge, and coming back for a while every winter." He leaned forward and spoke with boyish candor. "Now that the time has come to go, I am realizing for the first time what you have all done for me, what you mean to me. There's something about the old place that steadies a fellow. The people you meet batting about the world never really give a damn about you; it's the old associations, the early friendships that count. After I've pulled out, I want you to tell the others how much I have appreciated it. And tell them I'm coming back."

In one of his sudden transitions from repose to nervous activity, he got up and strode to the end of the veranda and back to Hollister. "Feel like going over and having a look at the ship?" he asked abruptly. "I'd feel easier if I was sure everything was set before turning in. And besides, I'd like you to see her."

In spite of his affection for Enfield, and the fact that this was his friend's last night in Exeter, Hollister inexplicably didn't want to have a look at the ship. He wanted to be free of everybody. Miriam had come in the roadster, and he had joined her at the club, driving over in the station wagon. Now he felt a deep, irresistible urge to get into it and take to the moonlit highway. To seize that moment of inviolable privacy that comes to one who drives alone and at night.

And yet, looking up at Enfield, he couldn't frame an outright refusal, and compromised on a halfhearted assent.

While Hollister got their coats and hats, Enfield

made a tour of the kitchen and bar, peeling green-backs from a fat roll, and telling the servants good-bye. Two of them remembered him as a small boy, and had followed his spectacular career through the sports pages. In the pantry, along one wall, were pasted pictures and clippings recording his meteoric transit of the sports firmament. Matthew, the griz-zled head waiter, exhibited them proudly, while behind him the negroes from the kitchen and bar stood in gape-mouthed adoration. Where had Mat-thew got them all? Enfield wondered. From the one, now yellow with age, showing a lad with a football clutched to his breast, plunging head on into the camera, to the most recent rotogravure of himself standing at ease beside his plane, they presented a fairly complete pictorial biography.

Standing there, seeing his life in graphic reca-pitulation, feeling again exultantly, but with a nameless nostalgia, the thrill of those early days, and sensing the encompassing pride and affection of these simple souls, Enfield was profoundly moved.

"Well, boys," he said, his genuine feeling in-fusing the hackneyed phrase with life, "after all, there's no place like home." Then he shook hands solemnly all around.

Casting club discipline to the winds, they fol-lowed Enfield and Hollister to the front steps and stood watching them as they disappeared across the moonlit course. Enfield turned to Hollister. "Did you ever see that absurd picture gallery in the pantry?" he asked.

Hollister nodded, regarding him quizzically. Enfield went on:

"Funny what that sort of thing can do to a

fellow. Funny that what a bunch of negro servants thinks of you can matter so much." Then, after a moment's silence, he went on, his usually easygoing manner giving place to a growing emotional intensity: "As a matter of fact, you'll never find anything else like it. It stays right on where a fellow's roots are, and sooner or later it pulls him back where he belongs."

He stopped walking and turned to his companion. "Felix," he said, "a while ago I told you I'd come back here for a while every winter. Well, you can tear that up now. By God, I'm coming back to live."

Hollister grasped his hand. "Good boy, Jerry," he exclaimed. "We'll shake on that."

After this, they had walked only a short distance farther when Enfield stopped again. His mood had changed, softened. He laid his hand on Hollister's shoulder and said: "You really didn't want to take a walk, did you? I'd have felt it before if I hadn't been so damned full of myself."

He turned Hollister about and faced him toward the club. Across the moonlit links, and with its clustered windows resting upon a gentle hill, it looked like a constellation half under the horizon.

Enfield gave him a gentle shove. "Get along," he said. "I won't bother with the ship after all. I'll take a run in the roadster later to set me for a night's sleep."

Hollister hesitated, turning back and extending his hand, but Enfield waved him away. "And no good-byes. They're bad luck when you're going into the air, you know."

CHAPTER 17

OLLISTER had parked the station wagon before the Gresham Arms and switched off his lights, before he admitted to himself that all evening, even during dinner, he had intended to see Leslie. That under the casual talk while he was with them, the even flow of his thoughts when he was alone, he had been deliberately shaping the evening toward that end. It had been this anticipation which had got him through the difficult and irritating ordeal of the dinner, transforming it into an exciting prelude to the hour which now lay before him.

Directly above where he stood, four flights up, he could see the two windows of Leslie's sitting room brightly lit, and in the moment that he waited before entering the building he saw a shadow pass one of them and pause. Then her silhouette appeared against the glass as she stood looking down into the street.

When he reached her door she was waiting for him. For a moment they stood, saying nothing, searching each other's faces, trying to penetrate the reserve that had fallen between them. It was useless to pretend that this was like their previous meetings. It had not been prearranged. Yet it was inevitable. To both of them came the thought that it had been predestined, inescapable, and that after it was over their old relationship would be ended, and in its place would be something wholly different but as yet unknown.

Hollister was the first to break the silence. He gave an embarrassed laugh that, essaying lightness, sounded false even in his own ears. "You don't seem surprised at finding me here," he said.

She answered him gravely: "Why should I be? We both knew you were coming." When he had entered, she closed the door softly and turned away, apologizing for the disorder of the room, and attacking it with her usual swift competence. "You must excuse the confusion. I've started to pack, you see. Not the actual packing, but there are so many things to be discarded before I go—"

"Regrets, for instance?"

"Oh, I've already thrown them out the window." She turned toward him with an armful of books. "I had to," she laughed, "so as to make room for a couple of memories."

He offered to help her, but she refused, and made him comfortable on the divan with a highball beside him. He sat forward with his elbows on his knees, his eyes following her as she moved about the room. She was wearing a negligee of raw silk, a deep sapphire in color, which was wrapped about her slender figure and bound at the waist with a garnet sash. Her legs were bare, and her feet were thrust into red leather sandals. In all of her movements there was a precision and economy of effort that, as she passed from one small task to another, seemed to bring order out of confusion as though in response to some natural law.

Hollister, watching her, was experiencing the sensation of being in a room which he had never seen before. The simple furnishings, even the sketch of himself, had taken on an air of taut expectancy, like objects which, brought together for a decorator's display and sharing no common personality, would presently be scattered and forgotten.

And then, observing Leslie as she moved about, he realized that she, too, had changed. And it came to him that the new taut quality in the atmosphere was an emanation from her and not a manifestation of his own overwrought imagination. The disarming child-quality that had made her always seem younger than her years was gone. She seemed older, and when she smiled he noticed for the first time that there were faint crow's-feet at the corners of eyes which had become larger and darker, and that her lips, parted slightly, seemed fuller and showed more color than he remembered. All of her movements were swift and restless.

With books in the curve of her arm, she stood poised for a second at the bedroom door. "I hadn't expected you for at least half an hour, or I'd have had the room ready," she said. She disappeared for a moment, and when she returned she added with a grin: "I might even have dressed."

A sheaf of papers on the desk engaged her attention briefly. She looked up from them and found his eyes appraising her. "Stop that," she commanded sharply. "I'm not on the model stand and I won't have you squinting through me."

"I'm sorry," he apologized. "I'm just trying to make you out. You're different. I feel as if I had never seen you before."

She crossed to him, swinging her hips in a deliberate swagger, and stood laughing down into his face, her own taking the direct light of a small lamp that stood beside his forgotten highball.

"Well," she asked, "how do you like it?"

He saw then that she was wearing make-up, and that it had been put on crudely, he could fancy angrily, the pastel softness of her face that he remembered going out under the sharp, almost hard, definition of line and color.

"Well," she challenged again, "how do you like it?"

Her proximity, and her manner, deliberately provocative, and in the air that vague foreshadowing, drawing closer now, warning him, set his pulses racing. "Technically," he told her, "it's the worst job I've ever seen. But somehow it says something. It convinces."

She accepted that gravely. "It's an outward and visible sign," she told him. "I'm on my own now and I shall do as I please." Then, searching his eyes, she bent slowly forward and pressed her mouth against his.

For a long moment there was nothing but a physical pressure, and a hunger, desperate, and fearful of its own defeat. Then in the act of parting an upsurge of emotion took them, fused them, and left them shaken.

Leslie turned unsteadily to the table and poured a drink from the decanter, holding the glass to the light and measuring with meticulous care. In the stillness, the small chattering sound of glass on glass was distinctly audible. She tossed it off, and with an involuntary shudder turned back and faced Hollister.

He was sitting forward with his elbows on his

knees and his face buried in his hands. His bony
length jutted into the sharp angles that drew sleeves
and trouser legs from wrists and ankles, and heightened the incongruous suggestion of adolescence
which was characteristic of him when faced with a
situation requiring decisive action.

It was this quality that had always disarmed
her. It struck at her now, infusing passion with a
soft, maternal desire to protect. Then, suddenly,
in a clairvoyant flash, the thought came to her that
it might be a conscious device. That some time during the evolution of his elaborate mechanism of
escape he had stumbled on this weapon against
which no woman was invulnerable. The suspicion
upset accepted premises. She had told herself that
this quality of immaturity, this perennial and en-
dearing boyishness that he had carried into middle
life, was a symptom of the emotional catalepsy in
which he had existed in Exeter. It had buttressed
her theory that if she could awaken him to reality,
he would be unspent, he would be strong to fulfill
his destiny. But so irresistible was his appeal that,
even now, with this suspicion in her mind, she
yielded involuntarily to it, turning back to him and
letting her hand linger on his bent head before she
seated herself quietly beside him.

His hand found hers blindly and lay upon it,
not in passion, but quietly, palm resting upon palm.

Presently, leaning forward and searching his
face, she forced him to meet her gaze. His eyes were
tragic, and she asked: "Did that make you very unhappy?"

"I don't know. I've never known anything like
it." He pondered for a moment, then went on. "It

couldn't have happened to a man when he was young. It takes the things that life does to you to bring out its beauty and its sadness."

Leslie covered his mouth with her fingers. "I won't have that," she said. "Love is a perfectly simple thing and has definite objectives. It's only a question of whether you have enough of it to win."

His hand closed about her own. "Listen," he said, "this isn't easy but I've got to say it. That might be your conception of love. Mine—right now, for you, is an unendurable hunger for something I know I'll never have, something I don't see how I'm going on living without."

She got up wearily and walked to the window, then turned her head and looked at him over her shoulder. "Your invincible Miriam," she said, "and the children. That's what's between you and life."

"No, my dear. It's more than that. It's the twenty years that I've finished and you haven't started."

She spun around on him in a fury, and involuntarily he got to his feet and faced her attack.

"You say that because you are afraid, terrified of your own shadow. You know that your family, your house, are something definite, tangible. That they can be left in one moment of saving madness by the simple act of boarding a train. And you're afraid—you've always been, that some day you'd go. But you feel safe now. You've rolled up your twenty years to hide in. Something that can't be run away from, that you can always pack along with you to stand at your elbow and tell you that the game is played out—that you are done for—that the easy chair and the cozy fire are best for age."

She crossed to him and stood looking up, her fists clenched and pressed into the softness of her breasts. "But if you believe that, you're believing a lie. Twenty years are not gone until they are lived, until all the adventure, all the passion, all the searching, that are packed into them, have been spent. Some people never know that. They die children. But you know it. For better or worse. And you can't escape it. And the time has come when you can't go on hiding."

Hollister seized her by the wrists, forcing her arms down, gripping, enjoining silence. She shook him off, and he stepped back, amazed at her vehemence and at the swift battering rush of her words.

"If you stop me now, you're done for. There'll never be anyone else to tell you the truth. When Miriam brought you here and fitted you into Exeter like a ready-made suit, you ceased to exist. It would have been a good life for some men, but not for you, because you had a special gift, and you either had to live for it, starve for it if necessary, or sell out and die.

"Well, you sold out—and what did you get? I'll tell you. Starvation for your own kind, for the thing you were born to do, for understanding. For the right even to fail wretchedly but honorably." She stopped, breathless, her eyes wild and dark, almost despising him. But before he could recover himself, she rushed on, her voice edged with hysteria. "I ought to stop now. I've said all that what you would call a lady should say. I ought to let you go home, tumble safely into bed and tuck your head under the covers. But I'm not going to be a lady. I am not even going to be decent, and for just once

you are going to see yourself from the outside looking in. There's another kind of hunger eating you.
But that's ironical, it's grotesque, because the com-
monest day laborer has a right to it. And I'll tell
you what it is: You haven't even got a woman."

Hollister turned suddenly from her. There was
a chair behind him and he blundered into it, knocking it over. After a while he asked, in a voice so low
that she could scarcely catch the words: "How could
you know that?"

"Any woman would," she answered, "who
loved you, and has seen as much of you as I have."

He turned and came toward her. His expression was puzzled, incredulous. "Say that again. I've
got to be sure I understand. Did you say you loved
me?"

From the outer hall came the sound of an opening door that poured into the confined space voices
lifted in farewell against a background of radio
music. Steps descended the stairs. The hillbilly bal-
lad beat against the panel of their door, insistent as
a pounding fist. Under the thump-thump of banjos
and shoe soles, a nasal voice droned:

"Put your arms 'round me an' feel my heart break—"

While it lasted they stood looking into each
other's faces, knowing it for what it was, not the
labored thumpings of a band a thousand miles away,
the good nights of an exemplary American home,
but the enemy at the gates. Watchful, tireless, the
enemy that had them almost beaten before they
started, and that now, even in this moment, was
thrusting itself between them, so that as they stood
gazing into each other's eyes their faces grew

blurred, like watchers from the deck and the pier-head as a vessel puts to sea.

When at last the door slammed, slicing off the song in the middle of a word, Leslie's eyes were wet. In the tense silence which followed, her voice sounded small and shaken. Across the short distance that separated them she flung out a hand to him. "Darling," she said, "come back."

She felt him responding, shaking himself free, and looming over her. His hands fell on her shoulders. "Answer me, then. Do you love me?"

"Darling—what can I say? I've been shouting it to heaven ever since you came in here, only you wouldn't understand."

Between them as they stood there a miracle was happening. A miracle in which, incredible as it seemed, Hollister was beginning to believe. More than that, quite suddenly and naturally he was believing in himself. There was nothing of the adolescent about him now. His hands bore hard on her shoulders, and his eyes gazing into hers gave her the illusion of expanding to her horizons, and rimming her world with blue fire.

"Do you mean," he demanded, "that if I took up life where I dropped it twenty-five years ago, you'd believe in me enough to come to me?—you'd share it?"

The fire in his eyes became intolerable. "Yes," she breathed.

His hands moved from her shoulders to her throat, and under his palms he felt the young life beating, rhythmic and strong. He tipped her face up, holding it between his hands like a flower on its stem. Then, with the word broken on her mouth, he whispered: "Now."

When she loosed her sash, the negligee fell softly to the floor. It formed a crescent of sapphire silk, and from its center her body lifted white and straight to the mouth that was crushing her into complete, if not altogether unpremeditated, surrender.

*I*T WAS strange, he thought, with a sort of detached wonder, how unsubstantial reality had become. The car driving steadily forward over the familiar road, the moonlight riding the telephone wires like a flight of luminous arrows, the home to which he was speeding, even Miriam and the children, all seemed like accessories of a life closed and finished, already a part of memory rather than the living present.

Leslie was reality—Leslie and the welding of their separate lives into a completed whole. It had happened not an hour ago, but already it seemed to extend far back into the past. All of their talk, each careless gesture, that had passed since he had entered her room, flashed up to him, sweeping him back to the momentous second when he had entered her door and found her waiting for him.

He tried then, definitely, to bring his mind face to face with the facts. To approach the hideous question of untangling the intricate fabric of his married life. But it could not be done—not on this night, at any rate. From the threshold of Leslie's room his thoughts, dismissing a quarter of a century as though it had never existed, soared back to the dingy studio in the Quarter, carrying him with them in a transmigration so real that he experienced it, not as memory, but as a sensation quickening his living tissue.

He had forgotten how utterly beautiful a

woman could be, and how much taller she always seemed when, free of clothing, she stood with the line of her body rising pure and unbroken from ankle to brow. It came back to him now out of the past, that never-failing sense of wonder, of sudden, almost blinding, revelation, that he had known in that earlier incarnation. It swept him back to the studio and to the girl, scarcely more than a child, who had posed for him. She would enter, he remembered, just a little slattern of the Paris streets. But she had had a real sense of drama. She would always take an extravagantly long time over her few buttons, then suddenly in a single fall her clothes would be in a huddle at her feet and she would kick them from her, springing like a young Diana to the stand. Her image—Leslie's, as she had stood so short a time ago—so much alike—only a few unimportant years between. Then they had seemed to merge, leaving only Leslie, and the intervening years had gone.

Clay—so deceptively submissive, lying in the palm of your hand, but swarming with stubborn devils when you tried to break it to your will. But it could be broken. There had been a time when he had almost done it. Once he had captured the soft solidity of a woman's breast, once he had caught the springing line of a tensed thigh. That was yesterday.

But now there was Leslie, and she believed he had it in him. And tomorrow was another day. His fingers gripped savagely, not on the hard rubber of a steering wheel, but on a soft resistive mass, forcing it out between his fingers, and in his nostrils was not the autumnal smell of the Carolina countryside, but the raw earthy odor of clay.

CHAPTER 19

AFTER Hollister left, Leslie stood for a time surveying herself in the pier glass. Then, working slowly, she removed her make-up, studying her image with grave absorption as her highly colored replica faded out leaving her familiar reflection to stare curiously out at her.

Since, now, this was not only herself, but a gift to another, she regarded it with dispassionate appraisal. It wasn't bad, she decided, noting the clear pallor of her skin, the mouth showing only a faint color, but full and sensitive—yes, even beautiful, between the firm little chin and the short upper lip; the eyes large and very dark under shadowing lashes. All familiar—too familiar, she concluded. It seemed to her that the mirror, habituated through years of use to her old reflection, had kept on repeating it, not realizing how profoundly she had changed. It was incredible that this night could leave her looking just as it had found her. That the ecstasy that had charged through every fiber had not left its signature visible upon her flesh.

The little gilt clock on her dressing table flung out a single breathless note, and she was amazed to find that it was only half past twelve. Only one hour and a half since Felix had entered her room, and the thought came to her how little the passage of time meant in relation to life, that it was emotional pitch that counted and not the dull mathematical progres-

sion of days into months, months into years, and
years into a lifetime. It demonstrated perfectly the
theory in which she had believed, and to which, tonight, she had won Felix. What if they had only ten
years ahead of them—five, even. The specter of the
twenty years that lay between them rose before her
then, the fear that he would go, and she live on. But
this she put resolutely from her. "No, darling," she
said aloud. "Not that—never that." And even if he
failed to win recognition, it wasn't going to matter.
That had been made clear to them in that clairvoyant moment when they had lain in each other's
arms. When they had spoken of it afterwards, there
it was, fully realized and accepted in the mind of
each. It was only following your star that mattered,
and success or failure lay only in your own ultimate
knowledge of whether you had been true or false.
And further, that happiness had nothing to do with
success in the accepted sense, but was a small, personal, and private adventure of no concern whatever
except to the two who had set forth upon it.

While he had been with her there had been no
discussion of future plans. It had been understood
that she would remain through the week to leave the
studio in order and dispose of her possessions. Now
she saw the impossibility of carrying out this plan.
To revert to their old relationship, to move about
the familiar setting under the eyes of Miriam and
the servants, and to pretend that there was nothing
between them was out of the question. The very
thought of it repelled her. In the life into which
they had entered there was a certain integrity which
must be maintained; there were certain articles of
faith to which they had subscribed and to which

they must adhere the more fervently since they violated the accepted code. With a sort of awe she realized how irrevocable was the step that they had taken, how much more binding upon them than marriage would have been, for each was answerable directly to the other and not to the vast abstraction known as human society.

And now, realizing this, she saw why the idea of returning to the studio had been unthinkable. It would have started their lives together with a deception.

Quickly she reached a decision. She would leave at once, tomorrow, or at the latest the day after. And she would not see him again before going. He would understand that. He would see that in that way only could their relationship be held inviolate until he came to her.

Acting swiftly upon her decision, she swept her toilet articles into their battered leather case and pressed the snap. The staccato click was an accent of finality in the midnight quiet of the room.

She was conscious now of a chill in the air that struck through the sheer fabric of her gown. Through the open door she could see the blue negligee lying where it had fallen on the floor of the living room. She had always prided herself on her lack of sentimentality about her possessions. Things could enslave you and tie you down, or they could go lumbering about the world after you making you work for them, and in the end possessing you. She had always said that when the time came to go, she would board a train and leave the auctioneer to clean up after her. But now, looking at the crescent of blue silk from which she had stepped into Felix's

arms, she was assailed by an emotion so poignant
that she paused in the act of going for it. She knew
that as long as she lived she would carry it with her,
bound always by the associations that this night had
woven into it.

Still under the spell of it, she turned back to the
room. Now, before it was dismantled, she must note
each detail, so that always she could close her eyes
and re-create it as it had stood tonight. So that she
could sense again at will that emanation, not a perfume; not a pattern of light and shadow that re-
corded the passage on the senses, but that more
subtle vibration that once captured would beat forever in the memory.

She saw then that Felix had left upon the chest
of drawers the small silver-mounted comb that he
always carried. How typical of him that he had forgotten it, and how impact of his personality it was.
She stood for a moment, holding it, then lifted it to
her cheek, pressing it until she winced under its
fierce sweet pain. When she turned and placed it in
the top drawer, it left a livid serrated line that stood
out for a moment like a scar on the pallor of her
skin.

She switched off the lights, plunging the room
into a warm gloom compounded of reflected light
from the living room and the cold whiteness of
moonlight. From among the blurred outlines the
bed, lying directly beneath the window and sheeted
in cold radiance, leaped with startling distinctness.
She noted that the moon had shifted slightly to the
southward and had climbed a little higher, so that
in falling through the panes it marked the bed off
in a pattern of diamonds, instead of squares as it had

done earlier. Otherwise everything was just as it had been. She stood for a moment making it her own, bringing to bear the trained observation of the artist. Then with an involuntary sigh, she turned and switched on the lights.

Now that her mind was made up, she would act at once. First she would write Felix a letter, making it plain why he must not try to see her again. Then she would work through the night. She knew that she would not rest again until it was finished and she was on her way. In her veins there burned a fever to be gone, to be done with Exeter, to plunge like a diver into the swift and uncharted currents that raced seaward from the known and finished into an unknown, a not even imagined, tomorrow.

Leaving the negligee lying where it was, and smiling derisively at her new softness, she took from the closet a robe, mannish and warm, and slipped into it. Then she went to the desk and picked up her fountain pen.

"Darling," she wrote. "By the time you receive this, you will realize as I do that we must not meet again here. The new world that we found tonight is too perfect. We mustn't step out of it. We dare not. I'll take it away with me and keep it until you come. I will write to you where to find me in New York.

"Darling, don't delay. We have missed so much already. And oh, darling, I am crying. Right now. All of a sudden. But I am so happy. It must be because, for the first time in my life, I am having to tell you good-bye. *I love you.* Leslie."

Through a mist she watched the paper absorb the tear that had fallen on it, making a cream-colored blister on dead white. Then she folded the letter and slipped it into its envelope. The practical business of addressing and stamping steadied her. She crossed to the bedroom window and raised the sash, and looked out and down. She could see the deserted street bathed in moonlight, and the postbox on the opposite pavement invested now with a mysterious and portentous significance. Into it had gone the dreams, ambitions, pitiful frustrations, of so many lives—and from it, like pebbles thrown into still water, they had extended in ever-widening circles, carrying hope, fear, despair, to the far corners of the world. And now she, too, must entrust it with her future and abide by the consequences.

For a moment, moved by these thoughts, she hesitated. Had she better see Felix again after all? Was there any chance of his misunderstanding? If you could follow the letter past that inexorable iron lid, the blurring thumb and finger of the postman, and watch the face of the reader. If, watching, you could reach forward and with your hand on his say, No, dear—these dumb things called words are trying to say *this* to you, not that. Then it would be well. But this blind, irrevocable committal, this staking of everything upon the long hazard that the subtle emotional essence of yourself would survive the intervening hours and convince beyond the limitations of mere words—that was something to wonder about.

She lifted the letter and studied it long and searchingly. In her bold, candid, but distinctly feminine hand she saw the words: Felix Hollister, Esq., Wingfields, Hatton Road, City. She held it for a moment, one hand folded over the other and the letter beneath them pressed between her breasts.

And then for the first time some deep premonitory instinct warned her. She felt it bearing down upon her, formless, and a little frightening. She had known fear before, but it had not been like this. Fear was something definite and directed, and it derived from some known source. But this sensation, starting with a vague prescience, and momentarily tightening about her heart, was different. It tensed her muscles and sharpened her perceptions until they seemed to plunge beyond the walls of the room from the clearly apprehended, the concrete, toward the terrifying abstraction that was menacing her.

She stood waiting, the letter still pressed between her breasts, her lips parted, and her eyes wild and dark. For a moment she felt omniscient, that if Felix should stir in his sleep she would hear and know. Across the moonlit gulf that lay between her and the other side of town she heard the chimes of the Baptist church striking one, silver ringing on silver, thin and ghostly. From a hilltop on the Wesley pike drifted the frantic clamor of a motor horn, softened and muted by distance. She perceived it not only as sound but as color, bright brass streaking like a comet through silver light. Finding her and spilling its beauty softly at her feet.

Then she felt the tension easing. And in a moment she decided what it was that she had feared. It was Miriam. It could not have been anything else. She could have laughed aloud in her relief. Yes, she was going away and leaving Felix at her mercy. But he was no longer the Felix whom Miriam had known. He was the boy who had lost his way twenty-five years ago, and had found it with her tonight. Nothing that stranger could do would detain him now.

Now her mood had changed, its horror ebbing swiftly, and in its place she experienced a still exaltation. "Darling," she breathed, "I could never doubt you. You know that—don't you?"

Saying it. Putting it into words. Hearing it with her own ears. And suddenly, in her strangely clairvoyant mood experiencing the profound conviction that waking or sleeping he had heard it too, she turned toward the door. It was settled now. The realization of it came to her translated into light that flooded her being and broke in dazzling waves against her vision. She opened the door blindly, and her feet followed the familiar way down the stairs and to the pavement.

CHAPTER 20

AFTER he had parted from Hollister, Enfield walked down the row of parked cars until he came to his roadster. Long and low-hung, with the top strapped down in its housings, it looked like some scaled and incredible monster crouched for a spring. Tempted by the beauty of the night and the knowledge that at this hour he would have the road practically to himself, he took his seat and stepped on the starter. At the light pressure of his foot the twelve cylinders gave a low snarl that shrilled to a menacing paean as he shifted to the accelerator and bore down on the pedal.

For a moment while the car stood in neutral he sat listening to the only music that he could understand, feeling as he always did a sense of physical power, a merging of his identity with that of the machine. He switched on the lights and the wash of misty moonlight that lay over the links was gashed by a shaft that flung the area before the car into sharp definition, giving the road, the receding avenue, an intense but theatrical reality and blotting out the surrounding landscape. He eased the car soundlessly from gear to gear, lifting the power in a controlled crescendo, feeling the responsive throb and surge until the two hundred horsepower of driving force poured out under his foot and the needle on the illuminated dial crept to seventy and hung there.

He had swung from the avenue into the turnpike and before him the road lay wide and straight.
On either side patches of woodland, occasional farm-
houses, a wayside store dark and shuttered, raced
past on a tide of misty half-light. It was a quiet early-
to-bed countryside, and at this hour the ribbon of
concrete that connected Exeter with the hamlet of
Wesley fifty miles away belonged to Enfield. He
settled himself in his seat, feeling with a conscious,
almost sensual, release, his taut nerves relax, his
hands grow light and sure upon the wheel.

He could remember well the time when he
never looked ahead of the living instant; when he
could take off for a flight concerned only, and with
complete absorption, with the business in hand. It
was, he thought, not more than three years ago that
he had acquired the disconcerting habit of suddenly
in the midst of a flight wondering what he would do
if such and such an emergency should arise. Or suffering a momentary obsession that in the familiar
song of the motor there was a false note, an unac-
countable syncopation. He was sure now that after
his months of rest at Exeter he was free from that
distracting habit. He bore down on the accelerator,
shooting the needle to eighty, then ninety, squinting
into the slashing wind, and feeling exultingly the
old sure sense of mastery, the excitement that lifted
him to a keen and tingling sentience.

Under the spell of the machine, that part of his
mind that was concerned with the routine of living
centered automatically on the road that poured its
miles smoothly and buoyantly between the headlights and under the soaring body. With his gaze
dreaming on the long hood he was aware of the life

that pulsed beneath it, the cylinders giving off a sound that was not so much a series of minute closely-integrated explosions as a flow of invincible power made audible. And playing against the voice of the engine, rounding out the symphony and giving it completion, he heard the whine of the suction cups on the big tires as they grasped the concrete then hurled it behind them.

Now thinking was like plunging into a swift stream that played among eddies and shot, with the thrill of the unexpected, down rapids and into tranquil pools.

Speed! He had made an eighty yard run once around Princeton's end for the touchdown that had cinched the game. A sky loaded with snow bellying down almost to the goal posts that had stood etched white against it. Cheering that had pounded in his brain like alcohol. Then when it was over they had found that he had done it with a broken collarbone. Yes, he had always had guts. They'd have to give him that at the ultimate class reunion when he would be reported missing and they'd be saying the best and the worst of him. Guts, and a straight shooter! He smiled grimly as he coined his epitaph. Not strong on brains, he'd concede that. If he hadn't had his own money life would have been pretty heavy going. But he had had it, and he had paid his way. And his friends liked him for what he was, not what he had. Getting them and holding them was one job he had put his heart into, and he knew he had succeeded. They'd still like him even if he went flat broke. He'd stake his last dollar on that.

Friends—the one he had just left—Hollister. Was it true that he was having an affair with that

washed-out little secretary of his? It had come up at
the club yesterday and Bob Pendleton had denied
it with such vehemence there might actually be
something in it. What an ass he was, likable, but still
an ass, with a wife like Miriam, grown children, and
everything set for a mellow old age. Women—funny
about men and women—in his whole life only
three whose names he could remember. Temperate
enough for a bachelor with twenty-five years of full-
blooded manhood to spend. And they had had no
complaint. Well, at least, two of them had none.
But Violet, the first—sometimes he wasn't so sure.
She had bewildered him by refusing to take his
money. He had been the first with her, too, but he
hadn't known that until it was too late. It had lasted
through his senior year, and when he was leaving,
feeling very much the man of the world, he had told
her that she needn't worry about finances, and had
stuffed a wad of bills into her little white handbag.
Silently she had forced it back into his hand, then
had turned quickly away so he could not see her
face. At the moment the thought flashed through his
mind that it was calculating of her, leaving him like
that with a sense of unfulfilled obligation, especially
when she knew the sort of fellow he was, and how
he would take it. He had said defensively: "Listen,
Violet. I've always been on the level about its not
lasting." And she had answered: "Sure, and don't
you worry about me. I'm all right. It's you I'm thinking about, and you're never even going to know
what you're passing up." He had thought that pretty
conceited of her, and had told himself that if she felt
that way about it they were quits.

But later, in France, he had kept thinking

about her, seeing her eyes as they had looked when he had said good-bye. Behind the clear look, the boyish bravado, a light had gone out. Now and then, in all the rush and change of the years, she had sprung into his mind with startling clarity, and he had wondered sometimes what it would have been like to have come back to her. There had even been moments when her words had returned to him, no longer conceited, but strangely prophetic. She came to him now on a wave of self-pity, not altogether unpleasant, like hearing Carrie Jacobs Bond on the radio when he was feeling lonely. He found himself wondering what had become of her during all the years that had rushed between them, and a soft, nostalgic emotion invaded his consciousness causing him to say half aloud: "Good kid, she always was a good kid." Yes, if he had it all to do over again, he'd chance it. He'd bet on her straight through to the finish, even if marriage did tie a fellow down. But that was all past now, and he had never been the sort who could act on impulse. Given time, he could reason things out, but somehow, what with this and that, there never was time.

The motor waked a roadside echo and suddenly he was between the rows of store fronts that bulked serried and ugly in the misty light and constituted the main street of Wesley. He glanced at the clock on the dash and gave the wheel an approving pat. Fifty miles in forty-five flat. He slowed down to twenty and circled the green. A solitary street lamp illumined the inevitable Confederate soldier standing precariously upon his shaft and gazing stolidly at his wasted horizon. Prankishly Enfield saluted him with a double toot of his French taxi horn.

From the granite seat that was hewn into the base of the shaft a figure lifted itself, yawned and stretched, the mouth forming a clearly visible O, and the arms raised as though in silent prayer to the figure above, then it shambled away into the shadows.

With a spin of the wheel Enfield swung back into the turnpike for the race home.

Fifteen minutes of exhilarating driving had passed. The car was tearing up a long hill beyond the brow of which, as the machine mounted and the horizon descended, the stars swirled up into the night with an effect like sparks blown upward from a titanic forge. Fascinated, Enfield watched the illusion, tricked out of his introspective mood by its dimly comprehended beauty. He topped the rise and halfway down the long decline that lay below him he saw the twin taillights of a machine. His response was automatic, and the needle crept from sixty to seventy-five, but to his surprise the lights held their lead.

This was evidently a challenge. Well, he'd be damned if he wouldn't show them. But he must resort to strategy. He would pretend indifference, idle along, and bring the two machines close together. Then, counting upon the lightning acceleration of his twelve cylinders, shoot around his rival and seize his rightful place on the road. He dropped to fifty, then forty, and was boyishly excited to see how quickly the other car responded, falling back to a lead of about a hundred yards and holding that.

He bore down on the throttle and bent forward over the wheel. The wind, mounting in a steady gush, battered his face and filled his eyes with water.

But, as though the cars had been connected by a cable, the other had got away with him and maintained its exact distance effortlessly in spite of Enfield's pace. After five minutes of furious driving Enfield again dropped back.

The slow-moving but mountainous pugnacity of the man was now thoroughly aroused. Reaching Exeter ahead of the other car became imperative, a fixation which drew all of his faculties together in a supreme effort. This was not merely a childish desire to prove his car the faster of the two. It had become a test of himself, of his ability to hold nerve and sinew steady, to take chances, sure of his complete mastery of the mechanism that fulfilled himself and gave his existence meaning. He must put this over without faltering, then he would carry the old, unconquerable certainty into the air with him again. He would know that he was whole again, whole and fit, that life would hit its old stride, swift and thrilling, and that he would have one more chance of riding it out to the finish.

And then for the first time it occurred to him to speculate as to what a car of such power was doing on that lonely road at that hour. Bootleggers, as likely as not, and they had probably taken his machine for a police car. That would explain their determination not to be overtaken. Or, suddenly, with a disquieting shock, it might be a police car pacing him for speeding, and merely leading him on into town and arrest. Well, he didn't care. Even the risk of a ticket could not deter him now. Five minutes more and they would be in the suburbs, and what was to be done must be done now.

They topped the gentle rise that looked down

upon Exeter. The town was there, waiting, and the first widely spaced arc lights were less than a mile away. Separated by a hundred yards of concrete that hurtled back to Enfield from between the taillights of his rival, the cars held to fifty.

Enfield knew that the moment had come. No vacillating now, no frustrating doubts, only the old certainty that started with a hard bright point in his brain and splayed out to flood his being with unconquerable power. He bore down on the pedal, driving the needle to seventy. Then he stopped watching it and concentrated on the car ahead.

His forward rush must have taken the other machine by surprise, for almost instantly he was behind it, pressing his klaxon in a peremptory demand for the road. Sluggishly the car pulled over. They evidently knew they were beaten. Now, for Enfield, the supreme moment, the orgasm of speed that, while his faculties functioned in an almost sensuous unity with the machine, freed his mind to a flood of vagrant images and impressions flung up out of his past. Strangely, it was Violet who flashed up to him now, stirring him to an old emotion suddenly warmed and amplified by his momentarily heightened sentience.

His radiator was on a line with the rear axle of the other car. He could see now that it was a large sedan. It clung to its own side of the road and took on speed—not enough to pull away again, but sufficient to assure him hazardous seconds before he could establish his lead and cut in ahead.

Then in a moment, shatteringly, he knew that he would never make it. His perfect co-ordination was breaking down. Beside him the sedan seemed to draw out interminably; the chromium bird perched on the radiator cap fascinated him. While the cars held their relative positions, it seemed to soar forward, drawing the sedan out after it like an express train and pre-empting the whole length of the road to town.

He wrenched his gaze from it to the road. The space between the sedan and the shoulder was suddenly appallingly narrow, and he perceived that the bulletlike trajectory of his car was failing, an almost imperceptible lateral variation creeping in, like a spent ball that begins to wabble in its course. Scarcely daring to trace this to its source, he glanced at his hands and in the faint light saw that they were shaking on the wheel. The shaking communicated itself to his entire body, breaking down the terrific muscular tension that he threw against it.

Some protective instinct that still functioned despite his complete demoralization must have prompted him to attempt retreat, for, automatically, he exerted a spasmodic pressure on the brake. The roadster gave a sudden premonitory lurch and the front fenders of the two machines began to sway toward each other. Fascinated, Enfield saw the distance between them diminish as they drew closer and closer in the grip of that fatal and irresistible affinity. Then, like the first shy kiss of lovers, they touched lightly and parted.

At that touch a dark and terrible ecstasy shook through him. He knew that this was the end, that they would draw together again to meet in complete disruption, and that he was powerless to restrain them. And yet under the spell of his inexplicable seizure he knew no fear, rather a sort of exaltation that this was his appointed time, and that he had ridden out his destiny to the end. He closed his eyes and, not as a prayer, but in a shout of savage triumph ejaculated "Christ!"

A sound, shocking in its irrelevance, brought Enfield back to reality. It was the loud, jeering, slightly drunken laughter of youth. He saw that he was driving slowly down the middle of the road. The sound came again, fainter now, and he turned and looked behind him.

The sedan had swung into a side road and was slowly gathering speed. From its open windows arms waved in his direction, and he flinched under a final derisive ya-ya-ya as the car plunged out of his field of vision.

The night wind struck chill through his sweat-drenched clothing. Now he knew that he had to stand up to it—take it on the chin. No use to delude himself. He was finished. The enormous drama of extinction that had loomed over him a moment before gave place to a frightened speculation as to what he would do with life now that it had been flung back at him.

Sensing with a sickly grin the grotesque contrast, his mind dropped from flying to golf. Hitting a piddling little ball around the ground from hole to hole. The thought awakened a feeling akin to nausea. Big game hunting? Yes, only he couldn't bear to see a living creature die. The war years had not helped that—they had only intensified it. He had known, though he had never admitted it to himself, that had he been on the ground, he couldn't have stood it.

Now if there was only a woman, someone he

could go to. Arms that would hold him, not in passion, but in that deep, silent understanding which, he had been told, followed passion, and for which he had never had time to wait. Violet could have given it to him. She had told him that he didn't know what he was passing up. She knew. Out of the past she rose, translated into an emotion compounded of self-pity and belated sorrow over her suffering. He gave himself to it, remembering her again as she had stood telling him good-bye, her face averted, her small determined hand forcing the roll of bills back into his own. The visualization was so sharp that, for a moment, it stood interposed between himself and the familiar street, blotting out the huddled bungalows, the uncompromising cube of the Gresham Arms which he was passing.

He was conscious of a slight jar, and instantaneously got an impression of an object flying back, feather-light, from his front right fender, across the sidewalk. Then he had passed, and before him the street lay, commonplace, familiar, and deserted.

He was not frightened, because about it all there was a sense of unreality. His mind, shocked and exhausted by the crisis through which he had just passed, rejected the event as a figment of the imagination. But immediately some deep, protective instinct assumed control, working behind the conscious processes of the brain, yet with complete logic. It forestalled an impulse to turn and look behind. It took swift cognizance of the fact that the street was deserted, and the flanking rows of cottages dark. Then smoothly, and with unpremeditated cunning, it directed the car around the first corner and slowed it down to a speed that would allay suspicion should any chance nocturnal traveler happen to see it.

Minutes passed before Enfield was faced by certain knowledge of what had occurred. It came battering at the door of his consciousness and could no longer be denied. That had been a woman. She had been standing at the edge of the curb with something white in her hand. She had been looking in the other direction and had stepped directly into the path of the car. Ordinarily he could have stopped, but tonight, shot to pieces by his experience on the road, it had been different.

For the second time that night panic possessed him, yet with its disruptive forces shaking him like an ague, he must make a decision. He must go back of course. But now a considerable time had passed, and while the street had been deserted at the moment of the accident, it was a populous district and if she had been seriously hurt, and this he would not admit, she would have been found and cared for already. If he returned now it must be with the admission that he had known and had not stopped.

With the steadying necessity for action upon him, he realized clearly for the first time where the car had got to. It stood upon the brow of a low hill at the entrance of a narrow lane. The lane led by a back way into the club grounds, in the vicinity of the parking lot. It was a way which he often used, and habit, prompted by the subtle exterior force that seemed to have assumed control of his actions, had directed him hither.

He switched off his lights and looked about him. He had, apparently, skirted the town by little used streets and had now only to drop down the hill and park. Below him lay the grounds of the club. The building itself, rising white out of the vast monotone of the links and roofed with twin slabs of frosted silver where the dew took the moonlight, was about to close for the night.

As he looked, the lights were extinguished in the cardroom, leaving only the bar illuminated, and the globe over the locker-room door. A group of late players stepped out on the veranda. He heard Jarvis Maxton, hearty and indefatigable, regretting the necessity of going home to bed. Miriam Hollister's contralto rose in answer, bell-like in the still air. She was saying: "Of course I'll have to go. Holly can't even be depended on to put out the cat."

The answering laughter of the crowd, indulgent but faintly derisive, threw Enfield's thoughts back to the sedan and its jeering riders, and again in a swift shattering wave the demoralization and disillusionment of that moment engulfed him, leaving him weak and shaken.

In the few minutes that remained before his friends reached the parking lot, he must arrive at some decision. Then he knew that he could not face them. He could not face anybody now. At the very thought his mind seethed into dark chaos, and he knew that if he told of the accident and tried to explain, he would break down and stand convicted before them. He remembered then that Miriam Hollister would pass the Gresham Arms on her way home, and that even if there had been a serious accident, and no one had discovered the unfortunate pedestrian, she would pass the spot as soon as he could, even if he turned back at once. She had quick eyes. Nothing escaped her, and in an emergency she would be infinitely more effective than he.

The necessity for immediate action had passed. Now he could wait until morning, get himself in hand, and face the music. His sense of relief at this respite was enormous. In contrast with the horror through which he had just passed, it made him feel almost his old self. He saw himself quite clearly as he would appear in the morning, suspected by no one, and admitting that while he was not conscious of having caused the accident, he had passed that way, and offering to pay a large indemnity on the off chance.

Yes, that was the idea. He needed only to collect his wits, then he would go and do all that was humanly possible. But first he must have a drink, three fingers neat, to break the tension and steady his nerves.

Below him, in the faint moonlight, Enfield could see the huddle of cars in the parking lot. He could drop down, he decided, park, and get to the bar through the locker-room, without encountering the group on the veranda. He put his car in motion, and dropped down the slight incline toward the club grounds.

The parked cars had not changed their positions since he had left them two hours earlier. Between Maxton's sedan and the Bedfords' roadster remained the vacant place from which he had driven his own car. He slid silently into it and switched off his motor, registering with a slight shock of surprise the fact that he had inexplicably forgotten to turn on his lights for the drop down the hill and into the lot.

Now suddenly, in a gale of high spirits, his friends were all about him, filling the cars, laughing.

Chick Bedford, warmed with good corn and an evening's winnings, lifted his voice in a paean of thanksgiving to his gods of chance:

> "Oh, there was a little hen,
> And she had a wooden leg"—

Maxton discovered Enfield. "Hello, Jerry," he called, reaching over the side of the roadster to slap him on the shoulder. "Just leaving, eh? Where've you been keeping yourself all evening?"

Miriam said: "I know. The old grouch, been mooning about the course with Holly—two of a kind."

Pendleton said: "Taking your constitutional, eh? Good job, too, at your age."

All laughed loudly to prove they didn't think Enfield old. Then there was a moment of interrogatory silence. Sudden anger flamed in Enfield. What business was it of theirs where he had been, what he did with himself? A man had a right to protect himself.

He said surlily: "Yes, just taking a walk."

Chick Bedford announced: "Doctors prescribe it." He shot his roadster out of the line, and the cozy little figure beside him giggled: "And babies cry for it."

Motors roared, lights splayed out garishly on road, avenue, whitewashed parking curb, then one by one the cars went rocketing down the drive. From the club came the sound of a slamming door, the globe over the locker-room entrance went black,

and the swift uneasy silence that follows in the wake
of gaiety possessed itself of the night.

The crunch of footsteps on gravel brought Enfield back to the present. It would be Paul the barman going home, and for a moment he pitted his
need of a bracer against his reluctance for human
companionship. He had only to ask and Paul would
reopen the bar for him. But was it worth it? The
footsteps paused, then left the gravel for the sand of
the lot. The man's dim figure rose before the car.
The negro was still wearing his white jacket, and
this, hanging between his black pants and dark
visage, gave the eerie effect of a dismembered and
faintly luminous torso suspended several feet from
the earth.

The man entertained an extravagant admiration for Enfield, and now the darkness above the coat
was broken by a flash of teeth.

"Dat you, Mr. Jerry?"

The eager proffer of companionship decided
Enfield. More than anything else in the world he
needed to be alone. He switched on his lights, and
said, with finality: "Yes. Good night, Paul."

Revealed now in his entirety, the negro stepped
forward, hypnotized as he always was by the splendor and size of the roadster. Above the sound of the
starting motor, he said hopefully: "Mr. Jerry, that
sho is some automobile. There ain't nothin' roun'
here can touch it." He had laid his hand on the
spare tire and looked up at Enfield. Then, daunted
by the unresponsive silence, but goaded forward
by a desire that could no longer be suppressed,
he tried again, humbly, his eyes raised in almost
comic supplication to Enfield's face. "Mr. Jerry,"

he begged, "you reckon sometime when you is goin'
some place, you could let me ride in de rumble?"

The appeal stirred the old Enfield into being.
He said, almost heartily: "Sure, Paul. Some other
time, you remind me."

Still reluctant to let him go, the man hung
there, looking down. Then he bent and removed a
small white square that had been caught between
the side of the spare and the tirewell. He held it out
to Enfield. "Dis here's a letter, Mr. Jerry," he said.
"Reckon it blowed out of your car."

Now, suddenly, in a frenzy to be gone, Enfield
snatched the paper and threw it on the floor of the
car. Then, seeing that the negro was at last clear of
the machine, he shot forward into the road.

Back in his room at the hotel, with a pint of
new bootleg corn on the table, Enfield commenced
to pull himself together. Four walls, a stout door, a
lock, between him and the aimless curiosity, the
blundering, amiable, incalculably dangerous stu-
pidity of friends. He half filled a glass with the
limpid whisky. It was all that he could get at that
hour from the sleepy boy at the door. The raw, oily,
odorous draft sickened him, but presently he commenced to feel the stimulant in a quickened pulse,
a feeling of renewed self-confidence.

The room was untidy with the litter of the recent packing, old letters overflowing the wastepaper
basket, a torn shirt in the center of the stuffy red
carpet, an empty pinch-bottle under the edge of the
bed. His trunk had gone to the express office. The
Gladstone, already packed, lay open on the stand,
waiting for the addition of his toilet things in the
morning.

The races—the thought of their tremendous imminence, to which he had looked forward with such confidence only this morning, broke his equilibrium with a slight premonitory turn of dizziness, and the hand that reached for pipe and tobacco fumbled the pouch loose and spilled the contents on the floor.

With a sound that was half oath and half sob, he got to his feet and stood, hands jammed in pockets. He hadn't the courage to pour the drink that he desperately needed, knowing the mess he would make of it and dreading the humiliation which even in the locked privacy of his room would engulf him.

He turned and faced the mirror, standing under the white direct light of the ground-glass globe in the center of the room. In a blind search for reassurance, he took the pose of the professional strong man, legs braced slightly apart, arms tensed with biceps bulging under the incongruous dinner jacket. But the old pagan delight in his body was gone. He could not delude himself. He saw the pose as ridiculous, theatrical, an illustration out of a physical culture magazine.

Then standing, and looking, at last, he met his own eyes. The look that they gave back was, he realized, different. It stared back at him with a certain defiance, the lids twitching slightly at the outer corners under the nervous strain. For a long moment he faced it out. Then with a groan he dropped on a chair and hid his face in his hands.

Until this moment, the inescapable fact of his physical collapse had loomed so ominously in his mind that the moral implications of his accident had scarcely occurred to him. He had convinced himself that it had been unavoidable. Reparation was something to be faced in the future, after he had got himself in hand. He would find some way of compensating, generously, as was his custom, through the medium of a checkbook. It might even be possible to close the matter out through a third party, without revealing his identity.

It seemed now, looking back upon the whole nightmare experience, that the chances of his actual identification with the accident were small, and his earlier visualization of himself going forward heroically and shouldering the blame was superseded by the conviction that a secret adjustment would be just as fair to the injured party, and that a quixotic exposure of himself would be foolish and useless.

He remembered having told Hollister when they had parted that he was going to take a walk before going to bed. Then the others, two hours later, had assumed that he had been on the grounds during the interval. His anger at being set upon by them with their infantile chatter had provoked him to corroboration, and they had accepted it.

Now, in swift retrospection, he checked over his movements from the moment of that ghostly impact, and was surprised at the clarity with which they presented themselves. It was almost as though he were watching the development of a photographic plate upon which inchoate masses of light and shade sharpened into vivid detail. He could have mapped his course to the hill behind the club, even though some of the unfrequented byways were unfamiliar to him and had been taken apparently by chance. He remembered, too, his drop down the hill to the parking lot, with his lights out, and wondered now for the first time whether it was a case of absent-mindedness, or what he had always defined as presence of mind—that automatic impulse which precedes thought and which, in the old days of flying, had pulled him out of so many tight spots. This idea brought him reassurance, steadied him.

He poured a drink, spilling only a little of the liquor on the table, and gulped it down.

And now into his field of consciousness surged the race that he would be missing, and the end of it all. Immediately his need for assuagement conjured up Violet. There was something miraculous, prophetic, in the way she came to him now, when his world was in dissolution and there was no one to whom he could turn. He rejected savagely the thought that she, too, was approaching middle age, that since she was so gentle, lovely, and desirable, she probably had, during the long interim, been possessed by other men. With fierce jealousy he isolated himself with her in an impregnable fastness of his mind and barred the door against the tragic happenings of the night.

The clamor of the telephone shattered his reverie, and still half dazed, he lifted the receiver to his ear. In the hazy borderland that lies between fantasy and reality, he distinguished the voice of the night clerk, apologizing interminably for calling.

"Yes, yes," Enfield cut in at last. "That's all right. What is it?"

"Dr. Pendleton. Said he must see you at once. He's on his way up. Said he hadn't time to let me announce him."

Enfield protested. He had said, "I don't want to see him; I can't see anybody," when the knock sounded on the door, cutting his remonstrance short. Almost immediately the knock was repeated, peremptory, urgent, yet discreetly muted.

Enfield unlocked the door and held it open. There was nothing he could say. He looked like a man who had been drinking all night alone, and the impression was strengthened by the spilled liquor on the table and the rank fumes that hung in the atmosphere of the room.

After a professionally appraising glance, Pendleton pushed past him and entered. Then he turned and locked the door behind him. "Sorry, Jerry," he apologized, "but this is a matter that couldn't wait. Perhaps you had better sit down." He looked sharply at Enfield. "What in hell have you been doing to yourself, anyway?"

Enfield stood for a moment without answering, looking from the locked door to the chair that Pendleton had pushed toward him. Then he seated himself obediently. He still had the feeling that Violet was in the room, but as his faculties returned, this faded out, leaving him face to face with a new, desperate sense of aloneness. Now he noted with vague incredulity that the night had passed. Beyond the windowpanes he could see the sky with its strange parody of dawn, black in the east where the massed factories belched morning smoke, and brightening slowly to the westward where the dawn winds streamed up clean and fresh out of the hills.

Pendleton pulled up a chair and sat facing Enfield. The ceiling light directly above them threw their foreheads into harsh highlight and sunk their eyes in cavernous shadows.

Pendleton leaned forward and gripped Enfield's knee. "Listen, Jerry," he said, "something very serious has happened. Pull yourself together and think hard. Now, tell me exactly what you and Felix did last night when you left the club."

Under the gripping fingers the knee began to shake. "Think, man," Pendleton insisted. "This is no time to give in to a hangover."

As, earlier in the night, Enfield had not questioned the premonition of imminent death, so now he knew that Pendleton was aware of what had happened, that he was at the breaking point, and that in a moment he would blurt out the whole story. But this ungovernable impulse was companioned by a terror so devastating that again he felt his consciousness lurch toward chaos. With a tremendous effort he got himself in hand, and then suddenly he was quite calm. He saw the whole thing from the standpoint of Pendleton, of anybody who would listen to the incriminating recital. The series of incidents following the impact, the flight, the elaborately secretive return to the club, the apparently unpremeditated alibi that he had given his friends, confronted him with their appalling logic. They were not the irrational manifestations of a diseased nervous system, but the cunning of the moral coward. For years he had thought himself one sort of person, and now he wasn't. Under the surface that everybody respected, the man with guts, the straight shooter, there had existed the potential hit-and-run driver.

In that first moment of revelation his self-loathing was so acute that he very nearly triumphed. He would tell the story without equivocation, and abide by the consequences.

He leaned forward and met the doctor's eyes squarely. His voice was low but controlled. "We had a couple of drinks on the veranda. You remember that; you were there. You and the others. Then we got up and walked down to the second tee. Felix said he was tired, so we turned back to the parking lot. He got in his station wagon and left. I couldn't relax. Couldn't get the races out of my mind, so I thought a drive would help me. I got in the roadster and drove out the Wesley pike."

Pendleton asked sharply: "And that was the last you saw of him? You are sure of that?"

Enfield rejected the interruption, hanging doggedly to his story, trying desperately to remember each minute detail. "I made Wesley in forty-five flat, and when I got there I circled the square. There was a man there, asleep on the bench under the Confederate monument—"

Pendleton's voice, sharpened by anger, cut him short. "Listen," he said, "I don't give a God damn what *you* did. It's Felix I'm concerned with. He's in trouble and his friends have to get together and help him."

Enfield stared. "Felix?" he asked stupidly.

"Yes, Felix. Leslie Morgan, that little secretary of his, was picked up dead under her window early this morning. The window was open, and she had evidently thrown herself out of it. But there was a man with her late last night and that damned preacher who lives in the next apartment heard him speak. He has reported to the coroner that it was Hollister. The coroner had the sense to call Miriam, and she called me. Of course Felix didn't have anything to do with it. As far as I know he's still asleep.

But if we let him get out and talk, he'll hang himself."

Enfield sat staring intently at Pendleton. His body, tensed and bent slightly forward, gave an impression of suddenly arrested motion. It was as though he had been caught back in the act of a fatal spring.

Pendleton continued: "There's bound to be a scandal; it's common talk that Felix has had intimate relations with the girl. But we've got if possible to forestall an inquest, or at any rate to keep Felix from appearing. We've got to save Miriam that." He leaned forward, and for a moment his composure gave way, his face contracted spasmodically, and he said brokenly: "God damn him!"

When he had recovered himself he went on. "We've both known her all our lives. There's nothing I wouldn't do for her. You understand that?— nothing. I thought that you would be prepared to make a statement to the coroner that you and Hollister had spent that two hours together."

There was a moment of silence, then Pendleton went on: "That's why I came to you at once. I thought we could run over there, and you could get it done in time to get off on schedule."

Pendleton's voice died away on a note of pleading, and Enfield began to think again. Oddly, his first thought was not of himself. Pendleton was in love with Miriam. He probably had always been, and that was why he had never married. He had gone on getting older, fat and pompous, there in Exeter—hoping for nothing, expecting nothing, just loving her. Well, he could understand that now. Hadn't he always loved Violet? The thought of her

steadied him, and then for the first time the full significance of Pendleton's words penetrated his consciousness.

"Where was she found?" he asked. "Tell me all
that you know about it."

Pendleton's temper bolted. "To hell with that!"
he said. "Time is passing. I asked you to do a simple
thing. Are you going to do it or not?"

"I've got to know," Enfield insisted.

"All right, then, listen. The girl lived at the
Gresham Arms. Her apartment was four floors up,
on the front. She was found on the pavement under
her open window. She was in her night clothes. Her
skull was fractured and death was probably instan-
taneous. If you want a motive, she was probably
crazy about Felix, and knew he'd never leave
Miriam. And she knew that Miriam would terminate
the situation sooner or later. Now you see why we
have to keep Felix out of it."

Enfield got to his feet, walked unsteadily to the
window, and stood there, hands braced against the
two sides of the frame. After a moment his shoulders
began to shake and laughter, hoarse and strangling,
filled the room.

Pendleton strode to him and swung him
around. "Have you gone crazy?" he demanded furiously.

Enfield staggered to the table and fell into a
chair, with his arms thrown out before him and his
face hidden in them. "Of course it's suicide," he
gasped; then his voice rose, edged with hysteria:
"Any damn fool can see that."

He raised his face but did not look directly at
Pendleton. When he spoke, his words came tum-

bling one after another, apologetic, yet defensive: "Of course I want to do anything I can for Miriam. You know that, don't you? Only I can't do this, Bob. You see I'm all shot to hell. I couldn't face people. I'd get rattled and spoil the story. And besides that, there's something else: you see, when I got to Wesley and drove around the square, there was that fellow asleep, and I woke him up. There isn't another horn like mine in the country. He'd know my car, and he'd spill the beans. They'd get us up in court and they'd *prove every damn one of us liars.*"

Once during this speech, Pendleton had attempted an interruption. He had said: "But, hold on, Jerry—at the club you told us you'd stayed there."

Then, leaning forward, he had got a good look at Enfield's face, his own incredulous at what he saw there. Lifting himself heavily to his feet, he had stood, while his expression changed from incredulity to disgust, waiting for Enfield to finish.

When the hysterical outburst had spent itself, and there was silence in the room, he leaned forward and delivered his indictment:

"So that's it. You're done with us—you can't be bothered to stay and do even Miriam a favor. You'd even lie to us to save yourself the trouble." His heavy face began to tremble, and the opaque, sloe-colored eyes narrowed and glinted fanatically. He raised a blunt forefinger and shook it in Enfield's face:

"We thought you were one of us. We counted on you. We were proud of you. Well, we're done with you, too. You can get to hell out of Exeter, and as far as we are concerned you can damn well stay out."

An hour later, Enfield was driving north along the highway. He was thinking of Violet. He hadn't thought of anything else since Pendleton had gone and left him in peace.

He had wired, scratching his plane for the races, phoned the airport to leave the ship grounded at Exeter until further orders, paid his hotel bill, and got out. And all the while she had been waiting to flood back into his mind and fill it. Now he could give himself utterly to the thought of her. He would go first to Cambridge and make inquiries. Wherever she was, he was going to find her and make it up to her. If there were reasons why they could not be together, at first, it wouldn't matter. He still had money, and money could fix practically anything. And he would be near her, making things easy for her. He would tell her that she had been right when she had said he didn't know what he was passing up. It had taken him over twenty years to realize it, but she had been right.

The weather had undergone an autumnal change. The sun, which had been shining brilliantly a moment before, had disappeared behind a low ceiling of clouds. A chill wind drove steadily down from the north, tossing the roadside trees, and sending a swirl of fallen leaves down the cement to meet him. It eddied in over the windshield and worried a small white square of paper out from under the projecting seat, then toyed with it, flipping it this way and that about the floor of the car.

Enfield reached down absent-mindedly and picked the object up, noting that it was a letter, sealed and stamped, but unopened. Then he remembered the barman, Paul. It seemed a lifetime ago that he had hung to the side of the roadster, resorting to any subterfuge to wangle a ride.

Inexplicably, as Enfield sat driving with one hand, and holding the letter in the other, the hand that held the letter began to shake, then suddenly the dark waters of panic were upon him, dispersing his faculties, obliterating time and place. He brought the car to a stop, and sat, conscious now only of the missive which he held and which seemed to cohere to his hand with some evil power of its own. It ceased to be a fragment of inanimate matter. Living, inexorable, freighted with its load of damning associations, it swept him back to the negro standing beside the car, telling him that it had been caught in the tirewell—then back, smashing the resistance that he threw against it, to a girl stepping bareheaded from the sidewalk with a white square in her hand. Moved by some force which he was powerless to control, he at last lifted the envelope and focused his gaze upon it. In a singularly candid feminine hand were the words: "Felix Hollister, Esq., Wingfields, Hatton Road, City."

Suddenly his face puckered up, and his eyes filled with tears. Then he apostrophized the cosmos: "God damn you," he wailed. "Why can't you let me alone!"

A great truck loaded with cotton droned by. The driver shouted genially, "Any trouble?" but getting no answer, shrugged and gave his attention to the road.

Enfield turned and looked behind him. There,

over a fold in the hills, a smoke pall hung suspended, marking the metropolis of Exeter. He drew out a large silk bandana handkerchief and dried his eyes. He was steadier now. Presently he fumbled out his pocket lighter, spun the wheel and, after a furtive survey of the barren countryside, got the flame to a corner of the envelope. When the encroaching line of fire burned his fingers he opened them, and let the small triangle of unconsumed paper flutter over the side of the car.

He put up his lighter, stepped on the starter, and got the machine in motion. At first there was a slight unsteadiness discernible in the driving, but this disappeared as the great car gathered speed and bowled away to the northward.

THE early-morning sunshine of late October poured level across the Wingfields lawn, and laid a thin lemon-colored glaze over the façade of the studio where it rose high-gabled and austere among its massed evergreens. It took on warmth among the chrysanthemums and late roses. It vaulted to the tops of alternate hickories and maples that bordered the highway, reaching the nadir of its beauty and sending them in a stupendous march of saffron and scarlet up the long incline and out into the blue infinity beyond. It was chill again, devitalized, and drained of color where it probed through the great east window of the Wingfields living room and picked up in merciless minutiae of detail the figure of a man.

He was medium-sized, squarely built, and was seated forward upon a straight chair, with a gray felt hat rotating monotonously between large embarrassed hands. He wore a black suit well shined at elbow and shoulder blade, tan shoes scuffed at the toes but scrupulously polished, a clean white shirt with soft collar, and a stringy four-in-hand of some dark undetermined shade.

He was excessively homely, his large thin-lipped mouth, receding chin, and slightly bulging eyes throwing off the inevitable suggestion of a frog. He was, in fact, the sort of person from whom Thomas always neglected to take his hat in the outer hall, even though he had been instructed to show the visitor into the living room.

For Thomas had a social instinct, and his belief in it was second only to his belief in a personal god. If he had erred in his judgment, he would have stood convicted of a lapse in etiquette. If his estimate had been correct—and it usually was—the breach would have been justified. For he had stumbled upon the incontrovertible fact that a hat held during a conversation tends to increase in size, and that eventually this phenomenon spreads to the hands which hold it, until, under the distressing prognosis of the disease, both hat and hands develop proportions which can be reduced to the normal only by precipitous flight into open air.

But in this particular instance the precaution was unnecessary, for it was evident that the man desired nothing so much as to find himself once again hatted and empty-handed, striding away under the open sky.

He was incongruous, even a little pathetic, as he sat there picked out of the mellow opulence of the room by that isolating and relentless shaft of light. And he was sinking beneath the weight of his embarrassment; embarrassment at the sumptuousness of the apartment, at the hat which now seemed to rotate under its own power between his huge and stricken hands, at the dimly comprehended menace to himself, to his integrity, that lurked in the impending interview.

For upon him, in spite of his homeliness, which was the more distressing because tinged with the comic, there was an air of transparent and appealing honesty. And it was this honesty which introduced

the note of pathos. It was not of the assertive profes-
sionalized type so common among politicians. It
was not a strength but a recognized inherent weakness. It looked out of the pale slightly-bulging eyes
not in self-righteousness, but in a pathetic mendi-
cancy, asking only that this final shred of dignity
might be left to a bankrupt self-esteem. Asking, yet
with a deeply grounded fatalism knowing that the
day would come when this, too, must go. For this
was Mr. Jed Harvey, Coroner of Exeter County, and
he owed his livelihood not so much to the electorate
as to certain people of importance who had en-
gineered the reform movement at the preceding
election and had launched him upon his political
career.

Facing the coroner, with her back to the window, sat Miriam. In spite of the early hour she was
dressed for the morning in a bright cotton print; her
hair, smoothly and firmly arranged, showed no de-
viation from its customary stability—her whole
appearance, fresh and crisp, taking its key from
her competent, carefully laundered and properly
starched person.

She occupied a deep lounge chair, and her long
shapely body, from her head which rested against
the cushioned back, to her crossed knees, and the
sandaled foot which swung free, almost negligently,
implied a detached rather than a vital interest in the
proceedings. But in her arms that rested, elbows on
chair arms, and hands that were tightly locked on
her breast there was a visible tension. And there was
a deeper, more compelling quality than was usual
in her voice as she said:

"I want you to know, Mr. Harvey, that I ap-

preciate your coming directly to me about this matter. We did establish an understanding of sorts during the campaign, didn't we?"

Her raised eyebrows invited a rejoinder. And
as she leaned slightly forward her face took the up-
flung reflection of light from the polished floor. It
was evident that she was pale, that there were shadows under her eyes, and that the casual accent which
she had given her body was belied by her eyes,
watchful, wary, alert.

Mr. Harvey rose to the lure with great caution.
"Why, yes, ma'am," he answered with ponderous
deliberation. "You might say as how we did. That's
why I came right to you after Mr. Salmon insisted
on an inquest. An' I ain't forgettin' what you an'
Mr. Maxton an' the doctor did for me."

"Not so much for you, Mr. Harvey," she assured him, "as for Exeter. Remember that. We
wanted a clean, honest administration, and we knew
that your department would be safe in your hands.
And let me reassure you now on one point," she
went on, drawing herself forward in her chair and
bringing her hand down in an emphatic slap on the
arm, "no special favors. We said that in the campaign, and we meant it. We will accept full and
friendly co-operation, but nothing more than any
citizen of Exeter would have a right to demand."

The coroner's eyes lifted from his hat to her
face, and lingered there for a moment in timid ex-
ploration. Then they dropped, and his expression of
fatalistic melancholy deepened. In spite of her words
of reassurance and the tombed chill of the room,
sweat burst out upon his forehead and glistened
there in the early sunlight.

"Thank you, ma'am," he answered with neither gratitude nor hope. He pinned the hat to a thigh with one determined hand, and finally locating a handkerchief with the other, mopped his face.

"Of course," Miriam went on easily, "this is a great shock to us. We were both devoted to Miss Morgan. Her position with us was more that of a daughter than an employee. But if, as you tell me, her window was open and she was found dead on the pavement below it, and in her night clothes, it was obviously a case of suicide, and I can't see why any inquest would be necessary or why we should be involved."

"You see, ma'am," he answered heavily, his brow furrowed by his effort at concentration, "while it's the law that the coroner has to decide whether or not there will be an inquest, circumstances can make it very dangerous to all parties for him to throw it out. He's got to have evidence to back up his judgment. Now take this case. It's suicide sure as I'm sittin' here, but there ain't no witnesses to the actual deed, and the body didn't leave no note declarin' her intention like they usually do. Bodies can make a lot of trouble," he concluded sadly, "by not exercisin' a little forethought."

Ignoring this generalization, and directing the conversation firmly back to the particular, Miriam asked: "Why do you suppose the Reverend Salmon wants to interfere? It's none of his business."

"If you ask me that, ma'am, I'll give you a straight answer. Because that's something I know it when I see it." He leaned forward and spoke mysteriously but with unwonted conviction: "Personal animus."

Miriam's laugh was exclamatory, mirthless. "But that's absurd. I've always been on the best of terms with him. He helped in our election. He couldn't have anything against me."

"Not against you, ma'am. It's Mr. Hollister. He said some very fine things about you. But he said he reckoned how you and him had come to the partin' of the ways. He said that as a man o' Gawd he had the moral welfare of the community in his keepin'. An' he brought Miss Mabel with him."

The coroner paused a moment, then asked in a tone of infinite weariness: "Do you know Miss Mabel, Mrs. Hollister?"

Miriam's self-control was shaken. "Mr. Harvey," she cried, "that woman's got the worst tongue in Exeter. You've simply *got* to keep her out of this."

"I can't, ma'am," he answered sadly. "You see, she discovered the body."

Miriam was thoroughly alarmed, and as always the emotion was translated into action. She abandoned the pose by which she had hoped to dismiss the incident as trivial, and irrelevant to the affairs of the Hollisters.

"What was she doing up at that hour of the night?" she demanded sharply. Then, before her visitor could reply, she hurried on. "You say that they identified Mr. Hollister as the visitor in the apartment. Well, go on. Start at the beginning, and tell me exactly what happened, and what she proposes to testify."

"She claims that there was company at her apartment last night," he began. "They was all in the sittin' room listenin' to the radio. She says something prompted her to go and look down into the street, and there in front of the building was Mr. Hollister's station wagon."

"There are other station wagons in Exeter," Miriam snapped, "but go on."

"Then, as she passed through the hall goin' back to the sittin' room, she heard someone at the Morgans' door which is just opposite. She says she can swear it was Mr. Hollister's voice. He said something about 'not bein' surprised to see me.' And Miss Morgan answered: 'Why should I be?' Then the door closed. She said that her family was worried about Leslie, as she called her, because—"

Mr. Harvey broke off abruptly, flushed dully, and examined the interior of his hat carefully as though it might reveal a hidden exit from his dilemma.

"Because what?" Miriam demanded.

"Because," he went on, without raising his eyes, "they claimed that Mr. Hollister had been goin' there often, and, since Mrs. Morgan's death, was stayin' in there alone till all hours. They said they loved Miss Morgan and wanted to protect her, and that Mr. Hollister bein' an atheist an' a *bo*hemian, he might take advantage of her."

Miriam's voice was level, controlled. "Did they say anything had led them to assume there was any such relationship?"

"Yes, ma'am. They both said that once when Mrs. Morgan was taken ill late at night, they went in to tend her, and the girl and Mr. Hollister came in. They said he was wearin' pajamas an' a bathrobe. They said she told them then that they had come

right from Wingfields where they was alone together, and that it was when you was abroad."

"All right," Miriam said. "I've got that. Go
on."

"Well, Miss Mabel says that last night after
their company went home she went to bed, but she
couldn't sleep account of her sense of responsibility
for that girl across the hall. At last, she said, she
couldn't stand it no longer and was just goin' to
wake her father an' ask him what to do, when she
heard the Morgans' door open. Then she heard the
girl and Mr. Hollister sayin' good-bye."

Again his vocabulary failed him, and the dull
painful flush of embarrassment surged upward from
collar to temples.

Miriam, still in that level and controlled voice,
said: "They kissed, I suppose."

"Yes, ma'am, thank you, ma'am, after a manner
of speaking; and then he said good-bye, and it
sounded to Miss Mabel like the girl was cryin'. It
upset her so, she said, that she was late gettin' back
to the front window an' when she did get there, the
car was pullin' away from the sidewalk so she didn't
see him get in. But she'll swear it was him from the
voice, she says."

Miriam said sharply: "So she'll swear it was
Mr. Hollister, will she? And that Miss Morgan was
alive when he left. Well, that lets him out—it proves
the suicide theory, doesn't it?"

"Oh, yes, ma'am." He fairly goggled at her.
"You didn't think it involved Mr. Hollister in the
death! What they want to do is to force an inquest
so they can get their story in the record. What they
say, if you'll forgive me, ma'am, is that he—he—took

advantage of her. And then put her away—as the sayin' is—an' that he is morally responsible, an' they's goin' to see that Exeter knows it."

Miriam rose and crossed to the window, and stood there with her back to her visitor, looking out into the polychromatic splendor of the autumn morning. Behind her the coroner's hat resumed its interrupted circling motion, moving slowly at first, then gaining momentum as the silence in the room lengthened.

At last Miriam broke the silence, staring before her out the window and speaking more as though she were thinking aloud than addressing her visitor. "It isn't only the Salmons," she said. "Except for a few intimate friends the people here don't like him. He was born here, he's a credit to the town. He's probably more widely known than any other man in Exeter. He works hard and minds his own business, and there is no malice in his heart for anyone. And yet," she went on, a note of bitterness edging her voice, "I sometimes feel that they resent him, almost hate him, in Exeter. Do you know why that is, Mr. Harvey?"

It was easier for him to talk to her this way, with her back towards him, and that note almost of appeal in her voice. "Since you ask me, ma'am, and it might help you to know, they don't understand him. They know he's smart but they think he's queer. He's cut himself off from the church. He has a way of goin' along the street, bumpin' into people he knows, and not even speakin' to them."

"But can't they understand that the man is an artist, and that artists *are* different? Their heads are always in the clouds. They can't take care of themselves like other people." She turned back to him, her hands out in an unconscious gesture of appeal. "Why, Mr. Harvey, I've spent my life taking care of him. He couldn't even get himself fed without me. Can't you see it's natural for him to be like that?"

He was quick to respond to her changed attitude with a more assured one of his own, and said, with a touch of patronizing smugness: "In Exeter we think it's natural to be friendly."

"I see," she answered slowly. "So that's it. They don't understand him, and what they don't understand they hate. And you're one of them, aren't you? And you really believe that my husband is the sort of man who could do a thing like this." She came close and stood looking down at him. Incapable of movement, he had to sit dumbly, and take it, while a slow fury burned through her words and scorched him. "And these are the people I've worked for, built hospitals for, given playgrounds to. And now they'd do this to me. Well, Mr. Harvey, I'm glad I know it. I'm glad I sat still and listened, because it shows me exactly where we stand. I could have disposed of the whole matter the moment you entered, but I didn't. Something told me to wait and listen. And now I am glad I did. It has taught me who my friends really are."

He sat with his eyes rolled up at her, fright adding the ultimate comic touch to his face. "I'm here, Mrs. Hollister, ain't I?" he stammered. "I came right to you. That shows where I stand. That shows I want to help you, don't it?"

She stood frowning down at him, letting her silence menace him, then she turned away, leaving him to slump forward, while he continued to watch her with his wide begging eyes.

"Well," she said at last in her crisp business manner, but with a shade of contempt in her voice, "if you are telling the truth, you are mighty lucky. How would you say Mr. Jerry Enfield stood in this town? Do you suppose his word would be as good as Mabel Salmon's?"

"Mr. Enfield!" he ejaculated. "Certainly, ma'am—"

"All right. You can go to your friends and tell them that Mr. Hollister was in Mr. Enfield's company at the Country Club between eleven and one last night. Mr. Enfield told me so himself. And so," she went on, "when you called me this morning I got Dr. Pendleton on the wire and asked him to get Mr. Enfield over at once."

She paused and looked at the mannish silver wrist watch that she always wore. "He should be here any minute now, to give you his statement. I hope you don't mind waiting."

Then they heard Pendleton coming, the swish of gravel as the motor took the curve and stopped under the porte-cochere, the heavy, deliberate foot-falls as he entered the room. The coroner scrambled to his feet, his face brightening at the interruption of his interview with Miriam, then sobering under Pendleton's forbidding scowl. He said: "Good mornin', Doctor"; then since the other stood silent, pondering, he added with nervous irrelevancy: "It's a fine time of year—now just before the first frost."

Pendleton's face cleared and he said: "Oh, good morning, Harvey," as though he had just noticed his presence. Then he turned to Miriam and behind the almost reptilian opacity of his eyes there was a sudden lighting. "It's all right, Miriam," he said. "They were together at the club from eleven until after one. There's nothing to worry about."

For a moment she stood searching his face, then she nodded toward the coroner. "I'll ask you gentlemen to excuse me then," she said. "I have a very busy day ahead of me." And she left the two men standing, facing each other.

The coroner was at once voluble. "You don't know what a relief this is, Doctor. I told the Reverent I knew there must be some mistake, but naturally he was all for takin' Miss Mabel's word for it. Now when I go to him with Mr. Jerry there won't be nothin' to it." He tugged at a heavy silver chain that spanned his vest and from which at regular intervals, like laundry upon a line, depended fraternal order emblems, a child's tooth set in gold, a small silver revolver. Drawing the chain through his fingers he at last came to a massive silver watch which he sprung open and consulted. Looking at it, drawing assurance from its unequivocal statement of fact, his embarrassment disappeared and he became the self-important, small-town official.

"It's eight-twenty-seven," he announced. "I'll be in my office in half an hour. When do you reckon Mr. Jerry can join me so's we can step over to the Reverent's?"

"Unfortunately," Pendleton began suavely, "as you doubtless saw in yesterday's paper, Mr. Enfield was leaving this morning to participate in the air races. When I got to him he was in his car starting without a moment to spare. He asked me, however, to tell you that he will return in a week, and that, if you wish it, he will make affidavit to the effect that Mr. Hollister was in his company between eleven and one last evening, the time during which Miss Salmon claims to have recognized his voice."

"But," exclaimed the coroner, taken aback, "we got to decide! We can't wait indefinitely for an inquest—the body—"

Pendleton stepped closer, demonstrating the power of bulk, of gross physical poundage, to impress and, by comparison, to diminish the moral resistance of a smaller man. But the coroner stood his ground, still holding the watch desperately like a talisman against evil, and looking up into the veiled immobility of the doctor's face.

Pendleton said: "Listen, Harvey," and his voice was gentle, almost caressing. "You are protected by my word that Mr. Hollister and Mr. Enfield were together. That's Hollister's alibi. There isn't going to be any inquest."

Slowly, sadly, with his eyes on the floor, Mr. Harvey closed and replaced his watch. There was a fleck of cigar ash on his vest and he dusted it carefully away. His hat was quiet now held in his laxed left hand. He had always addressed Pendleton formally, "Dr. Pendleton" or "Doctor." Now, with his eyes still on the floor, as though their relationship had entered upon a different phase, and with a laugh that was not altogether a success, he said: "Well, Doc, it's just as you say."

Pendleton made no answer. And in the brief silence Mr. Harvey buttoned his coat, one, two, three, with deliberate fingers. Then he looked up and met the other's gaze, curious and faintly ironic. "I quite agree with you," he said, his voice gaining

assurance as he got under way. "Certainly, with Mr.
Enfield prepared to make a statement upon his return and your own assurance in the meantime, there
could be no criticism of the conduct of my office."
Under his coat his chest swelled, straining the buttons and giving him the appearance, not of an apologetic, but of a rather pompous frog. He held out his
hand and said: "Well, Doc, it's been a pleasure to
serve you. There's just about nothin' that can't be
worked out when two friends get together and talk
things out."

Pendleton accepted the proffered hand but rejected the heartiness. "I understand then that the
request for an inquest will be dismissed at once."

"At once, sir. In fact I'll stop in at the Reverent's on my way to the office."

Pendleton stood staring abstractedly after the
retreating form of the coroner until he heard the
front door slam and the motor spin, then he went
into the small library that adjoined the living room
where of late Miriam transacted most of her business. She was sitting at the desk talking into the
desk telephone in an even uninterrupted flow. She
motioned with her head toward a chair and he
seated himself without shifting his gaze from her
face. Then he listened, watching her. The room was
alive with her voice, deep and musical with every
syllable perfectly articulated. She was saying: "Yes,
the party was in honor of my birthday. Yes," with
a ripple of laughter, "you may quote me as saying it
was my sixteenth—and in farewell to Mr. Enfield
who left this morning for the air races. The party
was in the nature of a reunion of our old Exeter
high school class, and we enjoyed ourselves so thor-

oughly that we didn't leave the club until one o'clock." A pause, then, "Yes, you may mention the hour. We are rather pleased with ourselves at staging one o'clock parties at our age. And the names—" A short listening pause, then: "That's right. Now that will be in the society notes this afternoon—you're sure?" There was a longer pause while she sat smiling into the mouthpiece. Then she said: "That's very flattering of you but I know story value myself and I do think it has the makings. Wait just a minute. Dr. Pendleton and Mr. Hollister are with me now. I'll ask them." Turning her face from the instrument she addressed the room. "Miss Butterleigh says that she will run the item in society this afternoon but she was flattering enough to say that it rates a Sunday feature article as well. She says that it is quite a coincidence that the same high school class should have given the state its leading sportsman, artist, surgeon, businessman and businesswoman. She would like to do brief interviews with us all. Do you mind?" Then: "They are highly complimented," she assured the invisible conversationalist. "You can call them later for appointments, and of course I'll be happy to have you drop in any time."

She replaced the instrument. For a moment she sat regarding her coup with a smile of sincere self-appreciation, then she looked up to meet Pendleton's unswerving scrutiny.

"By God, Miriam!" he breathed. "You're a wonder. By God you are."

"*You're* telling *me*," she laughed back. Her face sobered. She leaned forward, elbows on the desk, and chin resting on the backs of her interlaced fingers.

"Bob," she said at last, "no use lying to me. There's something wrong. If Jerry'd been with him he'd have come. He wouldn't have let me down."

"You don't know Jerry," Pendleton exploded. "I didn't either until this morning. He's yellow. I couldn't get a straight story out of him. I believe he was lying at the club and they had separated, but he's a dirty piker or he'd have come anyway."

She said: "But you came. You came and lied like a gentleman for me. I've got one friend anyway."

She reached a hand across the desk and he enveloped it in one of his huge unsightly paws. A silence fell and their strained and unnatural positions, reaching forward, stiff-armed with clasped hands, embarrassed them so that when they separated there was a restraint rather than a heightened intimacy between them. She returned to his last remark, facing it in all its implications.

"Bob," she said, "we've been through a lot together. You know me and you know that whatever it is I can take it. Was he with her last night or not?"

Pendleton's face and neck went a dull red, he gripped the arms of his chair and leaned forward to answer. "Of course he was. I haven't the least doubt he's been living with her, and the Salmons' story is straight. God damn him."

She turned that over in her mind, and her face cleared. "You mustn't say that, Bob," she reproved him. "Felix couldn't have deceived her. He isn't that kind of man and he's a complete innocent. He hasn't the slightest regard for appearances, and he's got himself talked about. I cautioned him about that myself after your last talk with me. As for

Leslie— Well, you never know about women. She might have wanted him. She probably involved him in a brief affair, but she would have known that she couldn't take him away from me. No, Felix didn't deceive her, and she didn't deceive herself. If she killed herself it was for some other reason. It's just an unfortunate coincidence that he happened to be involved at the time. There's going to be talk, of course, but we have the situation well in hand. Within a year the whole thing will be forgotten."

Pendleton regarded her with what incredulity his inexpressive mask could mirror.

"Great heavens, Miriam," he exclaimed, "you don't mean that after this you're going to forgive him, that you're going on living as man and wife!"

She smiled across at him indulgently as one might at a child. "Bob," she said, "you've never been married and you haven't the remotest idea what its all about. For that matter I don't think many married men have. They just muddle through. It's the woman's job and, if it's a flop, nine times out of ten it's her fault. What you call living together as man and wife hasn't much to do with it. At any rate not after the first twenty years. It's learning to pull together. It's an all-round partnership, children, the home, business. You don't junk a corporation just because there is a breakdown in one department— do you? No, of course you don't. You patch it up and you keep on doing business. Well, if a woman's wise, she does the same thing with her marriage." She paused and selected a cigarette from a silver box, proffering one to Pendleton which he accepted and lighted. Looking at him then through a haze of smoke she went on: "In the face of what has just happened it may surprise you to hear that I consider our marriage a success. Felix has a certain gift—so have I. We supplement each other. We're a going concern with a future."

She paused and tapped the ash from her cigarette, swinging her glance from Pendleton's face to scrutinize the diminished cylinder. "But we're more than that. We're reasonably happy about it. He's a difficult person to understand and it's taken me half a lifetime to master the job, and to learn to make allowances, but I know now what he needs and I give it to him. I am genuinely fond of him, and as for Felix— Well, I just can't imagine what would become of him without me."

She looked across at Pendleton but he would not meet her eyes. He had insulated himself with his negative aura and sat there withdrawn, impenetrable.

"I know you don't understand him," she accused. "Or he you for that matter. You've only endured each other on my account. There are times when I think you even hate him."

He looked up then and said shortly and bitterly: "Why in God's name shouldn't I?"

CHAPTER 22

*H*OLLISTER was awakened by the sound of a car
starting. There were three distinct stages: the slam
of the door, the spin of the starter, the growl of the
motor that dwindled out into silence. These sounds
nudged him out of a profound and dreamless beati-
tude, then, before thought had shaken itself free of
the vapors of sleep and assumed its mastery, they
dropped him to lie for a moment upon a tide of
pure sensation. In the air was the spell of autumn,
indefinable, nostalgic, but, now in his state of untrammeled sentience, he realized it, not as a commonplace of each recurring October, but a synthesis
of many odors, colors, sounds, each to be savored,
cherished, remembered. Grass, raw from its late
mowing and wet under a drench of dew, smoke of
burning leaves astringent in the nostrils, chrysanthemums, petunias, phlox—not a perfume, but a
rich polleny stain on the air. Light falling from a
clean, pale sky to blaze and smolder into prismatic
combinations in garden, woods, and fields. Music
like a soft rain sounding from the lawn where robins
strutted in their russet vests and scattered broken
minor chords.

Springing from his bed and tearing off his
pajamas, he threw wide the French window and
stood taking the morning chill in a million needle
pricks upon his naked skin, drinking through every
pore the freshness and beauty of the day. He was

exultingly conscious of his own body, the steady thump-thump of his heart, his lungs drinking deep of the sharp, revivifying air, his skin taking the bite of the cold north wind and glorying in the challenging sensation. He felt clean and taut and there was a vibrance along his nerves like the thrumming of a high-tension wire.

It was years since he had experienced such an awakening. Here in Exeter the process had been reversed; consciousness coming first in a vague premonition of something left undone, some omission to be rectified, a knowledge that the work had lagged and would have to be speeded up. Then later, if he had the time to give to it, the deliberately planned hour here or there to enjoy the garden or go for a hike through the woods. It was strange that when thought came to him it was not first of Leslie but of his work. Always in those student days his awakening had been like this, life stripped down to *feeling*, and a driving need to work. People hadn't mattered. Food only when he was spent, tired, and hungry, and its demands battered through his absorption. And on those God-given mornings getting out of bed and at it before it escaped him. Translating in some inexplicable way the strange weakening twist that a bird song gave him into a fluid line on the figure that he was modeling, a line that he may have sweated over all of the previous day and missed. Out of some closed and forgotten chamber of his memory there flashed into his consciousness the head upon which he had been working when Miriam's summons had reached him in Paris. It had baffled him, he remembered, the thing he had been fighting to bring to life hiding obstinately in the amorphous clay. Now, instinctively, he knew what it needed. One hand cupped behind the head, and with the ball of his thumb he made a slow flowing movement. Then Hollister laughed. The abandoned clay had been flung out by the concierge a quarter of a century ago, but it was real. It was more actual today than the stacked etchings waiting for the season's sales. And now the picture of the studio and its well-stocked shelves brought him up standing. His mind gagged upon the thought and rejected it. And suddenly in retreat from it he was in Leslie's arms again and she was telling him that it was over, done with. He sensed her then deeply and, for the first time since wakening, in her complete identity. She had been a state of being into which he had entered. She had been the source of that radiant element which had flooded his world, and she had given him again eyes to see, ears to hear. But only now, in a swift reliving of their hour together, did she become actual, the woman who had fed the long hunger of his flesh and spirit with her own body, her slender, unflawed beauty. The sense of her nearness was overwhelming, quickening his passion as though his hand had touched her flesh. He closed his eyes and saw her. He could have drawn her then, lifted her impression from that amazing pictorial memory of his and fixed it to the smallest detail on paper.

When he opened his eyes again he experienced the sensation that he had had when he left Leslie early that morning—the sense of unreality in the world that lay about him—the familiar suddenly worn thin, so thin that you felt as though you could walk out through it into the reality that lay beyond.

He took a cold shower. The lash of the icy water across his back made him flinch. Then he was out again, his body glowing under the rough, hard strokes of the towel.

Last night his mind had avoided the issue. He hadn't been able to drive it up to the task of facing Miriam, tearing his roots out of Exeter. Now, inexplicably he didn't mind. Vaguely he remembered that he and Leslie had agreed to wait out a fortnight, to leave the work in order. To tidy up before walking out. How utterly absurd. He would go to Miriam at once. It would be clean, swift, and final, and then he would go to Leslie.

Without waiting to dress he threw on his bathrobe and went out into the hall. The house was quiet, and this was strange, for while Miriam was an amazingly efficient housekeeper, one always heard the whir of the machinery. At this hour the house was usually full of brisk morning sounds. Sweeping, breakfast noises from the butler's pantry, Miriam giving an order to Thomas, Thomas giving an order to the cook, the cook giving an order to the maid.

He got to the tower and began the descent of the grand staircase. He had always hated, even feared, that pretentious adornment. The spiraling slabs of oak repeating themselves interminably as they descended into the decorous gloom of the hall, spaced too close for a good honest step—too far to be taken two at a time, they had either to be hurdled or minced. And the succession of descending windows, each framed coyly in ivy, and monotonously repeating the same picture of Piedmont countryside. God, how he hated it all, the efficient bustle, the cleanness, the iron routine of the life that it per-

sonified. Halfway down his irritation gave place to
anger. Undirected at first, it grew upon the thought
of his long servitude, then brightening and harden-
ing it centered on Miriam. Preoccupied with his
own plans, his own emotions, it had not occurred
to him to wonder about his wife's acceptance of his
revolt. He believed, now that he came to think of
it, that she would not care in the sense of losing
someone whom she loved. But there would be a
scandal, he supposed, and her whole plan of life
would be disorganized. She would suffer. That like
everything else here was thin, unimportant, uncon-
vincing. In fact, as he approached the library, where
he knew that he would find her at this hour, he was
conscious of a growing sense of malicious satisfaction. As he closed his fingers over the knob of the
library door, he heard Pendleton's voice on the other
side. The words were lost, but there was no mistak-
ing the heavy blurred sound, with its not unmusical
timbre.

Miriam would have been just Miriam, but they
were more than that—more than the sum of their
two parts. They were Exeter, and now in a moment
while this unaccustomed ruthlessness was upon him
he would enter and vanquish them. He would cease
to be what they had made of him, and become himself.

He opened the door and stepped into the room.
Pendleton's bulk surged forward in his chair, the
hands, gripping, half raised him from his seat. Then
recovering himself, he settled back, glowering.
Miriam, startled out of her habitual self-possession,
was at a loss and showed it. For the first time since
he had come to live under this roof Hollister felt

himself completely master of a situation. Yielding to the temptation of dramatizing it, he stepped forward, helped himself to a cigarette, and lighted it. Then he seated himself on a corner of Miriam's desk, bony legs dangling. He said: "I'm rather glad you are here, Bob. As Miriam's oldest friend you should be among the first to know, and I'm sure you'll be a great comfort to her." He turned to Miriam, looking down at her over his shoulder. Meeting her incredulous eyes, suddenly losing his pose, feeling his resentment against her going, he said, in a rush: "I'm awfully sorry to upset you. I didn't think I'd be, but I am. I'm quitting, Miriam. Walking out on the job. Leslie and I are leaving this afternoon."

They registered nothing. They sat there, themselves in effigy, their eyes fixed on him, and the silence lengthening.

He got up and leaned over to Miriam, his hands on the desk between them. He said: "I'm sorry. You don't seem to understand. I'm telling you that Leslie and I are going away together, and we're not coming back. I've got to get back to my modeling, and Leslie understands. She's going to help me."

He paused, and still they sat there saying nothing. "I've got to get on with my work," he insisted, his control giving place to exasperation. "I've wasted too much time already—almost my whole life. There'll have to be a divorce, I suppose. But if you don't want to give me one it won't matter. And some sort of settlement. We won't want much. You'll scarcely miss what we'll need. And so," he concluded abruptly, "Leslie and I have decided to go."

He had forgotten Pendleton. In this moment

when he had to make things clear to Miriam with
all of his faculties bearing down upon her in an
effort to make her understand, accept, the man had
slipped completely out of his mind. Now there was
a sound behind him that caused him to turn, startled
into awareness. The doctor was sitting forward, his
face convulsed and suffused with blood. His eyes,
small in the massy flesh of his face, glittered with
hatred. Words held too long in leash burst from him
in a shout.

"But you can't run away with her now. And for
a damned good reason. Because she's dead."

Hollister said: "Don't shout, please. And don't
interrupt me. I don't know whom you're thinking
of, but I'm talking about Leslie Morgan. I was with
her only a few hours ago, and I'm telling Miriam—"
Pendleton cut in roughly: "—that you're going away
with her. Well, listen—get this into your fuddled
brain. After you left her this morning, Leslie Morgan threw herself out of the window and killed herself."

Dumbly Hollister turned to Miriam. When she
met his look her face broke suddenly—the hardness
melting out—and her eyes filled with tears. Her lips
moved inaudibly. Then impulsively she reached out
to him, nodding her confirmation.

For an undetermined space of time Hollister
experienced death—heart and lungs frozen, veins
and arteries gripping his body in an icy mesh. Pendleton's words had smashed him at a point in space,
freed him from the pull of gravity. Beneath his feet
the earth went hurtling by on its orbit. Over his
vision it poured a blur of undistinguishable details.
The wind of its passage howled in his ears. The

backwash of its incalculable human agony caught
him, tossing him this way and that, almost sub-
merging him. Then at last it receded before physical
pain.

Dimly he became aware of his body, of his right
hand, a throbbing agony. The earth had snatched
him back, gripped him by the feet, and was hurling
him forward. Now the room, the effigies of Pendleton and Miriam, the library window, blurred but
recognizable, were moving with him. Then they
slowed and stopped, his right hand pounding like
a trip hammer, pulling them all back into equilibrium. He opened his fingers, disclosing a burning
cigarette crushed in his palm. He turned his hand
over, but it clung to the seared flesh. Very deliberately he picked it away with his left hand, dropped
it, and crushed it out with the toe of his slipper.
Miriam had taken the wounded hand in both of
hers. She was refusing Pendleton's offer of assistance, getting him out of the room, her voice flying
out at him in short fierce rushes. "Bob, you're a
beast. Get out and stay out. When I want you I'll
call you up." Then her hands, firm, sure, knowing,
cleansing the burn, applying an unguent, laying the
bandage on, twist and overlap. No bungling. No
hesitation. The room, free of Pendleton now, folding in on them. And Miriam's face, softer than he
had ever known it, and wet with tears. He felt her
arms go about him, and against him, the push of her
firm full breasts. No passion there, but sanctuary—
security for all time. A sure anodyne for the agony
that Pendleton's words had driven through him.
Peace. Deep inside him he felt a sob breaking loose,
convulsing his throat.

Miriam's arms drew him down. Her voice said brokenly: "My poor child." His need of her was a tidal wave, engulfing him. He had only to plunge his head between her breasts, feel them there, twin bulwarks against disaster, and let his grief have him. Howl it out like an animal in a cave. Sink into her and be comforted.

Then he was disengaging himself. Pushing from her with childish gestures. Thrusting, unthinking, with his wounded hand until the pain wrung a cry from him.

Her face, flinching as though from a blow, cried a question to him. And without conscious thought, from the dark chaos of his spirit, words flung out an answer. "I've got to be alone." Her hands dropped away, and with the blind unswerving look of a somnambulist he went to the door and opened it. Then he hesitated, habit, the schooling of all these years, plucking at him, urging upon him the appropriate gesture. His eyes, still with that lost unswerving look, swept the room until they picked up Miriam, standing motionless where he had left her. He bowed formally. "I hope you'll excuse me, Miriam," he said. "You understand that under the circumstances—" Then he turned suddenly and blundered out into the hall.

In looking back upon the hours which followed, Hollister was never able to separate the actual from the imagined. The blow, delivered with such telling force by Pendleton, reduced consciousness to the state in which in one moment the brain perceives and records with clarity, and in the next its function is usurped by the imagination. And the one

is indistinguishable from the other for they are
equally credible.

He knew there must have been a sequence,
cause leading inexorably to effect, this incident,
apparently trivial, assuming importance in relation
to its successor, the whole having continuity. But
he was baffled in his attempt to fit the haphazard
pieces into a definite pattern, because the time element was lacking. Certain happenings stood out
clearly in his memory, not by virtue of their relation to others, but as isolated incidents, burned, it
seemed to him, into the living tissue of his brain.

But while facts and actual happenings were un-
stable in his mind, there was a design which, in
looking back, he could realize was completely
ordered. There were areas of depression, through
which he had moved into a brighter terrain, then
back into shadow, at times so frightening that panic
would grip him and he would recoil in horror, not
daring to face what lurked there. And fearing for
his sanity. He fought, hour after hour, to hold the
darkness back. Sleep betrayed him, thrusting him
toward it the moment his tired eyes closed. And so
he had to hold himself wide-eyed, knowing that the
odds were against him, that his resistance was almost gone, and that once he yielded he would be
finished.

Holding himself awake. Telling himself that
Leslie had believed in him, clinging to that in the
face of everything, he could still make the intangible
real; he could still feel himself the Felix Hollister
who had awakened to a new earth that morning
before Pendleton had smashed him. If he doubted
for even a moment, if, drugged with exhaustion, his

resistance caved, the inevitable question would come thundering down upon him—*If she had faith, why had she done it?* Then the darkness would have him, the being whom Leslie had created out of himself —who had lived and breathed—and the world that he inhabited, would suddenly cease to exist. Miriam would be real again—Exeter would be real. It became an obsession with him. He could not plan his next move. While he fought to hold it, that state of being which was her very essence, the part of her which he had realized that morning even before herself had sprung clearly into his mind, still surrounded him. Still, miraculously, knowing he would never see her again, it filled him with this strange sense of exultation, this will to see it through. His struggle must have lasted all of that day and through the following night, because it was early daylight when Miriam finally got into his room.

He hadn't wanted to admit her, some instinct warning him that if he exposed himself again to the menace of her generosity, her willingness to forgive, his habitual dependence upon her would overwhelm him, and he would give up the unequal struggle, sink fathoms deep in her, and sleep.

But she had insisted and finally he had given in. For a moment they had stood, trying to read each other's faces. Then, alarmed by his failing resistance, Hollister had backed away, holding his bandaged hand behind him, sensing that she might take it, and that her kindness would break him.

She had, of course, misinterpreted his gesture. Her face had changed, the softness draining out of it. "Very well," she had said, "if you are determined to make it difficult, I don't know what I can do about it." She had been brief and to the point then and Hollister felt the menace lifting. She seated herself and said: "There are important decisions that have to be made. You have certain responsibilities, and if I am not to share them as I have always done, you'll have to face them alone. But remember, in spite of your habit of ignoring appearances, they are of the utmost importance. We are going on living in Exeter, and the way we pull ourselves through now will have a great influence on our future, and not only our own, but the children's."

He shifted his position, and she saw fear leap into his face.

"What do you want me to do?" he asked.

"There's Leslie," she answered. "It's got to be faced. Our position is that of being her only friends here. We'll have to go through with it together, just as though nothing had happened."

He turned abruptly and stood facing the window, with his back to her. The movement exposed his hands, the wrist of the wounded one gripped tensely in the other, and above them the whole figure straining forward away from her.

"Oh, Holly," she cried impulsively, "you don't think that I understand, but I do. I know that you want to go to her alone, and stay there, just you two together. But can't you see that it's impossible? That I'll have to be there, too."

He turned like an animal at bay. "I don't want to see her," he cried. "I can never see her again."

"Don't want to see her?" she asked incredulously. "Why, didn't you love each other? Weren't you going away together?"

He turned around and faced her. He felt her hold upon him weakening. There was a gap between them which, as he stood looking, widened. He knew that she would never understand him. That what he would try to tell her was untranslatable from his language into hers. And suddenly, facing this issue, he had certain knowledge that if he went and saw Leslie lying there, her still form would blot out forever the living entity that he held now, and which, even in her absence, filled him with the will to fight on.

He closed his eyes, and instantly she was there, her face lifted to his, her body falling away below it in sharp perspective—the full twin rondures of her breasts, the receding curves of thighs, slender doe-ankles, and feet spread delicately in red sandals. Behind her (a single brush stroke would paint it) the crescent of live blue silk.

His eyes opened and picked up his wife. He stood looking at her, his gaze shallow and myopic.

"My God, Miriam," he cried desperately, "can't you understand that if I do I'll lose her. She'll be gone, and I'll never get her back. Exeter'll be real again. You'll be real."

He stopped suddenly, arrested by the look in her face.

"Felix," she cried sharply, "don't you know what's happened, are you going mad?"

There was a long silence. Then slowly, almost judicially, he answered: "I don't know; perhaps I am. Or maybe I've always been like this and I'm just finding it out."

She said: "Then I've never really known you. I've always considered you a perfectly normal human being. Now I don't know you at all. You frighten me—"

Seizing his momentary advantage, he advanced a step toward her. "Hadn't you better leave me then?" he asked in a low, tense voice.

"But, Holly—"

He crossed to the door and opened it.

She looked into his face, tried to pick up her broken sentence, gave it up, and watching him warily, passed into the hall.

He could not have said how long a time it was before she returned. She knocked, and called to him, and finally announced that she would not leave the door without seeing him. And so he admitted her.

She came in and her eyes were shining. The room vibrated to her dynamic humming. She was a creature possessed. She crossed to Hollister and took him by the arm, looking up into his face.

"Holly," she said, "I wasn't going to intrude. I wasn't going to force myself upon you again until you were ready for me. But then I got the news. I thought suddenly that it was just what you needed. It would give you a big interest, help you to snap out of this. What do you think it is?"

She waited, undaunted by the blankness with which he regarded her.

"Maxton has closed," she exulted. "He's taken the whole works—the complete series." Hollister's expression was attentive, detached, there was a faint smile about his mouth. She rushed on: "I see you don't get it— Well, listen. It means a fortune—tens, perhaps hundreds of thousands before we get through, because I haven't the least doubt that it will be a go, and the renewal option will be closed.

For a while they'll be syndicated daily in the papers
—at five hundred a throw, then they'll hit the magazines about Christmas. We've four hundred plates in
the studio that are available—ready, waiting. Your
life's work, and crashing over big at last."

She paused, breathless, and gave him an exas-
perated shake. "Wake up, Holly, and get it. You
say you're good at visualizing. Well, visualize this—
presses from the Atlantic to the Pacific reeling out
'Hollisters.' And good reproductions, too—I'll see
to that. How about that—does it make sense or not?"

Then he heard them clattering and banging,
and he saw them ranked out to a vanishing point
like an image thrown back and forth between re-
ciprocating mirrors. And from them in an irresistible gush, signed Hollisters, pouring wave after wave
across the continent. Pulps and slicks stacked on
street corners. A bulbous girl in a bathing suit—a
Hollister, a smut weekly—a Hollister, a pink
screamer—a Hollister— He saw them caught up from
the stands, as though by a great wind, and sent
whirling away to settle upon the face of the land.
Lying upon library tables, dentists' tables, the seats
of prairie privies, the reading rooms of ocean liners,
the hurtling capsules of transcontinental planes. He
could see them boiling up out of garbage cans,
coursing down gutters when spring rains came to
purge away the filth of winter streets. He saw them
defiling the cleanness of the forests where picnic
parties and tin-can tourists had passed, leaving their
trail behind them. Charleston's famous Battery
—St. Augustine's coquina fort—New Orleans' quaint
wrought-iron balcony—the old Telfair Mansion.
And everywhere they went—Felix Hollister, the dig-

nified go-between, the ambassador of good taste in cigarette advertising. Telling the world that if a Southern gentleman had smoked Carolina tobacco "befo' th' wah, suh"—and found it good, why not the discriminating public now. He saw the submissive public, fed on him, gorged on him, sickening of him unto death, yet having him pumped into it until one year, two years, from now, nauseated beyond endurance, it would rise and vomit him forth into oblivion.

He saw all of this and, inexplicably, he didn't mind because it was happening to somebody else. He found himself not caring in the least what people said about Miriam Hollister's husband. And suddenly out of this not-caring came strength—and reason. His mind began to function, to reach out and grapple with what faced it.

Miriam saw his face clear and his eyes kindle.

"There," she said triumphantly, "I knew it would do you good."

Ignoring that, he asked abruptly: "Miriam, how much of an annuity would fifty thousand dollars buy from a good company?"

She gave a surprised laugh. "The news has done you good," she affirmed. "It's even making a businessman out of you."

Then looking across at him, shrewd and alert, she qualified the statement: "But not a very good businessman at that, Holly. I've looked into annuities. Pay you about five per cent at our age; then when you die, bang goes the principal. You can get seven out of a mortgage—and if you watch 'em they're good as bonds; then when you check out there's the original stake, good as new for the estate. Annuities, my son, are for widows and orphans, but not for us."

"Nevertheless, I want to know," he insisted.

Her face sobered, and after a moment she said: "Why, at your age I should say about twenty-five hundred a year."

He asked: "Two hundred a month—right?"

"And an extra hundred for Christmas," she told him.

"Very well," he said, "fifty thousand of Maxton's money in an annuity in my name, and I'll sign."

She stared in surprise. "Why, certainly," she said after a moment. "If you want it that way. It's poor business, but it doesn't really matter."

"Yes," he said doggedly, "I want it that way."

"But why, Felix? You're so unexpected. What's mine is yours—yours and the children's."

"I want it that way," he said slowly and very distinctly, "because I can exist on a hundred dollars a month, and it will take a hundred more for a model and clay. I'm starting over, Miriam. I'm pulling out of Exeter."

"But you can't," she cried, staring at him blankly. "You've got us—me and the children." Her tone became triumphant. "We're all you've got left in the world now—us and your career—"

Her conclusion struck him as amusing, and he smiled. "No," he said. "I've reached the peak. You understand that, don't you? It's time I started over."

He leaned forward, seized by the idea that was elaborating itself in his mind, shutting everything else out, even Leslie. "Why, Miriam," he said, his eyes shining, "it's amazing. It's incredible. This thing that is happening— Can't you see it? You

aren't losing your husband at all. You took him on,
a nobody. You made a tremendous success of him.
He wasn't me; he isn't now. He was your own creation. And now, look! Do you see what is happening? He has outrun me. He has forgotten me. From
my poor body he has soared out into big business.
America has taken him on. All you've got to do now
is to sit at the throttle. He'll go through Maxton,
then he'll be good for postcards. He'd make swell
movie shorts. They haven't got pictures over the
radio yet—but television is right around the corner—" He waved an arm in the direction of the
studio. "And there's Felix Hollister—all of him—
stacked five hundred deep, waiting to be sold—"

Miriam sat regarding him in stunned silence.
He sprang to his feet and strode to the window. His
shoulders were shaking. It was incredible, but the
man was laughing. He spun around again and saw
her face.

"It's true," he said, "what I'm telling you. He's
yours, all yours. That is, except for that annuity
he's throwing to me as hush money. In my private
opinion the man's a damned jackass, but he certainly
knows his business. And anyhow I wish him luck."

Miriam got to her feet and backed away from
him. She was obviously a little frightened. But, con-
trolling her voice, she said firmly: "I can see that
you are speaking and behaving in a thoroughly ir-
responsible manner, and that I cannot count on you
for assistance. Stay here and try to collect yourself,
and I will make all necessary arrangements."

Her words and manner arrested him and he
turned to her slowly, the light going out of his face.

After a while he asked brokenly: "You mean—Leslie?"

"Of course," she said, drawing assurance from a situation that called for action. "Something must be done at once."

He pondered for a moment, then looked up, meeting her eyes steadily. "You think I have lost her," he said, "but you're wrong. Do you think I could have seen everything so clearly if she hadn't been here? No," he went on, his voice gaining strength and conviction. "We're going away together." He came and stood over her. "And look here, don't you touch her. Don't you go near her." A spasm seized him, breaking his composure. "I ought to go to her," he said in a strangled voice. "I ought to be with her, but I can't. It's terrible, but I can't."

He closed his eyes for a moment, and when he opened them again he had regained his composure.

"She would understand," he said simply, "and Dr. Brice would. Of all the people living in this town he's the only one."

His manner changed, and he was again the stranger who had bargained her out of the annuity. He said: "Get Brice on the phone at once and ask him to come to me. He loved her. He'll take care of her now."

Miriam regarded him with an almost impersonal curiosity. "I want to get a good look at you," she said. "I'm not often fooled by people, and here I've been living with you all these years and never guessed what you really were. You keep telling me it's something I can't understand. Well, you're wrong. It's as plain as the nose on your face. You've got yourself into an ugly situation and you haven't got the courage to face it. So you are running away and leaving me to hold the bag. I'd have stuck by you and pulled you out of it. But you haven't got the guts. You're walking out on me, on your children, even on the girl who was silly enough to kill herself for you. Looked at squarely it's as simple as that. Any fool could understand it. That's the sort of person you are."

At last she had reached him, found his vulnerable spot—that faculty of seeing himself from the outside. She was, as always, unanswerable. There were the facts. You could click them off on your fingers. There was not one of them that could be refuted to the satisfaction of an impartial jury. All right he'd have to take that, stand convicted.

He became aware of her gaze. She knew that she had reached him. She believed now that she had him beaten. A slow fury burned up in him and its fires conjured Leslie and she was saying: "And you knew that you could step out of it in a moment of saving madness by the simple process of boarding a train."

While Miriam stood gaping in amazement, he opened the closet and, forgetting that his hand was injured, jerked down a suitcase. He flung it open on the bed, and glared across it at her.

"At any rate," he shouted at her, "I am what I am."

"You're inhuman," she shouted back. "You're a monster."

"Quite," he replied laconically, as she slammed out of the room.

THE studio on West Twelfth Street had no skylight, but there were two north windows that looked down upon an untidy back yard with a naked tree in one corner, and up at the exact amount of sky that one could expect for fifteen dollars a week. At one of the windows Hollister was standing, preferring the negative ugliness that lay beyond it to the necessity for action which would confront him when he should turn and face the room.

When he had left Exeter Miriam had told him that he was running away. That had been only four days ago, yet already when he looked back he experienced a frightening suspicion that she had spoken the truth. Not that he was fleeing the righteous indignation of Exeter, but a thing more profoundly menacing which was beyond her comprehension, and from which there might well be no escape.

He realized now that since the first night in the studio he had still been running away, still hiding. He had hidden behind each trivial detail, each task of arrangement and rearrangement that his wits could contrive, and when at last, physically exhausted, he would undress and lie upon the couch which was to serve as his bed by night, his thoughts would keep turning up trivial and irrelevant ideas upon which he would concentrate with a sort of isolating fury.

When he had shouted at Miriam, "I am what

I am," he had believed that in accepting her judgment, dismissing his past, everything that he had been was done with. It could be sealed off and forgotten. He need but look to the future. But there was one thing which in that moment of release he had forgotten. That the future derived from his conviction that Leslie had believed in him. And here, far from Exeter, alone, as one can be only in the thick of indifferent humanity, the question that had battered at the door of his mind during those first hours was filling the room and crowding in upon him:

If she had believed—why had she done it?

If he gave in for even a moment, closed his eyes and let himself go, there was Leslie, living and unforgettable, just as she had been on the morning of his awakening in Exeter. But now if he let his mind dwell upon her, drawing solace from a reliving of their few hours spent together as lovers, swiftly and without warning the darkness would envelop him, and in spite of his frantic rejections, his desperate denials, he would emerge shaken and beset with doubt.

He had wakened on this particular morning tired and unfreshed and with the ominous realization that every practical detail had been attended to. He had even written to Miriam giving the address to which the contracts should be sent for his signature. It remained only for him to purchase his materials and get to work.

This then was the day upon which he would pick up life exactly where he had dropped it. He told himself this over and over, but the sense of exultation that he had experienced in anticipation was absent now that he found himself face to face with the accomplished fact.

He had dressed slowly and with care, pausing over the selection of shirt and tie, debating with himself the question of whether he should wear tweeds or a blue serge. Then realizing how out of character this preoccupation with attire was, and that it sprang from procrastination, he had turned to the window, angry with himself, yet lacking the courage to take the momentous step upon which everything would depend. But in the end his own anger saved him, breeding a self-contempt that forced him to proceed.

He turned then and, with feverish haste, prepared to go upon his errand. While he changed slippers for shoes and shook himself down into his overcoat, he kept telling himself that he had already wasted too much time. Saying it, yet knowing that his haste sprang from an exterior need, rather than from the old inner urge that could not be denied.

He got coffee and a roll at a small tearoom, then found his way to a shop that dealt in artists' supplies. For a time he stood before the window, gazing at the dusty casts, the book of nude studies lying open for inspection, the armatures, and drawing boards.

An inexplicable timidity had descended upon him, and it required a conscious effort to cross the threshold and accost the bored young man who was arranging materials in a case.

He had decided to work with plasticine instead of clay. It would be more convenient and the same lot could be used repeatedly while he was getting into his stride. But he had never employed the me-

dium before and his unfamiliarity with it became
evident to the dealer. The man stood regarding
Hollister with an amused but skeptical tolerance
that made him at first painfully self-conscious, then
angrily defiant.

Moved by an impulse to put the fellow in his
place he said, with a manner at once patronizing and
slightly apologetic: "It may interest you to know,
young man, that I studied with Matisse in Paris."

The shopkeeper was surprised and slightly incredulous. "Really," he said, without warmth,
"that's quite interesting." Then, as he lifted a set
of modeling tools to the counter for his customer's
inspection, he added: "That was a long time ago."

"Oh, I don't know," Hollister took him up defensively. "It was the winter of nineteen-seven and
-eight. He had just entered upon his *Fauve*
period, as I remember, and he did his blue nude
about that time. I remember that on one occasion
he told the class—"

He had been talking on, not looking at the man,
but at a pair of calipers wondering if it would be of
a proper size for his work. Now something impelled
him to raise his eyes and he encountered an expression in which the sympathy of youth for age was dis-
counted by a trace of contempt.

Instantly he knew that he had blundered. That
the man probably doubted his veracity, or if he accepted the story it placed him as a failure with nothing of his own to stand upon, bragging to strangers
of the successes he had known.

Overwhelmed with embarrassment and anxious
only to be free of the place, he purchased wildly and
without discrimination whatever the clerk recom-

mended. Then he ordered the stuff sent to his room, and at last got himself into the street.

Back in the studio, with the equipment piled about him, he stood and regarded it. Well, here he was in New York, beholden to no one. Nothing but his work now. Waking and sleeping, he could live it, give himself to it, and let it possess him.

But it had taken him two days to set up the small armature that the dealer had sold him, and get started. First he explained the delay to himself on the grounds of his burned right hand. But the slight wound had healed nicely, and now, protected by a square of adhesive plaster, it was no longer a valid excuse. Then he got nearer to the truth. So much depended on the proper start, he told himself, that he kept waiting, piddling about, hoping that the old ungovernable urge would take him. But it hadn't, and finally with hands that shook he had set up the wire skeleton and had started to rough in a full-length female figure.

It stood there now after two days of uninspired plodding labor, an embryo with roughly indicated limbs, breasts, and head, rising from a litter of tools and discarded fragments of plaster. While back at his old stand before the window stood Hollister, his gaunt shoulders set forward in an attitude of supreme dejection.

Beyond the bleary pane the sky changed slowly from misty gray to misty blue. From uptown, muted by distance, came the voice of Manhattan, pervasive, undeviating. It was pitched in a graver key, and the rhythmic pattern was less clearly defined, but it was not unlike the chanting of cicadas in the Southern meadows, and suddenly, with a sort of terror, the realization of his complete aloneness assailed Hollister, and he saw for the first time how small a difference there is between freedom and exile. If you could stand alone, fight through and win, you were free. If you had overestimated your power, and failed, you were lost, an alien in a strange land.

$\mathcal{T}$HE knock had been repeated several times before it attracted Hollister's attention. Then, when at last he turned toward the door, it was opening hesitantly to admit Felicia. She stood for a moment regarding him while the startled look went out of his eyes and they recognized her. She was wearing a closely fitting gray coat that accentuated the slim vertical lines of her figure, and she brought autumn into the room with her in a heightened color and sparkling eyes.

She said lightly, "Hello, Dad," then stood feeling the atmosphere of the room, glancing at the worn, uncomfortable furniture, the embryo upon the stand, and lastly back to her father, standing irresolute before the window.

She crossed the room and tendered him the smooth coolness of her cheek. He kissed her awkwardly with his hands hanging at his sides, knowing instinctively that Miriam had written to her, and wondering how she was taking it.

He had planned to see her later and he had visualized that meeting. He would have waited until he had got a fair start with his work, and counted on that to speak for him, to justify his break with her mother. He had cherished the wild hope that the artist in her would make allowances, and that she would understand his motives. But now she had found him with his defenses down, beleaguered by doubt and, in the face of the evidence against him, incapable of speaking in his own behalf.

Now she stood, drawing off her gloves, taking her time about it, waiting coolly receptive for what he might have to say.

"Take a seat," Hollister invited. "The couch is the most comfortable."

He removed a soiled cup and saucer, a pair of calipers, and an overcoat, making room at one end for her. Then he seated himself facing her, leaning forward with forearms on his thighs, and his hands dangling between them.

He said at last, without looking up: "You've heard from Miriam, I suppose."

She sat regarding him as she had that day in the studio when the mass printing of his etchings had been discussed. Her manner implied that she was neither for nor against him, but that as a subject for abstract speculation he interested her. And when she spoke, her tone was casual, and gave no indication of the emotion that lay behind it.

"Do you want her verbatim," she enquired, "or shall I be agreeably vague?"

"I'll have her straight," Hollister answered grimly.

"She said: 'I want you to look your father up and see if he has come to his senses.' "

Their eyes met and a gleam of understanding flashed between them, but neither smiled.

After a moment he asked:

"She told you everything—about Leslie?"

"Yes," she answered, "everything. But I can't talk about that now. You'll have to hear Mother's message and decide what you want to do."

She dropped her eyes to her lap where she was smoothing a glove over her knee with scrupulous care. The withdrawal indicated that he should have privacy in which to listen to Miriam. Hollister was grateful.

"She said to tell you that everything had been attended to in Exeter, and that she is willing to forget your rudeness to her if you are ready to come home."

The message was so completely Miriam that he felt her presence. Not as a personality projected by written thought, but as a physical materialization. He felt her contempt for the room in which he sat, with its untidiness, its poverty, its odor of failure. And he felt the swift irresistible drive of her will, like a tide set always one way, mounting about him and turning the earth beneath his feet to fluid sand. He looked about him for something upon which he could lay hold, something done, some promise for the future, but this room housed nothing but humiliation and despair, and a loneliness that hung in the atmosphere and stifled him like a poisonous effluvium.

Desperately he raised his eyes and met Felicia's gaze. She was leaning forward studying him as she had done that other time, but he experienced the sudden warming conviction that now she was on his side, that from the middle ground of her neutrality she was holding out her hand to him. It gave him strength to face the issue squarely.

He knew then that if he returned it would be the ultimate disgraceful surrender, and that loneliness, poverty, even eventual failure would be preferable. And he found himself saying violently, almost without volition: "No. You can tell her—No. Whatever it's going to be I've got to take it. I've got to see it through."

Felicia got up and took his face in her hands. Then she bent down and kissed him. "I knew you wouldn't," she said simply. "I was betting on you and I'm proud of you."

When she had seated herself again she produced two loose cigarettes from her bag and handed one to Hollister. She said "damn" as the first paper match flared, scorched her finger, and went out. But the second got them lighted, and they smoked for a moment in silence.

She had a gift that Hollister now noticed for the first time and which is common among reticent people who feel deeply. This was the ability to express a profound emotion through silence, and without the embarrassment occasioned by words. He felt her sympathy now, comforting, yet demanding nothing.

She said at last, not looking at him: "Would you like to talk to me about Leslie, or would it hurt too much?"

He strode to the window and stood there giving her his back in silhouette. "Yes," he said, "I'd like to try."

He pondered for a moment, then proceeded, shaping painfully into words the thought that had pursued him from Exeter. "You see," he began, "even if I wanted to go back I couldn't. It would be too painful."

"But you can go forward," Felicia said.

"I've tried." He turned and gestured toward his workstand. "There it is, and it's dead." He broke off into moody silence, then started again. "There's something I haven't had the courage to face. When Leslie killed herself she must have had a motive. They will say in Exeter that I made love to her. That she took it seriously, and I didn't. And so—" His voice failed him, but in a moment he started again, the words coming thin and hard. "But of course that wasn't so, because we were coming away together. She believed in me. That last night she—she gave herself to me. After that nothing could have broken her. Nothing except losing faith in me. If that had happened—if after I left she thought it over and decided that I didn't have it in me, that I'd ever let her down, she wouldn't have wanted to go on living. And so, you see, that's the thing I've got to face. She gave me back my faith in myself. And now it's gone with her because if she did that—she must have doubted at the last."

Felicia said: "And you believe that she killed herself. What right have you got to think that?"

He turned slowly toward her. "They told me that—Pendleton, Miriam—everybody kept telling me."

Felicia looked at him incredulously. Her voice was scornful. "And you accepted it. You had been lovers. You knew her better than anybody in the world, and you thought that she was a quitter. That she could do that to somebody she loved."

Behind the opaque screen of his look as he raised his eyes to her she saw a light. "I didn't think," he said slowly, "I didn't dare."

"Listen," she commanded, leaning toward him. "I knew Leslie. We spent an evening together. We made the engagement in the studio that last day I was at home. Remember?" Hollister nodded without taking his eyes from her face, and she hurried on. "We sat up late, talking, and we found out a lot about each other. I knew then that she was in love with you. Not that she said so, but I knew. And I found out, too, how clever she was, and how clearly she saw things. Even if she had hated you she wouldn't have done a thing like that to you. She was too kind. But I tell you she loved you—so it was absolutely impossible."

She took a final draw from her cigarette, then flipped it into the littered fireplace. "She would have known exactly how it would have looked to Exeter, her going out just then, when there was talk about you. She would have known that it would ruin you. If you had thought you'd have seen that, and you'd have known that she did not kill herself. That she wouldn't have done it just then even if she had wanted to. But there's more than that," she went on with an intensity of belief that carried conviction. "I know what faith she had in you. She couldn't have changed."

He stood, regarding her for a moment, then suddenly the lethargy that had bound him vanished, and his face quickened. "Of course she didn't," he cried. "You're right. She couldn't have."

He commenced to stride about the room in his characteristic way, colliding with furniture, seeing nothing, absorbed in what he was thinking. And from time to time thinking aloud, shaping a pattern out of the chaos of the past week.

"Of course I'd have known if I had stopped to think. But I couldn't. Not then. I wasn't there at all after what Pendleton told me. I had to get away, and I was afraid to look back. I didn't dare." He stopped before Felicia. "I suppose we'll never know, will we? She was alone, and it happened. There was a full moon, and she loved moonlight. She may have raised the window to see, and suddenly it was all over."

"But your life goes on," Felicia reminded him. "You've got your work. You made a plan together and now you've got to see it through."

Her words brought him face to face with reality and he looked about the studio as though he were seeing the place for the first time. Then he went over to the figure on the stand and gazed down at it in bitter silence.

Felicia crossed the room and stood beside him, close, so that her shoulder touched his arm. "Dad," she said, "last month you gave me my chance. You asked if I would be willing to chuck college if it meant freeing you to do your work. And I let you down. Do you remember?"

Last month. That wasn't possible. It came to him like a memory out of his early youth. And with a sort of wonder he recalled the bitter intensity of his disappointment. It seemed small, remote now in comparison with all that had happened since.

He slipped an arm about her waist. "Forget it, Licia," he said. "I've been ashamed of myself ever since for forcing you into an unfair position. You are right to take what you want now while you have youth."

"I am glad you feel that way about it," she said quietly, "because I'm coming to live with you. That's what I want most to do."

Hollister turned and stared incredulously down at her.

"Don't interrupt me," she begged, "and don't let's get emotional about this. It's a perfectly simple and practical matter. I thought it all out before I came. And I'm not going to mother you, or anything like that. We'll get adjoining studios somewhere, and we'll both be free as air. I'll get a thousand times more out of studying with you, giving my whole time to it, than by cornering all of the liberal arts in Poughkeepsie. And in return I'll darn your socks and wash your coffee cups. And we can go places together, see exhibits—have fun." She pulled him around so that he had to look at her. Then rushed on excitedly: "Now don't say no, and don't tell me that you are going to think it over, because I might as well warn you that I have a trump up my sleeve and I'll use it. All I've got to do is to walk out on Mother too, then you'll have to take me in off the streets"—she laughed up at him and added melodramatically—"or else—"

His eyes kindled and he said: "This isn't charity? You really think I'm worth it?"

"I want to be with you, of course," she answered gravely, "but it's bigger than that. You're going to do good work. Leslie knew it, and so do I. I want to help."

Here it was—the complete solution. No longer the aloneness and singlehanded battle against discouragement and failure. He wanted desperately to agree. But he could not. Angrily he realized that there was a definite obstacle. He could not put his finger on it, but it lay there in the back of his mind barring the way to an assent. It tormented him. It stirred his mind, forcing it to quicken and meet the issue. At last he began to sense it vaguely. Then in a flash, with startling clarity, he saw it whole. It had been so insidious that he wondered how he had escaped.

He leaned down and kissed Felicia lightly on the cheek. "No," he said, "some day, but not now. Your wanting to come has given me everything. If we went through with it I'd be sold out again."

She drew back rebuffed, and he hastened to add:

"Don't feel hurt. Don't judge now. Wait until I tell you. I see it all so plainly. It's like—yes, it's quite like the coming of the Holy Ghost."

He strode across the room and back, hands jammed in trouser pockets, not looking where he was going.

"You see," he said, "I've been taking short cuts, and there's no such thing in art. There's no easy way. You can learn to draw— Yes— You can learn to model. That's not art. It's a voice talking and saying nothing. It's a beautiful gutless replica of life. The little galleries are full of them, and you leave without remembering one. But once in a while you come up short before a marble or a bronze, and you don't see the surface at all. You see down through the plaited muscles to the pulsing viscera. And beneath that to the human joy or agony of the poor devil who lived it and beat it everlastingly into the clay. Then you've seen something—but it wasn't an exhibit on a stand with people gaping about it, but a man who has given himself to life and let it eat him. A man who has explored the exquisite and illimitable resources of pain, and who has known joy, not as a bellyful of champagne, or a night with a beautiful prostitute, or the virtuous fireside for that matter, but as a sudden release from despair, when the thing that he has striven for breaks into life under his hands—"

He paused in his tirade and his gaze became cognizant of Felicia, sitting forward, gazing raptly up at him.

"And I took it the easy way," he went on scornfully. "For twenty-five years I've been welching. Not because what I did wasn't honest, but because it was not what I wanted. Now I've got to get back at it. I have to take sorrow, and despair, and loneliness. I have to start over where I left off. In the beginning I'll do work that a child would be ashamed of, but I'll break it up and start over. I'll be an old man competing with youngsters. I'll be dated before I'm started. But I'll keep at it. You see, it is the trying that matters after all. And it's wanting something terribly—something that no matter how good you are you'll never get. Because there's no such thing as perfection—"

He had lost Felicia now. His glance, roving the studio, lit on his workstand with the hated embryo rising from it. He strode to it and circled its vaguely suggested waist with his hands. Then he pressed in and upward, as a potter molds his whirling clay—

And then, for the first time since he had left Paris, he felt it, and the words that he had put it into when he had tried to make it clear to Miriam flashed up to him. "But clay is something that has life— you can take it in your hands and you can feel its heart beat."

Felicia gathered her things and prepared to depart without disturbing him. But when she opened the door the rusty groan of the hinges penetrated to his consciousness and he looked up, but without seeing her, and with his hands still kneading the clay.

"Get me a model, will you," he said. "A girl under twenty if you can, and slender. I know what I want to do."

"I'll try," she answered, "perhaps tomorrow—"

But in a frenzy of impatience he cut in upon her. "No," he shouted, "not tomorrow—today. Can't you understand I've got my work to do?"

THE END